Pilgrim's Progress

Eric Brown

📖

J. R. Nicholls

Published by
J. R. Nicholls
Denby Dale HD8 8RT

This paperback edition first published 2016

ISBN: 978-1-911347-01-9

1 3 5 7 9 10 8 6 4 2

Printed and bound in Great Britain by
CPI Group (UK) Ltd, Croydon CR0 4YY

Dedication

This book is dedicated to Ellie and Izzy.
You have both made me a very proud father.

Chapter One – The set up

Garlic is one of the easiest crops to grow and probably the most important for providing the flavour in almost every savoury dish we eat today. You can plant it in February; but to give it a good head start, it is best planted late October/November the year before harvesting. Give the soil a good rake to break it up. Stretch a piece of string between 2 pegs to get your planting line. Carefully separate out the individual cloves from a bulb of garlic; one bought from your local supermarket is fine. Keeping each clove the right way up – the same way up as it grew on the bulb - gently press each one into the soil until the pointed tip is just at soil level, at intervals of 6 inches. Gently firm round each clove with your fingers. Subsequent rows should be 12 inches apart. Keep weed free, water in dry weather and bingo! Harvest when the tops start dying back by gently lifting with a fork underneath to prevent the bulb breaking and use either straight away, or store the crop by hanging the bulbs in a dry place. Nothing beats the mouth watering smell of your own home grown garlic cooking in a pasta or curry...

Graham's mind wandered as his eyes tried in vain to penetrate the total darkness that surrounded him. He had no idea how long he'd been lying there. He wasn't sure if it was still minutes, or an hour or more had passed. An emerging ache in his stomach reminded him that he hadn't eaten all day, but he was now finally beginning to feel hunger again. Over the previous 12 hours he hadn't thought about food at all, which wasn't really surprising in the circumstances. Now, though, the lingering aromatic memory of garlic, herbs and spices from Dave's earlier takeaway began to work their magic.

Perhaps the return of his appetite was a sign that his initial panic and consequential adrenaline rush that had sustained his earlier flight from the police was at last beginning to subside and he could start to think a little more logically again. He would need all his wits and cunning to get out of this one.

He shifted a little, as quietly as he could so he didn't cause any suspicion in the rooms below. He needed to make himself more comfortable though. The beam he was resting on was beginning to dig into his head and he was beginning to itch from the glass fibres that had found their way down the back of his T-shirt. The ever present dust and fibres in the air began to irritate his nose and he fought the urge to sneeze – that would be all it would take to reveal his presence to the police below and this time, there would be no escape. The brutality of the murder would ensure they wouldn't let him get away so easily again this time.

His mind wandered back 30 years.

"Graham! Graham! Can you turn that bloody noise down... *please?*" Graham lay on his bed, staring at the ceiling, oblivious to his mother's voice calling from the hallway below. A few moments later the door to his bedroom opened and the less than happy face of his mother peered round the door. "Graham! Didn't you hear me calling?"

"Oh? No, sorry. Hang on, let me turn this down." He leaned over to the amplifier and turned the volume on Zeppelin's 'Black Dog' to a level he hoped would be more acceptable to his mother.

"Thank you Graham," his mother said with a smile and a touch of sarcasm. "I just wondered how long you were planning to stay in bed?"

"It's Sunday mum. Nobody gets up early on a Sunday."

"It's nearly midday Graham and you've got exams next week in case you've forgotten." She walked over to the window and pulled open the curtains. Graham hid under the quilt as the blinding light hit his eyes. She turned back to face him.

"Graham, get up now for God's sake! Your sister's been up three hours and has been revising ever since. Come on Graham, what's the matter with you? These exams are important."

"Annie's different to normal human beings isn't she? I can't think of anyone else her age that works like that. It's not healthy mum. A young person's brain needs plenty of rest. It's still growing and developing at this age."

"What am I going to do with you Graham? You don't seem to realise in two years you're supposed to be at university. You'll be lucky to get there if you carry on like this. What's that smell as well?" She looked at him quizzically.

"What?"

"There's a burning smell in the air."

"I can't smell anything. Maybe it's next door's chimney. Old Clarkie burns all sorts of stuff on that fire. Macca reckons he threw his cat on after it got run over. He wanted some sort of domestic cremation for it."

"Graham! You've got a warped mind. Anyway Mr. Clark's not going to be having a fire lit in May is he?"

"Maybe he's incinerating some other life form..."

"For the last time...?"

"Okay, okay. I'm getting up."

"Thank you Graham." She left the room, still sniffing the air as she departed.

Graham was just about to have his usual morning wank when his sister burst into the room and sat on the bed, crushing his left leg.

"You could knock first you know?" said a furious Graham, a touch relieved he didn't get caught in the act.

"You are a lazy tosser Graham."

"Don't you start as well! I've just had the lecture from mum."

"I know. I heard, and she's right. What's that smell?"

"What smell?"

"You know what I mean. You've been smoking weed again Graham. Are you mad? Mum and dad will kill you if they found out."

"Well they won't if you don't tell them."

"I'll make a deal with you bro. You get up and do some work and I might not."

"Most people would have asked for money. What is it with you?"

"Don't you have any ambition Graham? Don't you want to do anything with your life?" She looked at him with exasperation, shook her head and left with a dramatic flair.

Graham lay back in bed and stared up at the ceiling. *I'll give it ten more minutes. I'll just hear 'Stairway' first...*

*

Suddenly a crash and blinding light made Graham sit up sharply. Then pain, as he felt a blow to his forehead.

"For fuck's sake Dave, you scared the shit out of me! Why couldn't you have done that quietly? I thought you were the police." Graham glared at the head and shoulders of his friend Dave, peering at him from the displaced loft hatch, as he rubbed his head where it had struck the roof truss above him.

"Careful Grimy; you'll go through my bathroom ceiling! They've gone now and anyway, the hatch sticks. You have to give it a bit of wellie to open it."

"What did you say to them?" Graham asked, still nursing what was now becoming a rising bump on his forehead.

"I said I hadn't seen you at all since we heard about, well, you know what. I said that we were all shocked and couldn't believe it."

"Couldn't believe I was a murderer you mean?"

"No, we couldn't believe they thought it was you of all people."

"Do you?"

"What do you mean?"

"Do you think it was me that killed him?"

"No, of course not mate! Really, none of us do. This whole thing is crazy. Everyone knows you're soft as shite. It's just they are so convinced. They say they've got all this evidence".

"Well, she arranged that, didn't she? That flaming tart! She set me up. I can't believe I've been so bloody stupid..."

*

Graham had been divorced two years. A mediocre local government salary, coupled with the monthly payments to his ex-wife and a large rent for a small two bed flat above a launderette, didn't leave him much to play with each week. Thanks to his weekly gardening article in the Post though, 'Graham's Garden', he could afford to keep his season ticket. So every other Saturday there was the footy, followed by real ales in the Tap with the lads. That was his respite from the humdrum, the financial worries, and psychological pressure his ex-wife liked to occasionally inflict on him.

The Tap (or 'Tap and Spile' as it was officially known) was his second home. If you didn't know it was there, you'd probably walk right past it, located down an alley branching off one of the fashionable shopping streets of Leeds, within easy staggering distance of the railway station. It was a freak Victorian survivor of German bombing raids, monstrous city centre redevelopments and, worst of all, the dreaded wine bar conversion.

Light bulbs encrusted with years of nicotine bathed the bar in a subdued yellow light. The wooden tables that wobbled on the uneven, sticky floorboards were only made stable by the folded beer mats wedged under their legs. The recent smoking ban revealed an underlying aroma of yeast, hops and urine, supplemented in winter by fumes from the coal fire. Whether it was in or out of a smokeless zone was somehow immaterial. The juke box had no music post 1987. It was a rich sound archive that covered the late sixties and seventies, with the emphasis on rock. Graham loved it.

Those Saturdays in the Tap either started with a high after the match or, more often than they preferred these days, a low. Life wasn't easy being a Leeds fan in the early 21st century. The heady days of Champions League football a decade ago had been replaced with the misery of relegation, administration and football that wasn't always pleasing to the eye. Thank God for real ale though. It always numbed the pain. Soon they would be off the subject of shoddy defending and failure to take chances in the box. Then it would be their other priorities in life; the telly, their allotments, relationships with currents and ex's...

The one solid thing in Graham's life, the one really positive thing he had achieved, was Anna. Coming up to 16 (where had the years gone?) she was a real source of pride and for the half the week (one third, according to Kate's solicitors) that she was with him in the flat, he was really happy. She was bright, funny and always brought him down to earth.

Graham was beginning to realise he was drifting through life though, and had been for years. Maybe that's how he'd ended up in the flat. Maybe, like everything else in his life, Kate and he had also just drifted apart.

He'd never really been an achiever like his sister, the pride of the family. Not that he was jealous. They had always fought like brother and sister but, despite that, he adored her, like everyone did. Graham had always just got by though, did just enough at school, college and at work. He wasn't unhappy, but neither was he happy if he was honest with himself. And as the years passed, he knew in his heart he'd wasted opportunities, and time.

It was after an excellent Saturday afternoon at Elland Road in mid September 2010 though that life unexpectedly looked up. A group of around half a dozen women turned up in the Tap. There was nothing unusual in that. It was common enough for groups of attractive people to turn up and join the resident social outcasts for a final top up while waiting for a taxi, or the last train home. No, what was unusual this time was that one of the group, the tallest and most attractive by far, was looking in his direction.

Graham looked to his side. Often, the subconscious leering of Graham's friends could attract concerned glances back from visiting groups of women. But no, all the lads were facing each other, discussing the possibility that if we played like that every week, we might just have a chance of sneaking back up to the Premiership; though being Leeds, we would probably balls it up before the end of the season.

There was no doubt about it. This woman was definitely looking at him. It was his round so without too much prompting he stood up, subconsciously checked his fly, and headed towards the bar. He walked taller than usual, conscious that he was developing a middle aged stoop and associated waistline expansion as he approached his 45th birthday. He wanted to look good as he walked past this group.

He smiled as he passed them. The tall blonde smiled back. Things were looking promising.

"What do you want?" George, the fat landlord who excelled in the Tap's legendary brand of customer care grunted. "And I don't want any coppers like last time, just notes and silver!"

"What?"

"It takes bloody ages to count. What's the problem with you? Doesn't your mum give you enough spend?"

"Right, okay. I just thought the change would come in handy," Graham mumbled, conscious the tall blonde could hear him being patronised by the 5'4" bloated, and rather sweaty,

7

middle-aged landlord standing before him. "One from pump 1, three from pump 2, two from pump 3, and a packet of beef crisps please".

"One from what?"

"One from pump 1, three from pump 2, two from... look it doesn't matter. Six of those please." Graham pointed at a random pump, conscious that he was going red and looking flustered, like a man not in control.

The blonde approached. "Hi," she said, smiling the most attractive smile he'd seen in a long time. The last time he'd seen a smile like that was when he met Anna's new English teacher at her last parents evening. But then that didn't go anywhere. When he asked her out for a drink afterwards, her expression changed immediately and she looked at him like he was a registered sex offender, saying something like, "I don't think it would very appropriate Mr. Pilgrimm. Do you?" This one didn't look alarmed though. This one was interested in him.

"Hi," he replied, leaning against the bar, aware that his elbow was slowly absorbing someone's spilled beer. He shuffled slightly, moving his damp elbow to somewhere more comfortable.

"My name's Frieda and I hope you don't think I'm being forward, but... well... I have to be honest; I find you very attractive." A seductive voice said with confidence and the hint of an accent. Dutch, Scandinavian?

"Well thank you". Graham tried to sound and look cool, in control, but conscious that he was probably going to break wind. He'd always suffered a bit from a nervous bowel when under pressure. Fine when you're 10. Not great when you're 45. "I'm Graham, Graham Pilgrimm, and it's really good to meet you". Graham was sweating. This woman was out of his league – *but she liked him.* He held out his hand and she took it. The moment was broken when a gruff voice interrupted.

"That's six pints of cider. £16.80 and no fucking coppers please!"

"What?" Graham jerked his head round. What had he done? The real ale sampling strategy had been ruined. How was he going to explain that to the lads?

Frieda laughed. Graham realised that she'd seen right through him. But it didn't matter. *She liked him.*

*

"Anna, is that you?"

"Dad, dad, are you alright? Where are you?"

"I can't say. Look I'm fine. I've just got to lie low for a while. Anna I didn't do anything."

"I know. We all know it, mum as well. She's worried too. We can't believe it. What happened?"

"Someone framed me. They made the police believe I'd done something I hadn't."

"Why don't you go to the Police? Why don't you tell them?"

"They don't believe me Anna. That's why I've got to stay away for a while, to sort this out and prove my innocence. Look Anna, I've got to go but I'll keep in touch. I love you."

"I love you too daddy." She hadn't called him Daddy since she was 11. "Look after yourself, please!"

*

No, the police didn't believe him. It was obvious the moment the two uniformed officers knocked at his door above the launderette at five to six in the morning.

"Mr. Pilgrimm, Graham Pilgrimm?"

"Yes, what is it? Is it Anna? Is she okay?"

"Anna?"

"My daughter. Look what is it? What's happened?"

"Mr. Pilgrimm, there's been an incident and we believe you might be able to help us with our inquiries."

"What sort of incident?"

"A man has been found dead in suspicious circumstances. We believe you may know him and may be able to assist us. Would you mind coming down to the station please?"

"What, now?"

"Yes please, sir."

In hindsight there was something in the tone of the officer's voice that should have set off warning bells. But hindsight is a good thing in, well, hindsight, and Graham was never his sharpest at six in the morning.

*

"So, what line of work are you in?" Frieda asked, her smile lighting up the Victorian gloom of the Tap. Graham sat at a corner table with her, a safe distance from the lads who were more pissed off with Graham for having to drink their accidental pints of fizzy apple juice, than being abandoned for the company of an attractive blonde.

"I work for the Parks department, here in Leeds." He smiled back, a little nervously, sailing into uncharted waters with someone who was clearly out of his league. "I check to make sure plants are planted, grass is cut, trees are pruned; that sort of thing."

"Are you in charge of lots of people?"

"Oh yes. Goes with the territory." Graham lied. The truth was he wasn't. He did check parks and green spaces to see work programmes were being adhered to, but the last time he mentioned a minor oversight to a Beeston born gardener he was told in no uncertain terms to "Piss Off!" which, of course, he did.

"Sounds really interesting," she replied. And she did sound interested.

"And what do you do Frieda? Do you work?"

"Well, yes and no. I'm divorcing at the moment. My husband, or soon to be ex-husband, owns a construction firm and I used to help with the business."

"Oh, I'm sorry." Graham backed off a little.

"Hey, it's fine." Frieda smiled. "My husband, ex-husband, isn't a very nice man. He can be controlling, domineering. He didn't like it if I went against his wishes. You know..." Graham backed off a bit more. The idea of coming face to face with 6' 6" of jealous tattooed builder didn't appeal. Frieda read his mind and laughed. "Hey, don't worry. He's a short arse who can only stand up to women. Believe me, he's a coward at heart and anyway, he's more than happy to get me out of his life now and find someone who'll go with the flow. Anyway..." she looked at him with her incredible blue eyes, "wouldn't you think I'm worth fighting for?" Graham felt a spiritual and physical stirring.

"Oh yes, " he said, his mouth dry as he looked deep into her seductive blue eyes. "Yes, I think you are," he stammered.

"Tell me about your friends." She glanced at the distinctly hostile looking five as they plotted amongst themselves, with occasional glances towards Graham, then back down to the offending pints before them.

"Well, from left to right, the bald bloke is called Kev. We've known him around 20 years, so he's new to the group. Next, there's Dave, Tomo, Mac and Jim-Bob. We all went to school together except Kev. He's a librarian. Dave's a teacher, Tomo's in IT and so's Mac. Jim-Bob's in, well, sales... sort of."

"Are they all married?"

"No, not now anyway. Kev and Tomo were once, but are kind of in-between now. Dave's in a long term relationship, but they don't live together. He's got his place and Viv's got hers. I guess if you've been on your own a while you like your own space." He decided not to say much more about them, conscious none of them led particularly interesting lives except, perhaps, Jim-Bob. He thought he'd quit while ahead. The thrill of allotment keeping might have been just a bit too much for Frieda.

"Do you come here often? Sorry, cliché," he laughed.

"No, first time. I'm just on a girl's night out with some of the neighbours. We called in while waiting for a taxi. What about you?"

"Every other weekend we usually meet up here after the match..." He stopped. Had he crossed the line? Football was up there with religion and politics. Off the agenda until you knew who you were talking to.

"Do you like Leeds? My father did when he was younger. He followed them from Sweden"

"Really?" Graham couldn't believe his luck. "Seriously?"

"Yes, loved them right from the days of Don Revie."

"Wow!" They chatted easily now. The conversation flowed and Graham relaxed. Fifteen minutes later, the conspirators glanced as one to face them and raised their pints of cider in unison.

"Grimy is a wanker, a wanker, a wanker..." Graham hid his face in his hands.

"No!" he groaned, "Not now please".

Frieda laughed a loud and raucous laugh. "You know what? I think I'd like to see you again. Do have any days off this week?"

"I finish early Fridays, around lunchtime," Graham replied, peering through his fingers at her. He slowly pulled his hands away from his face, not quite believing what was happening.

"Do you have any nice parks you look after, we can walk round?"

"One or two." There were only one or two really. Most of his patch was grassy strips in housing estates which often cultivated interesting arrangements of used condoms, nappies and dog shit.

"Well, I tell you what, you name the time and the place, and I'll bring the picnic".

*

Friday couldn't come soon enough and what a glorious day. They'd arranged to meet by the lake and despite the heat of an unseasonable September day, there were hardly any people in sight. Then he saw her approaching.

She was carrying a small picnic basket and dressed for summer; pale yellow top and long, flowing white skirt, finished with a pair of flat heeled sandals. She looked amazing. Graham began to appreciate her figure for the first time. Not overlarge breasts, but hey, no problem, thought Graham. With such a slim figure and the most amazing legs, the combination worked.

"You look fantastic," said Graham, without the hint of a lie.

"Thanks," Frieda laughed. "You don't look too bad yourself." This wasn't strictly true. Graham had come straight from work, his worn cord jacket over his shoulder, tie off and top button undone.

"That's kind, but I didn't have time to change. I got held up at the office."

"I'm glad you're here now," she said as she touched his arm. They started walking. The conversation flowed easily.

"Do have any children? I hope you don't mind me asking," Graham enquired.

"No," replied Frieda. "We couldn't. We, Pete my ex, couldn't. Low sperm count. No surprise there," she said with a slight hint of bitterness. "We talked about adoption, but never got round to it. Just as well really in the circumstances. What about you?"

"One. Anna, she's fifteen now. She spends most of her time with her mum, but I get to spend time with her a few days each week.

"What's she like?"

"She's amazing. We've been so lucky. Bright, funny; you'd really like her." Graham went red, conscious he might be moving too fast.

Frieda slipped her shoes off as they left the path and walked barefoot as she followed him up the steep grassy slope that led to the viewpoint at the centre of the park.

"It's a lovely name," she said.

"We named her after my sister Annie. She was pretty amazing too"

"Was?"

"Yes, she died last year."

"I'm sorry. What happened?"

"Annie was my twin sister. She was, what you might call, an achiever. A first at Cambridge and a well respected ecologist. She'd been taking a break from studying the impact of excessive shark hunting on the Great Barrier Reef when she died in a climbing accident in New Zealand. She was really beautiful. It's kind of good that we can at least remember her that way."

"Graham, I'm really sorry." She gently held his hand and her warmth felt good. They walked and talked as they climbed the hill and then sat down when they reached the top, leaning with their backs against two trees as they faced each other.

"Wine?" Frieda enquired.

"Sounds good," said Graham, happier than he had felt in years. She opened a bottle from the basket. They drank and ate the nibbles she had also packed; the conversation flowed easily. Frieda looked around.

"You can see the whole park from here," she said.

"It's one of my favourite places. It's usually really busy, but I guess everyone's still at work and the kids are back at school now."

"Hmm..." said Frieda, as she rested her back against the tree and stretched her legs out. Graham looked at her. She had her eyes shut, a relaxed smile across her face. He took more time to take her in. Her long blonde hair, parted slightly off centre, framed a slim beautiful face. Her small mouth, which accentuated her large blue eyes when they were open, was in proportion to an elegant smooth neck and narrow shoulders. She had slim arms that tapered into long, feminine fingers. His gaze moved to her narrow waist and down to those incredible flawless legs, slim ankles and finished off with elegant, graceful feet.

Graham looked above, at the light flickering through the canopy, when he was distracted by a gentle pressure on his crotch. He looked down and saw the grass tinted sole of Frieda's right foot gently pressing on his groin, her long toes scrunched around a growing swelling beneath.

"Does that feel good?" She asked in a darkly seductive voice. It did. It felt really good. His manhood was also suitable impressed.

"Yes," he said rather weakly.

A quick glance around confirmed they were still the only people in this part of the park. She fixed him with her large blue eyes. "Hey, Mr. Pilgrimm, guess what? I'm not wearing any pants."

"Oh... oh my Lord," stammered Graham. He had honestly never felt as aroused in all his life and, with a swift movement, she was astride him. One look and he could tell she was a natural blonde.

"Oh my Lord," were the only words that came to him afterwards. He'd held on as long as he could. He'd focussed on Mary Whitehouse, Geoffrey Howe, Margaret Thatcher and Arthur Scargill (for political balance). All helped him hold the inevitable conclusion back... a little while longer at least. And then..."Oh my Lord!"

An hour later, they walked back to the lakeside in silence, holding hands.

"Graham."

"Yes Frieda."

"I want to see you again."

"I want to see you too. When though?"

"Why not here again? Next week, same time same place."

"That's great, yes. Can I call you in between?"

"No, probably best not to until I get everything sorted at home. But there is something you can do for me."

"What? Anything." And he meant it. He was floating on air. He was cooking on gas. He had the ball in the net against Man U at Old Trafford.

"I get off on texts, you know, dirty ones; the dirtier the better."

"What?"

"I want you to text me every day until we meet again. But I want them dirty, really dirty. Can you do that for me? I'll make it worth your while."

"Erm, okay. If that's what you want. Yes!" She gave him her mobile number and they parted, with a kiss and look that aroused him again.

*

The following Monday, Graham breezed into his somewhat dilapidated office in the Victorian park's old bowling pavilion and sat facing his opposite number, Geoff. Geoff did the same job as Graham, but covered a different geographical area.

Geoff was old school, a different animal in the new politically correct face of the council; a cynical 57 year old with a nicotine stained moustache and somewhat unfortunately ill-fitting glass eye that always peered down, the result of a golfing accident some 24 years earlier.

"Morning Grimy. Judging by the look on your face you had it over the weekend."

"Morning Geoff, I'm fine, thank you for asking and yes, I did meet an interesting lady and I think we have a lot in common actually."

"You mean you met a desperate old minger who was happy with your 3 ½ inch chipolata." He laughed a wheezy laugh at his own remark which he then promptly followed up with a 20 a day coughing fit.

"Thank you for your thoughts on the matter Geoff, but my private life is my own concern, thank you," Graham patiently replied as he flicked through the papers in his in-tray.

"Touchy. She must be fuckin' desperate though."

Graham ignored him. The rest of the morning proceeded without incident and little conversation between them. Graham checked spreadsheets of grass mowing regimes, plans for winter bedding plants outside civic buildings, and opened an invitation to judge the vegetables and flowers at a local show. Graham smiled. *That'll be nice* he thought.

At 12 noon Graham looked with derision at his colleague opposite as Geoff stretched and belched with a ferocity that startled a pigeon into flight outside the partially open front door.

Graham shook his head, stood up and took his packed lunch outside. He sat on a nearby bench to enjoy the September sunshine and somewhat fresher air. When he'd finished eating, he thought about what Frieda had said and took out his phone; after some deliberation, he texted a short message. An hour later, back in his office, the landline rang.

"Good afternoon, Graham Pilgrimm. How can I help?"

A familiar voice replied, "Good afternoon Mr. Pilgrimm. If you want to spend some more quality time with me again on Friday, you'll have to do better than that." The colour drained from his face. He started sweating, felt dizzy and had the beginnings of an erection.

"Hi... yes... I'll see what I can do."

"Good boy. I look forward to hearing from you," she said and hung up.

"What's up with you Grimy? You look like you've seen a ghost." Geoff's voice awoke him from his trance and brought him back down to earth.

"Oh, it's only Mrs. Granger from The Crescent again, about the fly tipping."

Geoff pushed his chair back and rested his head against the customer care charter on the wall. "You should tell her to sod off and clear it up herself. That's what I'd do. These old fuckers have nothing else to worry about. They make me sick. I'm going out for a fag."

Graham watched Geoff disappear out of the door, looked down at his phone and began to text...

*

The following Friday, they met by the lake again. Fuelled by a week of texts that pushed even Graham's imagination to its darkest limits, they had sex in the park again on the same spot, up on the hill. Back at the lake she turned to face him, put her arms around his neck and kissed him on the mouth, her warm tongue probing deeply. She gently withdrew and asked, "Where do you live?"

"Oh, not far. It's only round the corner really."

"I'd like to see it, if that's okay?"

"Yes... yes of course." Graham was suddenly pulled in two directions. Of course he wanted to get her back and into bed (where was he getting this energy from?) But at the same time, he was aware that his bachelor pad could have benefitted from a couple of days of serious deep cleaning to prepare it for the visit of someone like Frieda. Even with Anna there three days a week, it was very much a solo male residence. Nevertheless, his groin made the decision for him, and he took her home. If she was disturbed at the untidy condition of his flat, she didn't show it. Instead, once he introduced her to the bedroom, she didn't need a great deal of persuasion to test out the bed.

Later, as he lay on the now somewhat dishevelled bed, he watched her naked body through the open doorway as she wandered around the flat. She looked at his alphabetically arranged CD collection ranging from classic rock, through selective punk (not the rubbish stuff, but great bands like the Clash and Jam), through to indie and mid 90's Britpop. She smiled at his collection.

"Only a man would arrange things like this in alphabetical order and leave a sink full of washing up for, how long, two days? You are a dirty boy." She looked at him as she emphasised the words 'dirty boy' in a deeper sexy voice. It was four days worth of washing up actually – just about got away with that then.

He wandered through to the open plan lounge and kitchen area and found her staring at a small collection of gardening tools in a box tucked behind the large leather sofa, he'd managed to get custody of after the divorce.

"What's that?" she asked, looking at what appeared to be a small medieval hand held weapon.

"That's a billhook," said Graham as we wandered over behind her, putting his arms around her waist and pulling her cool, soft buttocks against his warm groin.

"A what?" Frieda said, pulling away slightly.

"A billhook. It's a tool for laying hedges."

"Are you taking the piss Mr. Pilgrimm? A tool for laying hedges?" She turned around, looking at him quizzically. Graham laughed at her comical expression.

"It's an old traditional country skill. You use it to cut most of the way through the hedge stems so you can bend them all over at the same 45 degree angle and then weave them through a line of stakes. It makes the hedge stronger and rejuvenates it. I used to do a bit of volunteer conservation work before I started working for the parks department."

"Nice tool," Frieda smiled and grabbed him between the legs.

*

Scud was big, not tall, but broad. Built like 'a brick shite house' as they used to say where he grew up. He had a large round head with close cropped red hair. In appearance he looked like an angry pumpkin. Scud looked at the nervous group of Poles in front of him.

"So what's the fuckin' problem, then?" He barked, slowly tapping the palm of his left hand with the pick handle in his right. A voice from the back replied in nervous broken English.

"We, err, were wondering. The money we were promised. It's not what we have actually received in our packets... Mr Scud... sir."

"Really? Well there's a fucking reason for that isn't there. We are more than two weeks behind on the job. You were supposed to have finished Phase One before the end of August and here we are mid September and...?"

"The materials. No good, you promised...!" A loud crack made them visibly jump as Scud struck the table in front of him with the handle. He then pointed it menacingly at the voice from the back.

"Now listen here Lenin, you and your mates fuck off out of this office and get back to work or I'm going to pick one of you at random and break his fucking legs, comprende? And you know I will, don't you?" Without a word, they backed off and left the office. "Fucking Hungarians," Scud growled to himself after they left. European geography was not one of Scud's strong points. To be honest, Scud was not the sharpest tool in the box, but did rather excel in the field of intimidation and actual bodily harm.

Simon Cudworth, or Scud as he'd been known since he was 11, was of uncertain fatherhood and born into a hard South Yorkshire mining community, when coal was still king. His career path, like generations before, was set out for him from the moment of his birth to Mollie Cudworth in 1979. He would go down the mines.

The problem was though by the time he left school, at the earliest opportunity it has to be said, most of the pits had closed. His options were limited, but a well meaning 'uncle' suggested an apprenticeship on a government training scheme to learn the building trade.

When Hyde Constructions got the scent of rich pickings via the development agencies investing in the former coal regions, they moved in to help create the new landscape of industrial units and retail parks where the pit heads and slag heaps once stood.

Hyde Constructions prospered. They were able to undercut their competitors and stole contracts from right under their noses. A big factor in this was the use of unregistered labour working cash in hand, overseen by charge hands who would not take any nonsense from the desperate and uneducated under their control.

One day Scud happened to be in the right place at the right time. He was a member of such a gang who just happened to be working directly under the nose of James Hyde, the man himself, while he was on a site inspection that day. Billy Brown was charge hand and made the mistake of picking up on an oversight in Scud's work. Scud turned, glared at him and without a word, he grabbed Billy by the throat, dragged him to the cement mixer and shoved his head inside, only releasing Billy when he begged for mercy and apologised. James was impressed and promoted Scud to charge hand that day.

Scud picked up the phone and called his boss. "It's me. I've told them. There won't be any problems now."

"Good." The deep, softly spoken, but rather menacing voice replied. "If we fail with this one, it's going to knock us back with Riverside and then we're all up Shit Creek."

"There won't be any problems," Scud repeated, with a slightly nervous waver in his voice.

"Let us hope not Scuddy Boy, let us hope not." James Hyde put the phone down and sat back in his well-worn leather chair in the gloom of his rather cluttered and dusty office in LS1, contemplating his next move. He puffed on a cigar and took a large swallow from a tumbler of whiskey on his desk. He fixed his gaze across the room at the bookcases and shelves, overloaded with musty files and documents. The limited natural daylight that managed to penetrate the grimy windows and yellowing blinds was soon sucked into the grey walls and the soiled brown carpet. Hyde's 'Dorian Gray' portrait was captured in the decay around his office space.

He was 62, slightly overweight and balding, but with a youthful complexion and shiny chubby cheeks that gave him an almost baby like face. He'd been a Freemason for 25 years and was a popular figure in civic circles for his company's support of the local arts scene and community projects. To those who didn't have the dubious pleasure of knowing him intimately he appeared a jovial man and kindly father figure, especially to the younger women who worked for him.

He'd recently been divorced after 28 years of marriage to a long suffering wife who one day decided she'd had enough. It wasn't just that he'd stopped caring; looking back, she didn't actually feel he ever had. No, she could live with that, it was the other things in his life that she struggled with; phone calls during the night to people she knew should have been behind bars, and those occasional visits to the house from furtive creatures whose eyes rarely met yours. Even worse though were the affairs with a succession of sad young women, fooled by his charm, wealth and obvious maturity; the sugar daddy, fatherly figure he was so good at portraying that offered them more than their 'immature' boyfriends. He would buy them expensive gifts, flatter them for a few weeks, screw them and then leave them.

So one day Barbara took the brave decision to leave, with the love and support of their son Sam who also had no intention of ever seeing his father again, except perhaps to dance on his grave. They'd found out that Hyde had paid a substantial amount of money to a private abortion clinic for a young woman, barely out of her teens. Barbara summoned the courage to confront him with this. He denied nothing.

So that was that. Barbara and Sam walked away to start a new life in Manchester, without a penny of his vast fortune. That didn't matter though. They were finally free.

Hyde didn't care either in the end. If Barbara had tried to claim any of his money though, or reveal the truth about his true nature, that would have been different. Wife, and even son, would more than likely have ended up blended into the concrete foundations of one of Hyde Constructions' monstrosities blighting the West Yorkshire skyline.

The only important person in James Hyde's life was James Hyde, with the possible exception of Frieda. Of all of the women he'd ever known, this one knew how to press all the right buttons. She gave him the best sex he'd ever had. The naïve young women he usually seduced all paled into insignificance with this woman who could blow you within an inch of your life. Once he'd met Frieda, there was no turning back.

They first met at a construction industry conference in 2006. She was there with her husband Pete and they were participating in the post dinner networking after the speakers and workshops had all concluded their business. It was obvious to Frieda at once that Hyde was interested. He couldn't take his eyes off her. When Hyde made an obvious move towards them, she was about to find an excuse to get away when Pete gently grabbed her arm.

"Look Frieda, it's James Hyde of Hyde Constructions, and he's coming this way."

"James Hyde? I don't think I've heard of him."

"He's only one of the biggest property developers in Yorkshire."

"Oh?" Frieda decided to stay instead.

Frieda and Hyde exchanged phone numbers that evening and two days later she slept with him. As far as he was concerned after that, there was nowhere else he wanted to stick his aging member. As far as she was concerned, he was the next stage on her career path.

*

Hyde Constructions had secured the massive Riverside project by unusual means. But if they weren't ready to deliver because of delays on this current project, even with friends in high places, this wasn't going to look good. Besides, there was the other more pressing matter to deal with.

Just at that moment, the phone rang and a familiar voice changed the expression on his face immediately.

"Hello there Mr. Hyde and how are you today?"

"All the better for hearing from you Fri. How are you my little sex kitten? I can't get you out of my mind." He instinctively reached down and unzipped his fly behind the desk.

"I bet you can't, and there's more to come later, believe me. First, though, I think I've found a solution to our little problem."

"Oh?"

"My inconvenient husband, of course, but we're going to have to move quickly. He's talking about going to the police."

"You don't think he suspects you are involved in all this."

"No worries for me there big boy, it's you he's after. Listen, I've got a plan, but I need a man."

"Don't you always."

"No, I'm serious. Are you alone?"

"Yes, why?" Hyde leaned forward and rested his elbows on the worn leather desk cover, instinctively looking around him, even though he was alone in the office.

"I want you to find someone who'll take my husband out."

"What? What do you mean?"

"You know perfectly well what I mean," the cold, Scandinavian accented voice clarified.

James Hyde had often employed violence, even the occasional terminal accident. Those were always carried out on his own terms though. He'd never organised it on anyone else's, especially a woman. This was risky.

"I've a plan. It's fool proof, listen..."

Five minutes later, James Hyde smiled a broad smile. "You are a genius, a bloody genius. Now get that sexy arse over here right now!"

*

The phone in Graham's office rang. "Graham Pilgrimm, how can I help?"

"Oh, I think we both know the answer to that." Graham stiffened in his chair, in both senses of the word.

"I want you to come over to my house tonight, about 7. My husband's away for a couple of days. I need to see you."

"Are you sure it's safe?"

"Absolutely. Now take down my address..."

At 6.55p.m., Graham stood at the entrance to the affluent cul de sac. He studied the houses. All were built of Yorkshire stone, each slightly different to give a semblance of individuality. Though not unattractive, each was still a victim of the high land values of the 1990s, having just that little bit too much house compared to garden.

Frieda's house was the last property at the head of the turning circle, facing him as he nervously walked towards it. *Why did she want him so early?* There was still too much daylight for his liking. Looking from left to right, he walked down the block paved drive and round to the back door. Looking around nervously, he swallowed, raised a sweating right hand and knocked, a little quietly at first, then harder.

Suddenly there was a piercing scream. Graham jumped back then, thinking Frieda was in trouble, he tried to enter the house. Was her husband here? As he tried the door he was pushed back...by Frieda.

"Go away! Stop following me! Leave me alone!" Graham was confused. *What was going on? Was she alright?*

"Wh...?"

"Leave me alone! I'm calling the police." Aware now neighbours were beginning to emerge from the surrounding properties he panicked and ran, as fast as he could.

That was the last time he saw Frieda. 48 hours later, his life would never be the same again.

*

Pete McArthur was 25 and fell in love with Frieda the moment he met her. In 2003 he'd just taken over the family business after his father had died prematurely at 59 of a heart attack, when he was invited to discuss a tender for the renovation of a dilapidated row of council owned terraces in Bradford. At the meeting, he noticed a young and rather attractive blonde secretarial assistant in the background, he later found out was called Frieda Olin. Born to Swedish parents, she'd moved to England in 1999, initially to study at Leeds

University, but later drifting into the sex industry. This part of her career history, she failed to divulge to Pete.

She had the face, the body and a natural gift. She was hot. The pay was undoubtedly good, but after a year of giving blowjobs to middle aged, overweight and frankly unattractive businessmen, she'd had enough. She had ambition and wanted to better herself via other paths. Her first "proper job" was administrative work for Bradford Council. She was on the lookout and spotted an opportunity at the terrace renovation meeting.

Pete McArthur was well off, but no millionaire, nor was he an oil painting, but he was a start though on her journey to a better life. They married in June 2005.

Pete adored her and wanted kids straight away. Frieda wasn't interested. This was never intended to be a long term relationship; it was just the first step on her career ladder. She had no intention of sticking around too long. Unfortunately for Pete, he didn't realise marrying Frieda would have serious implications for his health 5 years later.

In summer 2010, Pete heard on the grapevine that Hyde Constructions, a larger and more aggressive company than his own family business had, against the odds, secured the highly lucrative Riverside contract. This was a government agency backed project to renovate a large area of derelict warehousing on the south bank of the Aire, to create a new quality residential and retail development within walking distance of the city centre. It was worth millions.

No surprise then that a large company like Hyde Constructions should have been successful, except that the word on the street was that their bid was overpriced, incorporated poorer quality building materials and missed many of the finer important details a successful tender should contain.

Something was wrong. Pete did a little investigating and what he found shocked him. It was dynamite! He confided in no-one, except the one person in his life he could trust – Frieda. It was time to let the world know what had been going on. Unfortunately, Pete never got the opportunity.

On the evening of September 28th, 2010, around 8.40pm, there was a knock at the back door. Frieda was out at Zumba class and he wasn't expecting any visitors. He opened it and was greeted by the sight of a bulky man, around 30, with a round shaved head. It was difficult to see in the gloom, but it also looked like he was wearing gloves. That was strange, it was still warm outside.

"Yes?" said a confused Pete, "can I help you?"

"Are you Pete McArthur?" A gruff South Yorkshire accent enquired.

"Yes, that's right."

The man raised his right arm and the last thing Pete McArthur saw was a blade of some sort, descending towards him.

Chapter Two – On the run

Potatoes are an ideal crop for the beginner. If you only have a small plot, then concentrate on 'earlies', those that you can lift early in the season and enjoy as new potatoes when they are at their most expensive in the shops. Buy proper 'seed potatoes' in February and chit them before planting to help get them started quickly. To do this look for the 'eyes,' small bumps where the shoots will grow from, and then carefully put them in a container such as an egg box with the eyes uppermost. Keep in the warmth and light for 4 weeks and when the shoots are just under an inch long, plant them 6 inches deep with 12 inches between each potato, in rows 30 inches apart. When the shoots appear above the ground, start to 'earth up' by drawing up the soil around the shoots. This supports the stem, controls weeds and encourages a heavy crop. When the shoots start dying back, begin harvesting by carefully lifting with a garden fork. Boil with mint and add butter. Absolutely beautiful!

Down at the station a uniformed officer took Graham into a sparsely furnished room. Its battered plasterwork had been painted blue; to promote a calming effect Graham assumed. One small window of toughened glass high up the wall was the only source of natural light.

Two plain clothed officers were waiting there. The taller, slimmer and older of the pair, gestured for him to sit down opposite them at the table. Graham was getting nervous and was convinced he was going to fart. He managed to hold it in though, as he was aware the uniformed officer was standing directly behind him.

"Graham Pilgrimm?"

"Yes, yes, that's right." Graham replied nervously. The taller officer introduced himself and his colleague.

"I'm Detective Inspector Smithson and this is Detective Sergeant Hopkins." The shorter and stouter officer remained stony faced, with a heavy hint of hostility, thought Graham.

Smithson was 58. He still had a full head of hair, neatly combed and almost white. He had pale blue eyes, was dressed in a dark navy blue suit and matching tie. Hopkins by contrast was 49, with thinning dark brown greasy hair. He wore an ill fitting beige suit that didn't flatter his stouter figure and appeared to feel the heat more than Smithson, with a perspiring red face and noticeable sweat patches under the armpits of his suit. His menacing black eyes scrutinised Graham.

"Would you like some tea or perhaps coffee Mr. Pilgrimm?" DI Smithson asked pleasantly, with a clipped Yorkshire accent. It didn't put Graham at ease.

"Err, tea please. No sugar though... thanks."

"Would you constable please?" The uniformed officer left the room. Graham chose the moment to let a small pocket of gas slip out.

"Do you know why you're here Mr. Pilgrimm?" DI Smithson asked politely.

"No. Just that someone I know has been found dead." He was going to add *that's all*, but he thought that wouldn't be appropriate.

"So you knew him?" DS Hopkins chipped in.

"No, I don't know. Look nobody's told me anything." Graham sounded more aggressive than he intended.

"Mr. Pilgrimm," DI Smithson said calmly, "this is a very serious matter and I suggest you also take it more seriously." Graham noticed DS Hopkins' fists tighten.

"I'm sorry," he said.

"Sorry you did it? Sorry you got caught?" Hopkins interjected.

"No, sorry I... look what is this about please?" Graham pleaded.

DI Smithson continued, "On the evening of 28th September, a prominent local businessman was found dead in North Leeds, the Church Meadows development to be precise." The colour drained from Graham's face. He needed the lavatory. "You're familiar with the area?" Smithson noted, observing the visible change in Graham.

"Yes, my girlfriend lives around there."

"Girlfriend? Frieda McArthur by any chance?"

"Yes, that's right. Is she alright?" Graham started to stand up, but was gestured to sit down by Smithson with a wave of his hand.

"No Mr. Pilgrimm, she isn't. She returned home from an evening out and found her husband butchered by the back door."

"Oh my Lord!" Graham exclaimed in a shaky voice. "What happened?"

"We were hoping you would be able to help us with that Mr. Pilgrimm!" Hopkins growled, tightening his fists again.

"I don't know anything about this. Oh my Lord. This is terrible."

"Yes it is, isn't it Mr. Pilgrimm," agreed DI Smithson calmly. "Perhaps you'd like to explain your relationship with Mrs. McArthur in more detail please?"

"Well, we met a couple of weeks ago..."

"A couple of weeks?" clarified Smithson.

"Yes, Saturday 11th September. I don't know what time. We started dating then."

"Did she omit to tell you she was happily married Mr. Pilgrimm?" Smithson asked.

"She was separated. Her husband was a bully. She..."

"Liar!" Hopkins slammed his fists on the table. Graham jumped and broke wind again.

"What? No, it's true, she..."

"You saw her, she rejected your advances and you started stalking her." Hopkins challenged.

"I bloody did not! Who told you that?"

"Don't you speak to me with that fucking tone of voice you sicko!"

"What?"

Smithson ignored Hopkins outburst and continued in his measured clipped tones, "Mrs. McArthur told us all about it. She told you she was happily married and wasn't interested. You pestered her to go out that night, got hold of her mobile number and spent the next two weeks sending her abusive texts. Isn't that so?"

"No. She wanted me to. She liked it."

"How can a woman of that class and upbringing enjoy texts like that!" Hopkins slammed several sheets on the table. It was obvious at first glance it was a transcript of two weeks of his sexy messages to Frieda.

Oh shit, thought Graham.

"You are one sick fucker," Hopkins continued, "and if you don't start talking soon, I am going to lose my patience." Graham observed Hopkins tightened knuckles were now completely white. "What does that mean?" Hopkins asked, opening his right fist to point at one of the texts, "and that. That is fucking sick. That will cause internal injury. You should be put away for a long, long time you sick bastard!"

"Now look here. These were between me and Frieda. They are private. She wanted me to do it. She... got off on them." He winced as he finished, aware that Hopkins was losing it. Hopkins stood up, glared at Graham and gripped the sides of the table with both hands. He looked to be struggling to find the words. Graham was relieved that he didn't find them.

After what seemed an eternity, DI Smithson broke the silence. He said in his calm, but now not very reassuring voice, "The problem we have Mr. Pilgrimm, Graham if that's alright with you, is that your story somewhat contradicts Mrs. McArthur's version of events. Unfortunately, unless you can prove that Mrs. McArthur responded in a manner that collaborates with this story, I'm afraid you are on a bit of a sticky wicket." The last two words were pronounced with a staccato Rotherham accent, betraying DI Smithson's roots.

With a chilling realisation, Graham saw there was no evidence to suggest Frieda had asked him to do this, or going to be any evidence of a response on either his or her mobile. When she contacted him it was via his work landline, and received calls couldn't be traced with their Council's phone system.

Oh fuck, he thought as he felt a trickle of perspiration run down his spine.

The officer returned with the tea. As he passed it to Graham's somewhat shaky right hand, DI Smithson added, "There are one or two other issues of concern as well." Graham looked up mournfully. "Could you clarify please whether you visited Mrs. McArthur recently?"

"Yes," Graham replied, "three days ago."

"The evening of Monday 27th?"

"Yes, Frieda invited me round..." He knew as he was speaking the words, what was coming next.

"Unfortunately, that does not tally with Mrs. McArthur's version," DI Smithson corrected him. "She states that you turned up in an agitated state, in something of a frenzy, demanding sexual favours. To make matters worse," slight pause, "Graham," pause and a faint smile, "this has also been verified by several of her immediate neighbours."

Oh fuck. Graham put his head down into his hands and rubbed his eyes with his sweating fingers as he remembered Frieda's cries when he knocked on the door.

"Mr. Pilgrimm, there is another thing as well we thought you might be able to assist us with; the murder weapon, it was somewhat unusual. One of our uniformed officers found it in the back garden. It looked like it had been dropped in a panic. It seems to be some kind of gardening tool. We understand you are in the trade, so to speak, and wonder if you can help us identify what it is please?" He showed Graham a photo of a bloodstained billhook. Graham could tell at once from the marks on the handle, that it was his.

"It's called a billhook," Graham said faintly

"Is it?" DI Smithson said, with no surprise in his voice. He knew what it was. "Mr. Pilgrimm, we were able to lift a number of prints from the handle. All seem to belong to one man. It would be interesting to see a sample of yours please. Perhaps after you've finished your tea?" DI Smithson fixed Graham with a steely gaze with his pale blue eyes and said in that calm, precise voice of his, "in the meantime, Graham Pilgrimm, I'm afraid I'm going to have to inform you that you are charged with the following offence..."

The voice continued, but somehow flowed over Graham, like he was watching someone else in a live drama, as a member of the audience rather than the chief player. He was woken out his trance by a rather more familiar urge.

"I need the toilet," he said quietly.

"What!" barked Hopkins. "You'll fucking wait...."

"Mr. Pilgrimm, as I reminded you before, this is an extremely serious matter," interrupted DI Smithson.

"No, you don't understand. I occasionally suffer from an irritable bowel. I sometimes get sudden urges to go to the toilet, especially under stress."

"Are you taking the piss?" barked Hopkins.

"Most amusing Sergeant Hopkins," DI Smithson added drily.

"No, really. Look, check my medical records. *I have to go to the toilet.*"

There was something in the pained look on Graham's face that made DI Smithson reconsider.

"Alright Mr. Pilgrimm. Sergeant Hopkins, will you take him to the staff toilet just round the corridor please and, Mr. Pilgrimm, no funny business please. I hope you realise that you are in a lot of trouble."

DS Hopkins led him to the toilet without a word and stood outside while he entered. Graham lowered his trousers with shaking hands in the cubicle and temporarily enjoyed the feeling of relief as his bowel emptied. Despite the emotional stress he was under, he was aware of the heavy aroma in the air as he washed his hands afterwards. At least there's a window open, Graham thought.

A window!

He took a look. It was small but once he opened it to its full extent, a crazy realisation came to him. *I can fit through this.* He took a look down. He was on the first floor. Despite his fear of heights, it wasn't too high and there looked to be a pile of bin bags below.

This is madness!

But then what choice did he have? He was well and truly caught. He was going down. He had nothing to lose.

A voice barked through the door, "Hurry up. If you're not out in a minute, I'm coming in!"

The decision was made. He climbed onto the radiator and managed to get his legs through the window. He gently lowered himself, then felt a resistance. His trousers were caught on the window catch.

"Fuck!" He muttered. He wriggled and then felt his trousers tear as he slipped out of the window until he was just holding on to the window frame with his fingertips. *Now or never* he thought, and then he let go.

The bin bags were soft and he rolled off them. He got to his feet and ran. He wasn't sure where he was or where he was going, but he ran.

Hearing a commotion, Hopkins burst in and a quick look around revealed an empty toilet. He wrinkled his nose at the aroma as he went over to the window and looked down. He saw no sign of Graham anywhere.

"The little fucker...!" He growled and rushed to fetch DI Smithson.

Hurrying back to the toilet behind Hopkins, Smithson asked him, "Are you sure he's gone?"

"Well, the window's wide open and he's not here," Hopkins said with a hint of sarcasm in his voice.

"Have you not seen the 'Da Vinci Code' Sergeant?" Smithson asked. Hopkins had no idea what Pilgrimm's disappearance had to do with the Italian restaurant down the road, but he watched DI Smithson as he checked inside both cubicles opposite the sink.

"Sergeant, please organise a search of the building to check he's not still here, then put a call out for his immediate arrest. Tell them he's a cunning and dangerous man and, if they need to use force, then use it. He's the type who could kill again. I want him behind bars as soon as possible."

As soon as DI Smithson mentioned force, Hopkins smiled. *That's more like it.*

*

Once he realised he was a safe distance from the station he stopped, exhausted and aware he was attracting attention from passers by. This was partly as a result of being on his knees on the pavement fighting for breath and partly as a result of a large tear in his trousers which exposed his white boxer shorts underneath.

He took a look around and suddenly realised where he was. He couldn't go home. He knew that at least. His flat would be the first place they would look. But Dave lived less than a mile away!

At 1.35pm the same day, Frieda had her mouth around James Hyde's manhood when her mobile rang. She pulled away, subtly dabbed at her mouth with a tissue and answered it.

"Yes, that's right, who is this?" She listened intently. "Oh my God, no!" Something in her voice made Hyde listen. "How? When? Okay. You've got to keep him away from me. He's an animal."

"What is it? What's the matter Fri?" James asked when the call ended.

"That was he police. Pilgrimm's escaped from custody."

"What? How did he manage that? He's a fucking council gardener."

"Look, I don't know. James, I want him out of the way. If the police can't catch him, you find him, and get rid of him. I don't want him coming anywhere near me. You know people. Get him."

"Look, I will, my darling. Can we just finish...?"

"No. Nothing from me until you find him. I hope I've not underestimated him. What if he's dangerous? If he finds out the truth... if he spills the beans..." She bit the nail on her right index finger as she stared down at the bed.

"You mean no sex until...?"

"That's exactly what I mean." She looked up and fixed him with a steely gaze. "Wipe him out and you'll feel my lips around your dick again; until then lover boy, nothing."

Hyde watched her get up, get dressed and then drive away from his large Victorian country house. He was now seriously pissed off with this man he had never had the pleasure of meeting. Instead of lying down dead, he was fucking up their plans and, just as important, he was depriving him of the pleasure of Frieda's body. Pilgrimm was going to have to be disposed of and, the way he was feeling at the moment, his desire was to make it as nasty and painful as he could.

He wandered into the study and sat behind the antique desk in the middle of the room. Taking a key from his jacket pocket, he opened a locked drawer and took out a mobile phone. It was switched off. He turned it on and while he waited for it to warm up, he reached across the desk to a bottle of single malt and poured a substantial measure into a tumbler on the desk. He took a large swallow and then dialled a number in the phone's address file. It rang twice and a gruff voice answered.

"Yeah? Is that you Mr. Hyde?"

"Yes. Listen Scud, I've a job for you. I can't talk now, but I'll see you on site tomorrow, around 12. The pay will be good."

*

Graham tried to look as normal as possible, conscious that his boxers were visible to passing pedestrians, despite attempting to disguise the situation by wearing his shirt out of his trousers and strolling as casually as he could with his hands placed strategically over the tear in his trouser crotch. After what seemed an eternity, Carr Lane came into view.

Dave lived at number 19, half way down the row of Victorian brick terraces on the right hand side. He slipped into the gloom of the shared passageway that gave him access to the rear of the property and entered the back yard of Dave's house. It was then he remembered it was midday and Dave would be at work. *Bollocks*, he thought.

He was not going anywhere else now though. He realised the police would be after him and he needed to keep off the streets. At the rear of Dave's property was a disused out house, used as a tool store these days. Graham looked around, checked no one was watching him, then entered. He pulled the excuse for a door behind him, and waited.

What if Dave was going somewhere straight from work? What if he was going to Viv's and not coming back that night? He was just thinking of calling him on his mobile when he heard footsteps and tuneless whistling. Dave!

He waited until he heard him put his key in the door, then he crept out and touched him on the shoulder.

Dave yelled and spun around with his hands in the air. Graham leapt back in surprise and fell against the wheelie bins, and then to the floor with a clatter that set dogs barking and curtains twitching.

"Grimy, what the fuck are you doing? You nearly gave me a heart attack!" Dave gasped, clutching a take-away curry to his chest in a somewhat dramatic manner as he leaned against the back door.

"Look, just open the door and I'll explain everything. Quick, please! There's not a moment to lose." Graham tried to pull himself to his feet using the general waste bin, which suddenly gave way, resulting in another fall to the ground.

"Shit!" he muttered, standing up successfully this time, brushing the food waste and other unmentionables that had spilled out and on to him from the bin.

Dave could see the desperation in his friend's face and opened the back door, looking around the yard and over to the neighbours' gardens in a rather dramatic fashion for whatever or whoever had been pursuing him, as Graham pushed past him into the house.

"What's going on?" Dave asked once they'd entered the lounge, as he watched Graham close the curtains and sit down on a chair, exhausted.

Graham took a deep breath and, with the exception of one or two of the more intimate bits, started from the beginning and told him everything.

*

The first to be visited by the police were his parents. John and Mary were both in when they heard the knock on the door and, seeing the two uniformed officers on the doorstep, jumped to the same conclusion as Graham had earlier, that a member of the family was seriously ill or had had an accident. Annie's death was still raw in their memories.

"Mr. and Mrs. Pilgrimm?" One of the officers, with sergeant's stripes, asked politely as Mary opened the door.

"Yes, that's right. What's wrong officers? What's happened?" Mary asked anxiously. Her husband made his way from the lounge to the front door hearing his wife's troubled voice.

"Can we come in please?" She opened the door wider and they entered, looking around for any signs of Graham's presence as they went through to the lounge of 71 year old Mary and 73 year old John's 1930s semi.

"May we sit down?" The sergeant asked.

"Yes, yes of course. Officers what is it? What's happened?" John asked.

"Can I firstly confirm you are the parents of Graham Pilgrimm of St. Andrew's Parade?"

"Yes, we are. What's happened? Please tell us?" Mary repeated, even more anxiously this time.

"Mr. and Mrs. Pilgrimm, have you seen or heard anything from your son in the last 24hrs?"

"No, nothing. Is he alright? What's happened?"

"Mr. and Mrs. Pilgrimm, I'm afraid I have to inform you that we have a warrant for the arrest of your son... for a very serious crime... murder." Seeing the shock hit their faces he quickly added, "I am not at liberty to give too many details away at the moment, but he had been taken into custody this morning for interview and... erm... escaped, from a first floor window."

Graham's parents stared, open mouthed. Their son, *a murderer?*

No, not possible, not Graham.

"No, there's been a mistake. Not our Graham. You've got the wrong person."

"I'm afraid there's no mistake Mrs. Pilgrimm. I'm sorry if this has come as a shock to you, but the thing is we need to find him as soon as possible. We have to get to the bottom of this quickly. Can you give us any clues as to his whereabouts, perhaps the names of friends he may go to for help, or places he may hide out, feel safe?"

Graham's parents, both stunned, just stared and said nothing. The second officer spoke for the first time. "Mrs. Pilgrimm, if you believe your son is innocent, it will be in his best interest that he returns to custody as soon as possible. The longer he is out there, the more people will believe he is guilty and that won't help his case."

The parents looked at each other. Mary bit her lip and, after a long pause and glance at her concerned husband, started talking.

*

"That was a result." Sergeant Davies said, looking with some satisfaction at his notebook back in the car. I'm sure we'll have our man by the close of play."

Constable Stoker stared ahead. Something wasn't right. He was only young, had been on the force for less than 5 years, but he had a good instinct for people, for situations. This didn't add up. *Something was wrong.*

*

Something's wrong here, Becky thought. She sat near the back, well down the press pecking order at the conference, but as she looked up at the detective speaking, Smithson or something like that, and at the grieving widow to his side, she couldn't put her finger on it just yet, but something was wrong.

Becky Andrews was average height with shoulder length dark brown, almost black hair and attractive large brown eyes. Quiet and often overlooked, she usually ended up with the stories that nobody else was interested in, the leftovers after the rich pickings had been grabbed by her pushier colleagues at the Post. Still, she was thorough and diligent, and usually got to the bottom of what was going on. Under normal circumstances, it would have been highly unlikely she would have been here at all, the story of a local stalker, turned murderer, on the run. No, definitely one for her colleagues, especially the male ones she thought, looking at the attractive grieving widow in front of her. Fortunately for Becky, the short notice of the press call, resulted in her being the only available reporter that day.

She watched Frieda McArthur, firstly when the detective was addressing the gathering with the important information that nobody should approach Graham Pilgrimm as he was believed to be dangerous and could kill again, and then when she tearfully pleaded to all in the room, and beyond, to contact the police if they had any information leading to the recapture of the monster who had taken away the only man she had ever loved. It was an incredible, powerful and moving performance. Her voice was shaking and the tears flowed on more than one occasion, yet when the police offered her the chance to pause and have a break from the ordeal, she persevered.

And then, when she'd finished, Becky caught a fleeting glimpse from Frieda to someone at the rear of the room, just for a fraction of a second. A look of recognition and, was she reading too much into it, a fleeting look of satisfaction?

Becky peered behind to her left and looked towards the corner of the press room where Frieda seemed to be looking. It was difficult to identify the precise location and there were a number of people gathered, taking notes and photos, but one man was conspicuous by not writing anything down. He looked to be late middle aged, plump, with thinning hair. He was watching and yes, yes he was. He was smiling!

A few seconds later he was gone, but she'd seen him before. Where? Who was he? She had an extensive knowledge of the local media and his face didn't ring a bell. If he wasn't from the press and he wasn't the police, why was he there and how did he get in? Something told her he was involved in this and, judging by that fleeting look, perhaps Frieda was as well. *Something was definitely wrong.*

*

After Graham had finished, Dave let out a long slow breath.

"Oh my God Graham. What have you done?" He rubbed his temples as he stared at the ceiling.

"Nothing! I've done nothing other than fall for a woman who's used me. How can I have been so stupid?"

"Well, we did think you were punching a bit over your weight when we saw her in the Tap." Graham gave him a glare of contempt, a sliver of pride survived despite the seriousness of the situation. "Mate, I just don't know what to suggest. Look, I think you've got to go to the police and tell them everything. If you're innocent, the truth will come out…"

"What do you mean if I'm innocent? Of course I'm fucking innocent!"

"Okay, okay, I'm sorry. I mean the truth will come out. You can't keep running. They'll catch you sooner or later. Look, stay here tonight and then go to the police tomorrow. Do you want anything to eat? I picked up a chicken jalfrezi on the way home."

"No, no thanks, I can't eat a thing at the moment." Graham calmed down as he spoke. "Look, thanks Dave. I'll stay tonight and think about my next move."

Later that evening, they watched the police press conference on TV. Both stared open mouthed, transfixed by the visual spectacle. A couple of times Graham sensed that Dave was looking at him with a hint of anxiety. *Did Dave believe this woman?*

Then the phones rang. The West Yorkshire bush telegraph had kicked in. Most of the lads had seen it; hose that hadn't soon heard about it.

After the last of the current wave of callers was dealt with, there was a knock at the door.

They looked at each other. They knew if it was the police, both of them were in trouble. Another stern knock woke them from their trance.

"It might not be the police," suggested Graham.

"It is mate!" Dave replied after peering through the curtains. Then with increasing panic in his voice, "there's a police car in front of the house. Quick, upstairs! The loft!"

"What?"

"It's the only place I can hide you here. Quick, upstairs!" Dave repeated, urgently.

They ran up the stairs and Graham looked anxiously up at the tiny loft hatch almost half a mile up in the high ceiling of the Victorian terrace.

"I can't get up there! Even if I could there's no way I can get through that tiny hole!"

More banging on the door below. Dave rushed to the bathroom, opened the window and called to the officers below in a somewhat shaky voice, "Won't be a sec, be down in a moment!" Then, back on the landing, "look, I'll crouch down and you climb on my back."

"What? Haven't you got any ladders or something I can climb on?"

"No! Get up on my back!" Dave crouched down. Graham looked up, took a deep breath and then climbed on Dave's back. Wobbling precariously and with the occasional "oh... ow... fuck...

bugger!" from Dave, Graham just managed to balance on the unsteady platform below him enough to reach the hatch. He pushed. Nothing happened.

"It won't shift!"

"Ow, shit. Give it a push!" Dave hissed through gritted teeth. Graham pushed and as he strained, he broke wind, the stress proving too much for him.

"For fuck's sake Grimy!"

With a final push, the hatch moved.

"It's okay, I've got it!" He got his hands on the framework surrounding the hatch and pulled himself up, somehow managing to squeeze his middle aged spread through the hatch. As he put the hatch back into place, Dave rushed downstairs to open the door...

*

Graham emerged from the loft, brushing the dust and glass fibres from his clothes.

Checking for non-existent blood after banging his head on the roof truss he asked Dave, "Do you think they believed you?"

"I don't think so. To be honest, I think they saw right through me. I don't think they thought you were here, but they knew I was hiding something from them. Mate you're going to have to go."

"I can't go tonight. Besides, they'll be watching outside." Dave saw the logic, but he wasn't happy. He'd never broken the law, never done anything more criminal than 34 miles an hour in the 30 mile an hour limit, where the High Street became a dual carriageway (which should be 40 anyway looking at the width of the road). Anyway, harbouring a suspected murderer was something else.

"First thing in the morning. Sorry mate, but I am getting seriously stressed and I have a responsible job."

"Cheers Dave. I promise I'll be out, first thing."

*

Graham had a largely sleepless night. At least he'd managed to eat, even if it was just a bland cheese sandwich (he regretted not taking up the earlier offer of the jalfrezi) before he'd crashed out in the spare room. But at the sound of every car driving down the road outside, he listened anxiously on the off chance it was going to pull up outside the house and release more officers, keen to follow up the initial visit to his obviously nervous friend.

However, there were no visits that night and the next morning Graham felt like shit.

"I've got to go to work Grimy. Where are you going to go?"

"I don't know. I'm so tired I can't think straight. I'd better phone work, let them know I'm not coming in."

"Are you serious? You're an escaped convict. What are you going to say to them?"

"I'm hardly a convict. Look... I don't know. But I should ring."

"I'll leave you to it. I've got to go. You'd better get a change of clothes. Have a look through my wardrobe and take what you need. Have a shower first though. You're a bit... you know..." Dave paused and continued, "and you can stay here till I get back if you want. Keep out of sight and don't go near the windows."

"Cheers Dave. I appreciate that. I'll sort something out today. I'd better make a few calls first."

*

It was a normal Friday morning and unseasonably warm when John Edwards, Graham's line manager, received a call on his landline which made him jump out of his seat and spill his tepid coffee over his keyboard.

"Shit!" he said desperately mopping up the mess. "Graham, is that you? Where are you? What the bloody hell have you done lad?"

"Hi John. I've done nothing. It's complicated, but I've been framed and that's the truth. I've got to sort this out. John, bit unusual this, but I need some time. How do I book this off in the circumstances?"

"What...? Have you lost your marbles? You're on the run from the police for murder, not going for a week in Spain with the wife and kids!"

"Look, I know, but I don't know how to count this. I mean is it annual leave, sick time. What does it go down as?"

"Fuck me. I don't know. Maybe I'll consult the Terms and Conditions file and see where murder and escape from custody fits in with absence from work. Bloody hell Graham!"

It wasn't very productive, but Graham felt he should at least have made the call and felt better for it, even if it left John a little bewildered. His next call was to his parents – that was going to be a much more difficult conversation.

*

"Funny how no one knows anything, isn't it Sergeant." DI Smithson pondered, sitting back in his chair, not really expecting much of a response from DS Hopkins who was staring at the ceiling and absent-mindedly picking at his nose.

"That friend of his, Dave Butterworth did," Hopkins replied. "He knew something and he knew we knew it. I want to go back and put the squeeze on him."

"All yours, Sergeant. We appear to be drawing a blank everywhere else."

*

The day passed slowly for Graham. Feelings of frustration, boredom and anger entered his head randomly. He knew he couldn't run forever. He didn't want to. He had family, Anna, friends, a career of sorts. He wanted his life back. At the moment it wasn't his. He was standing on shifting sands. He was losing what little control he'd had on his life and it was deeply unsettling.

This was the first time he'd really taken stock and thought about his life, its lack of direction, his lack of ambition. He came to the unsatisfactory conclusion that his journey through life had not really been determined by his own decisions at all, but by the decisions of others. He'd allowed himself to be blown in the wind like a dandelion seed. Wherever it dropped him was where he took root. If he had ever had to make a decision about his life, it was always to go with the flow, take the path of least resistance.

So was this current situation really so different from his life prior to Frieda? To be at the mercy of others, relying on them for the decisions that mapped out the course of his life?

He looked in the mirror upstairs and saw the lines on his face that reminded him he was getting old. He'd never really felt like he'd grasped the responsibilities that go with age. In his head, he was still 25, not really long out of college and with all the time in the world. But this wasn't the case now. More than half his life had probably already gone and, if this situation didn't get resolved in his favour, a major part of his remaining years on the planet would be spent behind bars. He looked at his hair. At least he wasn't balding, not like Kev, but he was greying; distinguished, or just old?

For the fiftieth time that day he cautiously peered out of the window as a car past the house. This one pulled up a few doors down. The tinge of anxiety turned to relief as an Asian family got out. The kids piled out of the back as the parents argued in Punjabi.

He made himself another cup of tea and another sandwich. He was definitely getting his appetite back at least. He sat down and thought. He was going to have to do something about this. He couldn't run forever. He had to clear his name. He just needed a plan, a strategy of some kind; that and somewhere safe to stay. The answer would come later that evening and it was pure genius.

Dave returned around 6pm. "Grimy, we've got to sort this out."

"Damn right. I just need a place to stay, and then figure out how to get to the bottom of this and clear my name."

"No, I mean I've been thinking. I think you ought to go to the police. I'm... we... you, are going to be in deep shit if the police find out you've been staying here. The lads all know you're here. They could all go down for this as well if the police find out."

Graham felt the wind leave his sails. He needed help and he realised that to get that help, others were going to have to take risks on his behalf.

"Yeah, yeah, you're right. I don't know what I was thinking, I..." There was a knock at the door. Graham and Dave looked at each other nervously. A quick look out of the curtains didn't reveal any obvious police car or any vehicle Dave couldn't link to one of his neighbours.

"Who is it?" Dave asked the back door nervously.

"It's me, Tomo. Can you open the door?"

"How do I know it's you?"

"Of course it's me you wanker now open the fucking door!"

Dave opened the door and was flattened against the wall as Tomo burst in followed by Mac, Jim-Bob and Kevin.

"Look, it could have been the police for all I know."

"Bloody hell Dave, put the kettle on and let the dog see the rabbit."

Graham walked into the lounge and they all stared, momentarily speechless.

"Hi all," Graham said a little anxiously and delivered a half hearted wave with his right hand.

"God. You look awful Grimy." Mac broke the ice.

"Thanks Mac. I thought I'd dress down for dinner tonight."

"So what the effin' 'ell have you done Grimy?" Tomo finally addressed the elephant in the room.

They sat down and with a feeling of déjà vu and a deep sigh, Graham started at the beginning again.

*

DS Hopkins and a uniformed officer pulled up outside the brick built Victorian terrace on Carr Lane and, despite the curtains being closed, saw shadowy movement framed by the subdued lighting within. They approached the door and Hopkins knocked, licking his lips and smiling in anticipation.

Graham had just reached the end of the story, relieved to see that his friends actually seemed to believe him, when they all heard the knock.

"That's not fuckin' Avon calling," suggested Jim-Bob, momentarily pausing the rolling of a joint.

"Not the loft again, please," asserted Graham, raising his hands in a defensive mode.

"Open this door, now!" Hopkins barked.

"There's no time anyway," Dave blurted out in a panic.

"Look, if they haven't got a search warrant, we don't have to let them in," said Jim-Bob, who was more experienced in legal matters than the rest of the collective. He licked the joint, sealed it and placed it in his denim jacket pocket.

"If we don't let them in, that's just going to make them suspicious." Mac said.

"Mac's right," said Kevin. "Graham, just get behind the sofa and Dave, open the door." As if in a daze, Dave opened the door as instructed.

"Can we come in?" asked DS Hopkins with more than a hint of demand in his voice.

"Yes, I mean no. Look what is it? You asked me everything I knew this afternoon and I told you."

"Well Mr. Butterworth, I'm not sure I believe you. And if you're not telling me everything you know, you could well go to prison for a very long time. Do you understand me?"

"Perfectly officer, thank you," a calm voice clarified from within the house. It was Jim-Bob, who continued, "and may I ask, do you by any chance have a warrant to search this house?"

"No, I don't, but if Mr. Butterworth has nothing to hide, then he'll let us in!" Hopkins hissed through gritted teeth.

"Sorry officer, I understand where you are coming from but it's the principal you see. Now if you return with a warrant, I'm sure my friend Dave will be more than happy to let you in," he smiled warmly at DS Hopkins as he stepped into the light of the doorway and gently placed his hand on Dave's shoulder.

"Now you listen here you little fucker...!"

"Sir!" a voice interrupted DS Hopkins, "I think we'd better leave." Constable Dirker had seen his friend and colleague get into bother before for crossing the line, even been implicated in the occasional 'he-accidentally-fell-down-the-stairs' situation before. A tactical retreat seemed like a wise move. Reluctantly and after a significant pause, Hopkins turned and left, turning back briefly to glare at Jim-Bob.

"I'm going to have you, all of you. You've made the biggest fucking mistake of your pathetic tiny lives."

"He's a charmer, isn't he?" said Jim-Bob after the car had driven away.

"Fuck me we're in trouble now" gasped Dave.

"So not a moment to lose," said Tomo, clapping his hands together and settling back in the armchair by the fireplace. He pressed his fingers together as if in prayer. "Kev if you'll present our friend Graham with your idea please?" He gestured to Kevin in a somewhat regal way to continue.

Kevin coughed and began, "Graham, you need somewhere to stay while you... we come up with a plan of action."

"Yes?"

"Well, how about Shed Heaven?"

"Shed Heaven?" Graham paused, then repeated, "Shed Heaven, yes. Bloody hell, you're a genius." Shed Heaven was the 'magnificent erection' as Tomo like to call it down on Kevin's allotment plot. It was simply the mother of all garden sheds, built by the previous tenant who'd just completed the structure before conveniently dropping down dead with a major coronary immediately afterwards; legend has it as the last nail was driven into the final piece of timber cladding its regal form. Kevin, being next on the council waiting list, was lucky enough to inherit it, together with its 10x20 yard plot. Located at the far end of the allotment site from the main gate, close to the canal, it was the perfect retreat from the day to day and an ideal refuge in the closing stages of Kevin's turbulent marriage to Jacqui.

"Shed Heaven." Graham nodded as he repeated the name.

Tomo continued. "What we've agreed is that each day, one of us will come down with supplies and a charged battery for your mobile. Mac's got a camp bed and sleeping bag in the back of his car which he'll lend you. We need to move fast though, Mr. Plod will be back soon, possibly tonight..."

"Oh God," moaned Dave wringing his hands. Tomo looked at him briefly with contempt, then turned back to Graham.

"... So, the sooner we move, the better. Pack some food and all your stuff. Leave nothing behind and Mac will take you down to the site. His car's round the corner. Me, Kev and Jim-Bob will leave now and move out in opposite directions. We'll make sure the coast is clear and then give you a call before you set off. Good luck mate."

Graham, for the first time since his visit to the station, realised he was not alone. He had friends who were prepared to fight his corner and that felt good, temporarily at least.

"Thanks guys. You've been amazing. I owe you big style."

"No problem Grimy," said Jim-Bob, pulling the joint out of his pocket as he spoke, "next time I'm up for murder, I'll call on you for a favour."

One by one they departed and each checked vehicles and people hanging around Carr Lane as they went off in their various directions. Tomo and Jim-Bob rang after a couple of minutes to give the all clear. Mac and Graham were about to leave when a call from Kevin stopped them in their tracks.

"Don't leave yet. They're in a car at the top of the Lane, near the junction with High Street, watching the house. I don't think they noticed I'd spotted them, but if you are leaving now they've got you!"

"Oh God," cried Dave again, dramatically raising his hands in the air as if about to surrender to an invisible enemy.

"What do we do now?" asked Mac, ignoring the outburst.

"The wall at the back of your yard, what's on the other side?" Graham asked Dave.

"Oh, I don't know, a timber storage yard I think. Why?"

"If I go over that way, can I get out onto a road?"

"I don't know. I've not been in their yard before funnily enough." Dave replied with a hint of sarcasm.

"Don't be like that Dave. Look, I don't think I've a choice. I've got to give it a go. Mac, can I meet you in about 10 minutes near the crematorium gates up the lane."

"No problem, see you there. I'll give you a five minute start and I'll bring your stuff with me."

"Cheers Mac. And thanks for everything Dave."

"No problem, anytime," said Dave, not too convincingly. Graham did a quick final check to see that he'd got all of his few possessions together for Mac, including some spare clothing from Dave.

"Good luck mate," Dave said, more convincingly this time.

With a last look back around, and a nod to Dave, Graham was off.

Scaling the wall at the rear of the yard wasn't too difficult; dropping into the dark on the other side did create some anxiety. But it couldn't be as bad as a drop from the first floor of a police station toilet window.

He landed easily. A quick glance around indicated the coast was clear and he made his way past assorted piles of sawn timber of various lengths until he glimpsed a street light in the distance. He made his way towards it, hoping it would ultimately guide him somewhere close to the site entrance.

As Mac left for his car with Graham's small bag of possessions, something niggled at the back of Dave's mind about the yard behind his house.

Oh bugger yes. He knew he'd forgotten to tell Graham something...

*

There was a substantial gate at the yard entrance, difficult to climb, but not impossible. Graham was just pondering his next move when a sudden noise and movement grabbed his attention from the right.

Oh shit, thought Graham. *Oh fuck.*

It was some sort of hound. It contained a substantial amount of German Shepherd, plus one or two others of the angrier varieties of breed. Whatever its genetic makeup, it was seriously pissed off and judging by the way the growling mound of hair and teeth was running towards him, he probably had less than 3 seconds to make his move. Unfortunately, he was probably around 10 seconds off the gate. His only hope was a small, square brick built storage shed to his left. Realising he couldn't get in or climb on top of it, he ran behind it.

The beast veered around it to locate its prey, snarling, with jaws opening to get a mouthful of Graham's flesh. High on adrenaline, Graham began to run in a frantic clockwise direction around the building, with the beast in hot pursuit. This carried on for what seemed like an eternity to Graham, but was probably less than a minute.

It was clearly not a sustainable form of avoidance. Graham began to realise his middle-aged body could take no more. He was going to have to give in and surrender to the beast.

As he made his way round the shed for what he decided would be the final time, he became aware of a piece of timber on the ground, roughly 3 feet long by 2 inches across. He stooped and grabbed at it as he passed. Gripping the weapon firmly with both hands, he turned to face his tormentor with the idea of striking it firmly on the head.

Instead, as soon as the beast saw the stick, its mood changed dramatically and it started leaping up at it, barking and wagging its tail. It wanted to play.

Graham thought fast. "Here boy, fetch!" He threw the stick in the opposite direction, with the giddy beast quickly in pursuit. Graham ran to the gate, with a slight wobble in his legs, his head spinning as a result of spending the last few minutes running round in a circle.

Graham got to the gate, and was just about to leap up and climb over, when the beast returned with the stick. It dropped it at Graham's feet and began barking at him to throw it again.

"Good boy. Fetch!" Graham threw the stick again, as far as he could, and started climbing the gate as quick as his tired body would allow.

He made it to the top and began scaling down the other side as the beast returned. It barked for more. Graham was safe from its jaws, but anxious the noise could attract the attention of passers by. He tried to climb the final five feet to the ground as quickly as possible, but couldn't. He was being impeded by something. A quick check round revealed that the trousers Dave had provided to replace his torn pair, were caught on the gate.

"Oh bollocks, not again!" he exclaimed as looked down. He couldn't free himself so once again he let himself drop to the ground, hearing the familiar rip of trouser material. Once on the roadside, he ran with what little strength was left in his legs, to the rendezvous with Mac.

"What took you so long?" asked Mac, once he'd piled into the back of the waiting Audi.

"Just an appointment with the Hound of the Baskervilles, but I think we're friends now."

"Oh, okay," said a bemused Mac as he started the car.

*

The entrance to the allotment site was kept padlocked to prevent theft, vandalism and nocturnal lovemaking within the treasured plots of the current holders. Graham, like all the plot holders, had a key to the gate and luckily kept it attached to his house keys, which he had with him.

He gathered his things together, including the camping equipment his friend had provided. With a quick check around that the coast was clear, Graham thanked his friend, unlocked the gate and entered the site.

He waited for the Audi to disappear. Then, with another quick look around, he locked the gate behind him and headed off into the night towards Kevin's plot. Despite the lack of lighting, he was familiar enough with the layout of the site. He had walked this route several times each week for the last 12 years or so and could probably have done it blindfolded. It helped that his plot was located in the same vicinity as Kevin's. Although he'd packed a torch, he did not risk drawing any attention to himself from any passers by beyond the security fencing surrounding the site.

The track continued in a straight line for around 200 metres, lined on both sides with standard sized ramshackle plots separated by a herringbone pattern of mown grass paths that gave access to plots beyond the ones immediately lining the track. The track then stopped at a small car park, surfaced with crushed stone to prevent cars getting bogged down in bad weather. Graham turned round and could just about still make out the locked gates in the glow of the street lighting beyond. He turned back and continued along the track as it left the car park to his right and continued in that direction for 20 metres. The track then turned a sharp left, continuing through the site in roughly the same direction again as the initial track from the gate. A quick glance back from here confirmed the gate had disappeared from view altogether now.

He continued down this track for another 200 metres until it ended at a second car park, not quite as well surfaced. Beyond this was a fence that backed on to the canal. Prior to his current circumstances, he would normally have branched off to the left, some 100 yards or so back, to find his own plot, located 20 yards down one of the grass access paths. Tonight, though, he was heading for Kevin's. To get there he turned off to his right, just before the car park, and headed down a path, passing two further plots on either side until he came to his destination.

It had a neatly mown grass path down the middle with beds on either side and at the end of the path stood the impressive timber structure known to all on site under the age of 50 as 'Shed Heaven'.

Facing Graham was a bank of windows on the east side of the shed which caught the first rays of the sun in the morning, perfect for warming those fragile seedlings on the shelves inside. The door was found at the south side of the shed, to Graham's left as he faced it. He carefully made his way round in the dark and let himself in.

*

"James Hyde's office, can I help you?" Sharon, the 22 year old and occasionally groped receptionist enquired when the call came in first thing Monday morning.

"Is Mr. Hyde available please?" A softly spoken, educated voice enquired, a touch agitated.

"I'm not sure. Who shall I say is calling please?" She asked with a somewhat disinterested tone in her voice as she browsed the catalogue looking for some suitably expensive gift for Hyde to buy her, as payment for the extras that seemed to go with this job.

"Can you tell him it's Councillor David Neil and I need to speak to him urgently please?"

"I'll see if he's available. Can you hold please?" She pressed a button on the phone which put her through to Hyde. "I've a call for you Mr. Hyde. Are you available?"

"Can you tell them I'll ring them back? I'm in the middle of something."

The 'middle of something' was James Hyde sat behind his desk with his flies down, surfing pornography on his PC. Frieda had not been joking when she'd threatened to withdraw favours until Graham was encased in the foundations of his next building project and now, even after only a couple of days without a visit from Frieda, his walnut sized scrotum felt the size of a melon. He was getting desperate.

"It's Councillor David Neil, Mr. Hyde, and he says he really needs to speak to you now." At these words, James Hyde pondered for a moment then exited the website.

58

"Alright, I'll take it now... Hello David, how are you?" he spoke as he cleared his search history. Well, you never know do you?

"Fine, fine. Look what's happening with Riverside? You were supposed to have confirmed deadline dates and returned the contract paperwork we sent out two weeks ago. The office has heard nothing. People are getting nervous."

"Sorry David. We just had a couple of hitches with the current project, but that all seems to be sorted and we're back on course. The workforce is pulling out all the stops now. I'll get dates and paperwork out to you this week."

"James, please don't mess me around with this. I stuck my neck out for you. You know what I mean..."

"Don't try that one David. You've done alright out of me over the years and we know who's going to end up with a nice little nest egg at the end of this one as well, don't we?"

"Look, James. Please... no later than Thursday..."

Councillor David Neil was seriously regretting ever getting involved with James Hyde in the first place. He'd met him at a regeneration networking meeting six years ago. Neil had been having a few personal financial problems and was vulnerable. A recreational gambling habit had become a serious addiction that he'd only just managed to keep secret from his wife and colleagues.

Hyde had been doing the rounds and testing the water with a few people of influence, when he finally got round to Neil. After a few pleasantries, Hyde steered the conversation towards his thoughts about a possible two way business arrangement. The temptation was too great for Neil. His palms were sweating as they spoke about how much money he could earn.

It was too much for a weak and vulnerable man and greed soon poisoned Neil's mind. He looked beyond the simple payment of gambling debts, to the extra benefits the money could provide; cars, foreign holidays and more, much more.

From that meeting he was hooked. A matter of weeks later he received his first payment for a small scale construction project in the Wakefield area.

Shortly before Riverside though, Neil decided he was going to cool the arrangement with Hyde. A construction worker had fallen four stories when some sub-standard scaffolding had collapsed. It had been erected by an unqualified work team working cash in hand. The worker survived, but sustained serious leg injuries that would stay with him for the rest of his life. Of course, there was an investigation, but palms were greased, Masonic favours called and the injured worker received a private settlement from Hyde's company. They got away with it... just.

If Hyde would have accepted Neil's resignation a few months earlier, it was out of the question now. When Riverside was proposed, Hyde knew at once he was in reach of the ultimate prize. This would not only offer him the greatest earner he was ever likely to receive, but he would also become a legend in the construction industry if he pulled this one off. Hyde needed Neil's support more than ever.

When Neil approached Hyde with his 'resignation', thanking him for such a successful arrangement that had benefitted them both so much, but he'd rather draw a line under that part of his life and move on now... he was met by a stony silence. Hyde simply looked at him and took a large swallow of whiskey as they sat at their table in the fashionable city centre bar. After a pause, Hyde expressed his disappointment and suggested they reconvened their meeting the following day in Hyde's office.

The next day an anxious Neil turned up on time, not sure what to expect. He was admitted into the office by a couple of short but bulky men. They led him into Hyde's inner sanctum where he found him sitting back in his chair behind his desk and smoking an expensive cigar. Hyde greeted him warmly and gestured for him to sit in a chair next to him. Neil looked nervously at the two men who also occupied the office, one who stood behind them as they sat at the desk, while the other stood by the door. On the desk in front of them was Hyde's PC. Hyde clicked with the mouse.

Within two minutes, it was clear that pulling out of Riverside wasn't going to be an option for Neil. It wasn't just the substantial amount of money that was going to be transferred into an offshore account that was going to persuade him to support the Hyde Construction tender for the Riverside project. No, unfortunately for Neil, the deciding factor was 25 minutes of footage of happily married with 2 children Councillor David Neil, chair of the regional development agency, recorded in unusual circumstances with an attractive Swedish blonde in a hotel bedroom, after the concluding night of a conference in Harrogate.

The footage showed Frieda, dressed in leather and carrying a whip, leading the naked form of Cllr. Neil as he crawled on all fours around the luxurious hotel bedroom on a dog's lead.

It was grainy and jumped a couple of times, but there was no mistaking the similarity between the 57 year old councillor who sat staring at the screen grim faced and the figure on the screen, at one particular moment having his backside tapped with a whip and the words, "If doggy wants to show me his bone he's going to have to do what mistress says," coming from the mouth of the Swedish mistress.

"What? How? When...?"

"Oh Cllr. Neil, or do you mind if I call you David as I think we're going to be good friends again now, despite last night's little episode; so many questions. I'm sure you remember the occasion. A rather good speech I recall at the close of the conference. Words along the line of *the development board leading the way out of recession*. I think you were the one being led there don't you think?" Hyde chuckled as he gestured at the screen. Scud and his accomplice joined in.

"You can't... you won't..."

"We can and we will. However, this footage will only come to light if Hyde Constructions fails to secure the Riverside redevelopment or if you are foolish enough to go further with this. And don't try and take the disk. I have copies," he added as Cllr. Neil moved towards the laptop. "If everything is successfully concluded, there'll be a nice little bonus for you, as usual. Everyone's a winner." Hyde sat back in his chair, put his fingertips together and smiled, his cigar clamped between his teeth.

*

Graham woke just before 7.30 am to a sunny early autumn day, after the best night sleep he'd had in days. Arriving at Shed Heaven in the dark, he'd set up his camp bed as best he could with only the light from his mobile to help him. Despite the tools and stored boxes of recently harvested vegetables, there was still plenty of room to set the bed up in the remaining space. He'd crawled into his sleeping bag exhausted and fell fast asleep, almost at once.

As he lay in his sleeping bag he put his hands behind his head and took in his surroundings that first morning. The windows on the east side, illuminated by the morning sunshine, offered excellent views over most of the site to the fenced boundary with the elevated road beyond, as it rose to meet the bridge carrying it over the canal.

The downside was he would have to be careful as it could also work the other way, offering the curious a view of him in the shed. The door faced him and had a lock on the inside. *I might need that*, he thought.

The timber walls supported a rustic and somewhat random pattern of shelves filled with tools and pots, interspersed with harvested vegetables; mainly onions, shallots and garlic, hanging and drying. There were numerous cardboard storage boxes piled around, most containing potatoes as far as he could tell. *He's done well with his spuds this year*, thought Graham to himself. In the corner of the shed was a stack of miscellaneous garden chairs and seating for those moments when the lads got together to take a break, have a beer and the occasional smoke.

He lay back, conscious he needed a wee, but too warm and comfortable to move. As he lay back, he thought about what he would normally be doing today? He thought about the football. He'd missed the last game – didn't even know the result. That was a first.

A memory popped into his head. Frieda. He remembered the feel of her astride his manhood and before he knew it, he was up. There was nothing else he could do. He reached down into the sleeping bag and was almost there when the door burst open.

"Bloody hell Kev! You could have knocked!" He said pulling his hands out of his sleeping bag with lightning reflexes.

"What are you doing?" asked Kevin, looking suspiciously at the sleeping bag.

"Nothing. Just stretching."

"Hmm..."

"Anyway, it's good to see you mate."

"How did you get on last night?"

"Slept like a log and feel okay, in the circumstances." He stretched and yawned.

"Well, look, I've brought a bacon butty and a flask. Thought a cooked breakfast wouldn't be a bad start to the day. And I've brought you some reading matter."

"Oh cheers Kev. That's really appreciated. I've got to get this sorted though, as soon as possible. I'm going to need some help."

"How about a gathering of the clan this afternoon, say 2pm here in Shed Heaven?" There was no footy that day for the lads, so 2pm would probably be an empty slot in all the lads' diaries.

"Sounds excellent Kev, thank you." With that, Kevin departed and left Graham to his bacon butty, flask of tea and porn mags.

*

Becky wasn't due in the office that day, but she took advantage of the empty and, for once, quiet office to check the Post's image archives on her PC. *Where had she seen that man at the back before?*

She had an excellent memory for faces. Remembering their names and when she'd first seen them, well that was another thing. So trying to recall where she'd seen this one before wasn't easy, but she knew she'd suss it. She usually got there in the end. She'd definitely seem him somewhere before. *Where though?*

She squinted and wrinkled her nose to one side, a habit she had when thinking. Her male colleagues used to make fun of her when she did this, not in a malicious way. Taking the piss was part of the culture. One or two used to watch her though when she did this, laughing outwardly with their colleagues, but inwardly falling for her. She was attractive, and a lot more attractive than she really believed herself. Coming out of a long term relationship in the manner she had done, had seriously affected her confidence. As she searched the archive, fragments of a memory returned to her. It was one of the last conversations she'd had with Andy.

"Why?" she pleaded with him, her eyes stinging with tears. "Why did you do it Andy? How could you? I loved you. I would have done anything for you. We had all those plans for the future."

"I'm sorry Becky. I'm really sorry." He looked down at the floor. He couldn't meet her eyes. Despite all he'd done, all he was still doing, he felt for her. He didn't love her and there was nothing he could do about that and Becky knew it. These things happen. You can't help your feelings. What hurt more was finding out that he'd been sleeping with the other woman for nearly two years.

A noise outside the office drew her back to the present. She was aware she'd been crying and reached for a tissue to blow her nose. As she did, something entered her mind about her mystery man. He was a business man. It was some sort of event, a launch, conference – no it was a charity do.

That was it! It was last Easter at that arts centre. His company, Hyde Constructions, had just donated £5,000 towards a performing arts project targeting underprivileged kids. James Hyde. That's him. So what's the connection between him and Frieda McArthur?

Far from satisfying her curiosity, this only raised more questions. She went to the drinks machine in the corner of the office and drew out some tepid brown sludge pretending to be coffee, fixed her large brown eyes on the PC monitor and wrinkled her nose again.

*

After his breakfast, Graham cautiously opened the shed door and checked the coast was clear. There was no sign of anyone around. He picked up the wash bag Dave had lent him and, looking around him as he went, made his way round to the back of the shed to the compost heap.

After enriching its fertility he found the water tap at the boundary of Kevin's plot that he shared with his neighbour, an ancient being called Joe. Graham had a wash, cleaned his teeth and immediately felt more human again.

Hearing the metal gate bang shut at the far end of the site alerted him to the arrival of the first of plot holders of the day, so he reluctantly left the early morning sunshine for the shade of Shed Heaven and awaited the arrival of the lads.

As he waited, he peered through the windows to see if any of the morning shift were working on the plots in the vicinity of Kevin's. He made sure he was far enough back in the shadows of Shed Heaven not to be spotted by anyone getting too close.

A few minutes after he heard the gate, a middle-aged Chinese woman passed the plot on the left hand side as Graham looked out. Mrs. Lin had been a widow for four or five years. She held the plot immediately behind Kevin's. Graham made a mental note to interview her one day, if life ever returned to normal. She grew some exotic vegetables that even Graham had never seen before. He thought one day it would be really interesting to do an article on how allotments were shifting away from the traditional flat cap working class image they used to have, into the multicultural melting plots their site represented. As well as the Chinese community; Asian families, Africans, Caribbeans and recently, eastern Europeans, rented plots on the site. Graham loved the diversity and the new plant varieties and growing techniques that came along as well. There was always something new to learn. Perhaps it might even become a book one day. Graham smiled an ironic smile to himself. He knew what he was like – full of ideas but how many ever became reality.

A movement to his right caught his eye. The stooping figure of an old man with a thick head of white hair came into view. It was old Joe. He paused as he passed Kevin's plot and lit a roll up. He coughed a deep chesty cough, caught his breath and moved out of view and on to the plot next door. *They'll be the death of him one day*, thought Graham. He needs to watch himself at his age.

The rest of the morning passed without incident. Graham read a little and dozed.

*

Anna opened her black Toshiba laptop, booted it up and checked her messages. There was the usual rubbish on Facebook. She learned that Vicky from her class was a slag and that her cousin Maisy's status was 'hung over' – *silly girl* she thought. Maisy was the same age as Anna. She brushed her straight mousy blonde hair out of her eyes and checked her Hotmail in-box.

Result! That was what she was waiting for, a message from Laura. Laura was Kevin's daughter. She spent most her time with her mum Jacqui in Wakefield after they sold the family home in Leeds, but she still went to the same school as Anna and they remained close friends.

While visiting her dad, she'd done some investigating on behalf of Anna and, after listening in on a few whispered conversations her dad made on his mobile, she finally made the breakthrough.

*

As the morning passed slowly by, Graham's mood changed hour by hour and minute by minute. His emotions fluctuated between frustration, relief to be free and then to anger at how he ended up in this situation in the first place. Why him?

He supposed if it wasn't him it was going to be somebody else. Frieda just needed a fall guy to pin a murder on. He'd fallen for it alright and, unfortunately for him, her too, big time.

Above all, he worried about what he was going to do next.

Just after noon, he made himself a cheese sandwich. He realised he'd nothing to cook on. A mug of tea would have gone down well. He made a mental note to ask the lads for a small camping stove. That triggered another thought. How long was going to be down here?

He stared at the shed wall, his mood slipping towards depression, when a sound brought him round. It was a slow and steady thumping noise. He initially wondered if it was someone at the shed door. No, it was too faint for that. He listened hard. The sound stopped. Graham was just returning back to his thoughts when it started again. This time he thought he heard a low cry, a woman or a child. Where was it coming from? He picked up a direction for the sound. It was Joe's plot, more accurately Joe's shed, by the sound of it.

It was out of sight of Shed Heaven's windows, but on the blind side of Shed Heaven, a knot hole offered a glimpse of Joe's plot. He peered through and confirmed the sound was indeed coming from Joe's shed. A fear crept into his head that Joe could be having a seizure or heart attack. But then there was that cry that didn't sound like Joe's voice.

The noise stopped and there was silence. Graham stayed glued to the hole for the next five minutes. He was just about to dismiss the event as a figment of his imagination, when he heard the sound of Joe's shed door opening.

Graham's jaw dropped as Mrs. Lin appeared at the door, checked that the coast was clear, and adjusted her clothing. She turned back to face the shed's interior, said something Graham couldn't make out, then left.

Well well well. The dirty old sod! Graham smiled to himself.

The encounter between Joe and Mrs. Lin in Joe's shed cheered Graham up enormously and he was in a much better mood when the lads turned up later.

A couple of minutes past 2pm, Graham heard a tapping at the window. He jumped up and was immediately relieved to see Kevin looking in. Kevin pulled back from the window and tried the door, but it was locked. Graham didn't want to take any chances, so he'd put the catch on. He got up and opened it to see Tomo, Kevin and Jim-Bob standing outside.

They came in and sat down on the varied pieces of garden furniture piled in the corner that Kevin had accumulated over the years - none of it matching any of the other pieces there.

"How's it going Grimy?" asked Tomo. "You've made it look a proper home from home."

"Very funny," replied Graham. "Where are the others?"

"Dave's gone to stay with Viv for a couple of days," said Tomo. "He's majorly stressed. That arsehole of a copper came to see him again and we told him afterwards to get out of the house or he was going to crack and give the game away if he came again."

"It'll do him good to stay with Viv and empty his sacks a bit more. That should relax him a bit," added Jim-Bob helpfully.

"Mac's coming down later," said Kevin. "He'll ring when he's at the gate." Mac and Dave weren't plot holders, but regularly called down when the lads were around to share a beer and the occasional smoke.

Jim-Bob reached into his jacket pocket, pulled out a tin and rolled a couple of joints as they chatted. Jim-Bob was their main provider. He'd acquired contacts while at university who'd kept him regularly supplied with consistently good grass in the years since.

"Oh, that is good," said Graham. The stress evaporated instantly and he felt in a much better mood after only a couple of deep drags. He passed it on to Tomo and barely noticed as the door opened and a leathery brown face with pure white hair and a couple of day's stubble on a wrinkled chin peered round.

"Now then lads – I thought you must be in. I saw the smoke signals coming out of the roof from Sitting Bull there." Old Joe gestured towards Tomo. Joe then noticed Graham, who immediately tensed as he sat on the bunk. Joe raised his hands. "Before you say anything kid, I saw the news and what's been said, well it's all bollocks. You couldn't even kill that rabbit you cornered in your plot last year, never mind kill a man. You don't need to worry about me son. My lips are sealed."

"Cheers Joe. You're a good one," said a relieved Graham.

"Pull up a pew and rest your rickets Joe," said Tomo. "Here have a drag on this. You'll last another hundred years with a good lung full." Tomo passed him the joint which he took in his knobbly old fingers, drew it to his stubble and took a deep pull.

"Ahh. I can feel the aches and pains melting away. That's good shit."

"Who do you think you are, Bob Marley?" laughed Tomo. "Anyway, there's nothing like a good smoke when you've just had a Chinese takeaway. You sly old fox."

"How did you know about Su?" said a visibly surprised Joe.

"Sheds have ears Joe," said Tomo conspiringly.

"There's nothing wrong in offering a little neighbourly support to a grieving widow." Joe said, with the hint of a smile on his face.

Nobody had any idea how old Joe was. He never told anyone his age. He even remembers bits of the Second World War, according to one of the other plot holders.

"Old Arthur down by the canal reckons he fought in it," Kevin once told the lads. Whatever his age, he was down every day; tending his plot, rain or shine; and was always welcomed as one of the lads.

With everyone feeling relaxed and at ease, the conversation changed to the small matter of Graham's predicament.

"The only real starting point is this Frieda," said Tomo. "What do you know about her?"

"I know where she lives, but that's really it. Her husband had a building firm. Despite the picture she painted of him, he was probably an okay bloke. And then one day he was found dead with my billhook stuck in his head."

"I thought they found it in the garden?" Kevin queried.

"You're splitting hairs," said Graham.

"Bet that billhook split a few," added Jim-Bob.

"Thanks for your input," Graham replied then continued. "We need to find out what we can about her, who she associates with and... what was that?" Graham heard a creak on the decking outside. All eyes turned to the door.

Jim-Bob stubbed the remains of the second joint out and crept to the door, picking up a marrow with his right hand on the way. He reached for the handle and flung the door open. Graham wasn't sure who was more surprised, him and the lads, or Graham's daughter Anna standing there.

"Anna. What the Hell are you doing here?" Graham gasped.

"Dad? So you are here after all." She looked at Jim-Bob. "Are you threatening me with a courgette?"

"It's a marrow," clarified Graham, "and anyway, how did you know I was here?"

"Laura told me. She'd heard you on the phone," she said, looking at Kevin, who looked a little sheepish at betraying his friend's hiding place. He shuffled awkwardly on the old piano stool serving as his seat.

"Oh Anna, I am really pleased to see you though." He hugged his daughter and she sat down with her dad on the camp bed.

"Anna, you can't say a word to anyone you know about your dad being here." Tomo said firmly. "This is really serious stuff."

"I'm not a kid. The last thing I'm going to do is betray my dad." She sniffed the air. "Have you been smoking weed?"

"No, it's... err... slug pellets," said Jim-Bob.

"Do slug pellets usually give off smoke?"

"Look Anna," interrupted Graham, "we've got stuff we need to sort out today, so I can get back to having a normal life."

"And how are you going to sort it out?"

"Well, that's what we've got to figure out. Anyway, you're best going back to mum's Anna."

"No way. I want to help."

"Anna you're too young. This isn't a game. It's serious stuff."

"Dad, I'm not stupid! I'm going to help and there's nothing you can do to stop me."

Graham knew his daughter. He had no chance. Reluctantly, he looked at the others and they all looked back with expressions of resignation, confirming they would have to accept whatever help this 15 year old girl could give them.

Quite a lot, as things turned out.

*

James Hyde poured a measure of whiskey into one mug, then another. He pushed the cracked one across the battered old Formica desk in the Portakabin towards the bulky form, squeezed into the ever-so-slightly-too-small plastic chair opposite. Outside were the noises of a hard working, bullied workforce, ensuring that Hyde Constructions was almost back on schedule and ready to take on Riverside.

"So Scud, what do we know about our Mr. Pilgrimm?"

"He's a nobody. He's a few friends round Leeds, drinks in a shit-hole called the Tap near the station. He's divorced and works for the council."

"For a nobody he seems to be a doing a good job avoiding the police and us. Any clues to his whereabouts?" Hyde looked at his reflection in the window, checking his jacket and tie before heading off to another photo shoot for the latest presentation of a cheque to support yet another community project.

"No, not yet," mumbled Scud, nervously pulling at his lower lip.

"Not very helpful these contacts of yours are they? Am I wasting my money paying them do you think? I'd hate to find out they didn't exist and you were simply pocketing the money. That would never do, would it?" Hyde looked at Scud as if he were a naughty schoolboy. Anyone else talking to Scud like that would have ended up in a wheelchair. Not James Hyde though.

"They're looking. I'll make sure they come up with something soon," Scud muttered. "There is one other thing though. He's got a 15 year old daughter, lives with the mother."

"Oh? That could be useful to know." Hyde rose, swallowed his whiskey in one go and went to the cabin door. Before he opened it, he looked back at Scud, still wedged in his chair, sipping whiskey from the cracked mug. "If I don't find out where he is by the end of the week, you and I are going to fall out Scud." With that he left and headed for his Range Rover. He looked at his watch and figured he'd enough time to see one of his whores for a quick blow job on the way to the community centre. The sooner this was resolved, the sooner normal service could resume with Frieda.

Who the fuck does he think he is. One day, thought Scud as he watched the Range Rover drive away. Nevertheless, if he was going to get a decent payout, he was going to have to put the squeeze on a few people to find this Pilgrimm. He decided to start at the Tap.

Chapter Three – Cat and mouse

Onions can be grown from seed or by planting sets. Sets are 'baby' onions and are by far the easiest way of growing them, especially for the beginner. They grow quicker and produce a heavier crop. Rake the soil to a fine tilth as for garlic and use 2 pegs and string to mark out your planting line. Plant each set flat end to the bottom and pointed tip uppermost by gently pushing each one into the soil until the pointed tip is just at soil level. Plant the sets at intervals of 4 inches. Gently firm round each set with your fingers. Subsequent rows should be 12 inches apart. Keep weed free and water well in dry weather. Harvest when the tops begin to die back. Carefully lift the bulbs with a fork on a dry day and leave them to dry before storing them by hanging in a dry place.

Onions are a vital ingredient of so many savoury dishes. Try them chopped raw in salads too. Good for the blood!

At 8.35am, Becky parked her blue Fiesta a safe distance from the entrance to the cul-de-sac, far from the prying eyes of the residents who would be sure to notice a stranger's vehicle in the neighbourhood. She gathered from the interviews her colleagues had carried out with Frieda's neighbours, that everyone knew each other well down on Church Meadows. There was a good social life, probably a bit of wife swapping in and amongst, but certainly any unusual faces or vehicles would be noticed at once.

She wandered around to the entrance of the cul-de-sac and looked down towards Frieda's house at the far end. All looked quiet. A black Saab was parked down the drive. Becky assumed it was Freda's.

It had been a week since the murder. Graham Pilgrimm was still out there somewhere, doing a remarkable job of evading the police. Becky had never met him. She was vaguely aware of him from his 'Graham's Garden' articles and eventually found a photo of a not bad looking man in his mid 40's at a recent Green Flag award ceremony in one of the council's parks, smiling in the background as a local councillor raised the flag, celebrating the achievement. She'd found it while trawling through the archives, where she'd identified the mystery man at the press conference as James Hyde, a wealthy local businessman. Hyde was a puzzle. He seemed whiter than white. A pillar of the community who put much of his hard earned wealth back into local arts and youth projects. Yet somehow he was connected to the murder, her instinct told her this – and it was rarely wrong. It wasn't just his presence at the conference. She'd caught a glimpse of an expression on his face.

Graham Pilgrimm, the killer on the run, was causing panic around Leeds. He wasn't to be approached. He was a danger to society; public enemy number one, according to the papers. Schools were even considering closing until he was caught - Anna suddenly found herself more popular than ever as a result.

Was this man a murderer? *I don't think so*, thought Becky. *Not our Mr. Pilgrimm.* So if he's not a murderer, and it's his word against Mrs. McArthur about their relationship, then perhaps there's more to Mrs. McArthur than meets the eye.

It's certainly possible that she's guilty of nothing more than lying about their affair because she wanted to keep it out of the media; the murder carried out by a person unknown, with a motive unknown, and she simply wanted to be seen as the loyal and loving wife. Perhaps she really believed Graham Pilgrimm was the murderer; killing her husband in a jealous rage, perhaps...

Becky lost herself in her thoughts for a few moments more, when signs of movement in the house suddenly snapped her out of her trance. A curtain was being drawn back. She retraced her steps and left the entrance to the cul-de-sac for her Fiesta.

She had almost reached her car when she became aware of a figure crouched down behind some dogwood and Buddleia at the landscaped entrance to the cul-de-sac. The figure was watching Becky.

Unnerved, she opened the door to her car, then paused and looked back. The figure was no longer looking at her, but down the cul-de-sac towards Frieda's house. She got in her car, closing the door quietly, and watched the figure through the windscreen, peering over the rim of the steering wheel. The figure wasn't tall, maybe 5'4". It was wearing a green combat jacket that blended in with the vegetation and red Converse trainers that didn't. The face was difficult to see. It was obscured by the vegetation and a grey scarf.

Becky was mesmerised by the figure and only distracted when the sound of a car engine brought her back to reality. Looking back towards the cul-de-sac she saw Frieda in the black Saab, heading out onto the main road. Frieda paused at the junction before setting off, as she also noticed the figure in the shrubbery.

The figure climbed out and stood in the road, staring at her. Frieda stared back; probably as unnerved as Becky was when the figure had looked at her. The figure stood its ground out in the open and stared at Frieda, as if making a point. Becky then noticed it was a girl, no more than 16, with medium length light brown hair, tied back in a pony tail. After a pause, Frieda sped off up the road.

Damn, thought Becky. She had hoped to tail Frieda, inconspicuous in her modest Fiesta. But she was off, obviously spooked by the figure in the shrubbery. Becky was incensed. This annoying girl had nearly blown her cover. She drove up to the girl.

"Who the hell are you!" she shouted out of the window.

"Never mind who the hell am I, who the hell are you!" The figure retorted. They stared at each other. Becky's large brown eyes fixed on the equally large blue eyes of the stalker.

"What are you doing here anyway? What were you up to?"

76

"None of your business. I don't have to explain myself to you."

"Look. I haven't got time for this, get in the car."

"Shouldn't you be offering me sweets, or showing me some puppies? Isn't that the usual routine?"

"Look, get in the *fecking* car will you?" Anna, thrown by the driver's assertiveness and also curious to her motives for being there too, climbed into the Fiesta and Becky hit the accelerator, in the hope of catching the Saab somewhere further along the road into Leeds.

*

It was early doors in the Tap. George was alone and passing the time by polishing a glass, well, trying to remove the obvious signs of a dried on cheese and onion crisp from the side before replacing it on the rack.

He was vaguely aware of a bulky figure standing the other side of the bar.

"Yes?" He grunted, not looking up.

"Are you the landlord?"

"No, I'm Spiderman. My costume's in the wash." A hand reached across the bar and grabbed George by the collar. The glass fell to the ground and smashed on the grimy floor.

"Listen fat man, I haven't time for this. I want some information about one of your regulars." The response came back in a strained mumble. Scud looked at George and realised that he was probably pulling the collar a bit too tight. George's feet had left the ground and he had developed a purple hue.

He released his grip just enough so that George could put his feet back on the ground again. His shoes crunched on the glass.

"Now I'll ask again. I want some information about one of your regulars. Tell me what you know about Graham Pilgrimm."

"I'm... I'm not sure I know him." George wheezed. Scud leaned over the bar until he was nose to nose with a terrified George.

"Now listen. You think hard big man, because I am not messing around. Tell me what you know about Graham Pilgrimm!"

"I don't know the name." George whimpered.

"He's the one on the run for murder. Does that help?"

"Oh, yes. Yes, I know him!" said a relieved George, now eager to please and hopefully pacify the terrifying figure before him. "He meets his friends here after the Leeds home games. He's a pain in the arse, but he doesn't seem the murdering type." As George said the words he wondered a little anxiously if the man facing him might be.

Scud finally released George and patted him firmly on the cheeks with both hands. "Good boy. Now tell me everything you know about him and who he hangs around with."

*

It didn't take Becky long to catch up with Frieda's black Saab.

Becky drove like a maniac and Anna quickly lost her cockiness. In fact she was terrified. She'd never seen driving like this. Becky made sure there was enough distance between her and the Saab to avoid the risk of raising any suspicion, but ensured she was still close enough to keep the Saab in her sight.

They hadn't spoken since the Fiesta had set off. Once she was sure she had the Saab in her sights, Becky broke the silence.

"So who are you and why were you lurking in the bushes?"

"My name's Anna. And that woman is the reason my dad is on the run."

"You're Graham Pilgrimm's daughter?"

"Who are you and how do you know my dad?" asked Anna, now feeling quite unsettled through a combination of Becky's driving, and also because they were now discussing her father.

"I don't know your dad in person, but I know what he's supposed to have done. My name's Becky and I work for the Post. I also think your dad could be an innocent man."

*

As the days began to pass, Graham began to feel more and more frustrated. His only human contact was the 10 minutes or so each day when one of the lads popped down with fresh supplies.

To avoid giving him a major coronary by just turning up unannounced, they rang him on his mobile as they were entering the allotment site. Joe occasionally called in to check he was okay, usually first thing in the morning. Joe never rang first, of course, so his taps on the door usually did cause a little anxiety. Nevertheless, it was still good to see his ancient face and get news of the ever distant outside world. Joe would then tend his own plot until lunch time, with the occasional break for a smoke and a cough and then, every other day, a fifteen minute interaction with Mrs. Lin in his shed.

To retain some degree of sanity, Graham formulated a daily routine to give a structure to his days and occupy his time. He usually rose at 7am. At that time of the year there were no plot holders on site. The first to arrive usually came between 8.30 and 9am. The clang of the security gate at the site entrance gave him a warning of their arrival.

He went to the rear of the shed and after visiting the compost heap there, had a wash using the tap next to Kevin's plot. He'd have a walk around the paths and plots close by, never venturing too far just in case he needed to beat a hasty retreat back to the shed if someone turned up early.

He breakfasted around 9am. This was usually bread and jam. Mac had come up trumps and dropped down a single ring camping stove that meant he could have a cup of tea as well now. After that he would lie back on his bunk and surf the net using his phone, not just to check the news reports around the search for the 'Compost Killer' as he was quickly named by some wit in the press, but also to keep in touch with the outside world. Any news, however trivial, made him feel part of the human race again.

He'd read the paper and magazines that were dropped off by the lads, and listen the radio. Unfortunately, although he had an FM radio built into his phone, he could only access that with headphones and that meant compromising his sense of hearing, vital in alerting him of someone's impending arrival. Instead, he used a cheap wind-up radio that was fine, except it took the best part of 5 minutes to charge it for around 30 minutes max of listening time. Lunch, perhaps a sandwich or tin of soup, was usually followed by a siesta.

The afternoons were the worst. Time passed slowly. The more he looked at his watch, the slower it went. Sometimes, if the weather was bad, he got the chance to venture out for a while when the other plot holders gave up and went home. He had to be careful though. If he got too wet, he had little chance to dry off properly in the shed.

He started to pick up after 5pm. He'd cook a light meal and rest up on the bunk, listening to the sound of the gate as, one by one, the plot holders went home for the day. Fortunately the growing season was coming to a close. There was still produce to harvest, and would be for weeks to come, but the frenetic summer programme of planting, watering and weeding had eased considerably.

After dark was the best time. Knowing he was alone, he'd get out and walk around the site, venturing much further than he'd have dared earlier in the day. After a couple of days, he started jogging around the site. Years ago he used to run. He'd even run a few half marathons, at a decent pace as well. From 35 onwards though, the combination of a sedentary lifestyle, real ale and occasional smoking had taken their toll and he'd given up. However, the allotment runs he was undertaking now reminded him of how good it felt afterwards, the natural high that only running leaves you with. Back at Shed Heaven, he'd do a few sit ups and press ups. Five of each was more than enough to start with. But at least, it was a start. He'd relax with more reading, surfing, or the radio, and have a glass or two of supermarket budget whiskey, his one luxury in the shed, that helped prepare him for sleep. And so his daily routine began to take shape.

The meeting they'd had in Shed Heaven, the day after Graham was installed there, concluded with the following proposals in no particular order:-

1. Remove Anna from the shed as soon as possible so there was less chance of her getting into trouble if she knew too much, reduce the risk of her giving the game away inadvertently through knowing too much and to allow Jim-Bob to roll more joints away from her judgmental eyes.

2. Not discuss the location of Graham with anyone else, however trustworthy, including close family, partners and women they may be lucky enough to share an intimate moment with in the near future.

3. Prepare a daily rota to supply Graham with essentials including food, clothing, personal hygiene items, a topped up mobile battery, pornography and other general reading matter to pass the time.

4. All to scrutinise the press and media to keep up with fresh developments that might give clues for further investigation.

5. Investigate Frieda McArthur. Graham knew where she lived and little more. She needed to be watched and followed, with all associates and destinations recorded.

"I can do that." Anna suggested.

"No way!" challenged Graham. "That is far too dangerous and you've got school to think of as well."

"Not a problem. My Head's been really understanding and given me time off if I need it. It will be good to get away for a few days. I just feel I'm being watched and talked about all the time. Dad, I'll keep a low profile and have my mobile with me all the time just in case..."

Graham sighed. He knew he'd have to give in. "Just for a couple of days and if anyone..." he repeated, "anyone spots you down that road, get out quick. Don't talk to anyone and any sign of danger, get out."

Anna smiled broadly. "Thanks dad, love you." She kissed him and got up to leave. "You can talk about other stuff now and smoke some more weed if you want."

With a wave she was gone, leaving the group somewhat lost for words.

That had been the last major development for days now. Graham lay on the bunk, staring up at the roof, having returned to the shed as the morning shift of plot holders started appearing. He felt they were getting nowhere and fast.

Meanwhile, five miles to the north, a black Saab was being pursued by a somewhat erratically driven blue Fiesta.

*

"How do you know my dad is innocent?"

"Don't you think he is?"

"Of course I do, but everyone else in the papers, on TV, they're convinced he's a killer, that he's going to strike again at any moment. No one is safe from the 'Compost Killer'," she said with a hint of bitterness in her voice.

Becky smiled. Despite her initial hostility, she was warming to Anna. She had guts, wasn't afraid to stand up for what was right and speak out, even if others looked the other way. Anna reminded Becky of her own youth, the reason she wanted to be a reporter in the first place.

"It doesn't matter what the reporters, or the people who write for the TV believe. A lot of them think he's innocent. The problem is they want to sell newspapers. They want people to watch their TV programmes. The more your dad is seen as a danger to society, the more viewers and readers they get. Sorry kid, it's the way it is." Becky sometimes felt she had to apologise for her profession.

"You think he's innocent though."

"Yes, yes I do. And I'd like to prove I'm right."

"FUUUUUCK!!" They yelled together as they swerved to avoid the elderly black lady who wandered into the road, straight in front of them.

They turned to check she was alright, just in time to catch her flashing a finger at them as she mouthed something beginning with 'F'. Anna had seen enough episodes of Match of the Day at Graham's to be able to lip read certain choice phrases. "The old folk of today, no respect," she muttered. Becky smiled.

*

Frieda was oblivious to the commotion 250 yards behind on the Leeds Outer Ring Road. She was looking for a familiar turn off that took her north up the A61 towards Harrogate. Half an hour later, she came to a small village, little more than a row of cottages, and then slowed down at the entrance to a private lane that headed off to the left.

She turned in and stopped at the iron gates that barred her way after 15 yards. Frieda wound her window down and pushed a button. A moment later, spoke into a microphone, oblivious of the Fiesta parked opposite the drive on the other side of the A61 with its two shadowy occupants.

The gates opened and the Saab drove in. Before Becky and Anna decided what they were going to do next, the gates closed.

"Now what?" Anna asked.

"Well, I'm not climbing up those gates... and neither are you!" She caught a glint in Anna's eye. The girl had guts, but there was a time and a place. "No, I think we need to work a little smarter."

Becky started the car and pulled a little further along until she came to a small general store. "Wait here," she told Anna, and then got out.

"Excuse me," she smiled at the elderly lady behind the counter. "I wonder if you can help. My name is Jane... Jane Tate." She spotted the bag of sugar behind the counter. "I'm afraid I was turning around in the entrance to a property down the lane and my foot slipped off the clutch. I think I've left a bit of a dent in the gate. It was some kind of security gate. I tried ringing a buzzer, but didn't get a reply. I can't just drive away. I need to apologise and if there is a cost, reimburse the owner. Do you have a name and address for the property? I feel really embarrassed about this." She smiled and looked her appealing best, pleading with her big brown puppy eyes.

"I think that's really admirable of you love. There's too many that would have just driven away. Is it the gate set back with a high wall on either side?"

"It is." Becky said, looking sheepish for doing such a silly thing.

"My Barry would be quick to go on about women drivers, but I bet if it was a man who'd done that they would be off, quick as a flash." She emphasised the point with a sweeping hand gesture. "That leads to 'The Beeches', home of a gentleman called James Hyde. Oh... have you heard of him?"

Becky didn't mean to make it obvious. "I think I do. Is he a builder, something like that?"

"He's not just a builder love." The old lady laughed. "He's built most of Leeds over the last 10 years and it looks like he's about to build a lot more soon, sounds like he's going to re-develop a big part of the old city waterfront. He's doing very well for himself and I'll tell you something as well, it couldn't happen to a nicer person. He's done a lot for this village and he does a lot for poor kids and the arts in Leeds. We need a lot more like him."

"Well, I'm glad I called in. It's the least I can do then to pay him something back for all that hard work. I'm sure I'll be able to get his contact details through his company. Thank you. Goodbye."

"Thank you and goodbye Miss Tate. I'm sure Mr. Hyde will be fine about the damage. He'll appreciate your honesty." Becky smiled sheepishly and left.

*

It was early doors in the Tap. George rubbed an emerging bruise on his neck with his left hand as he rubbed a grubby cloth on a stubborn beer stain on the bar top with his right. He heard footsteps approaching and a voice.

"Are you the landlord?" Without looking George muttered, "No I'm Superman. I'm wearing my pants on the inside tonight." A hand reached across the bar and grabbed his collar, pulling him over the bar. *Oh bollocks, not again,* he thought.

"Now listen here sunshine, I don't have time for this. Are you the landlord?"

"Yes," wheezed George, once again struggling for air. "How can I be of assistance?"

"What?"

"Sir, I think you're holding him a little tightly by the throat," Constable Dirker suggested helpfully.

"Are you the police?" gasped George, regaining his breath.

"No, I'm Batman and this is Robin." DS Hopkins replied.

"Look, I could have you for police brutality!" George challenged, once he'd regained his confidence and the ability to breathe.

"Try it son, and I can arrange for some unpleasant visits to this establishment over the next few months. I'm sure a thorough investigation of your health and safety procedures, customer's smoking habits, not to mention food hygiene standards will reveal a few things of interest?" Hopkins threatened, prodding a limp excuse of a cheese sandwich on the bar with his forefinger. "Now, sir, let's start again shall we? I understand you have a regular here who goes by the name of Graham Pilgrimm. We'd like to know everything you know about him; who he hangs around with, conversations you've overheard... Just tell me everything you know."

With an unpleasant feeling of déjà vu, George started talking.

*

The Saab drove down a long winding drive, fringed by mature beech trees, inter-planted by laurels and rhododendrons.

The drive led to a fine Victorian stone house, surrounded by manicured lawns and evergreen shrubbery. Flower beds were noticeably absent in what was effectively an extravagant bachelor residence.

As the car pulled up outside the front door, it was opened by an unusually dishevelled James Hyde. Frieda got out of the car and eyed him up and down.

"You look like shit this morning Mr. Hyde."

"It's lovely to see you as well Frieda."

"Are you going to invite me in?"

Hyde pulled the door open and disappeared back inside, followed by Frieda.

They went through the tiled entrance hall, past the staircase with the worn red carpet that led up to Hyde's bedroom, normally their first port of call, and instead went into a rather gloomy oak panelled study through a door to the right. A coal fire burned in a splendid Victorian fireplace.

"So James? How's the search proceeding?"

"I've got my best men on the case," he replied, pouring a couple of tumblers of whiskey.

"Are you hoping to get me drunk so you can take advantage of me?" She eyed him with a mixture of suspicion and mild amusement. Hyde banged the bottle down. Frieda barely moved.

"I need you Frieda. For God's sake woman, just give me five minutes, that's all, and I won't ask again, not until he's caught. Just give me a quick..." He looked down at his fly, a subtle invitation for a blow job to ease the tension that was slowly driving him insane.

"Not a chance boyo. Not until our friend is disposed of and if by your 'best men' you are referring to that Cro-Magnon you employed to dispose of my husband, we've no chance. His idea of strategic thinking is deciding whether he takes a shit before or after he pulls his trousers down. Up your game Mr. Hyde. The longer he is out there, the greater the chance he's going to figure something out. And then Mr. Hyde..." She stretched a long leg out and tapped the toe of her heeled boot on his bulging crotch.

*

Jim-Bob opened one weary eye, wondering if he was still dreaming. His throbbing head told him he wasn't. No, there it was again, the sound of knocking on the one door that gave access to his upstairs flat in Headingley. He looked at his mobile next to the bed and looked at the time in disbelief. It was 6.28am and he had the mother of all hangovers.

It might be a mistake. Whoever it was, they could have the wrong address. He rolled over, closed his eyes, and hoped they would go away.

Then it started again, a definite persistent knock. "Oh fuck it," he muttered to the world in general, threw back the sheets and wandered over to the window. Peering out, his blood ran cold. A police car with a uniformed and plain clothed officer stood below. He recognised the plain clothed officer at once. It was the one they'd encountered at Dave's house – the one with the serious attitude problem.

He wondered whether to ignore them, looked anxiously at the bathroom door and, as the knocking started again, decided to take a chance and walked down the stairs to open the door. He put the chain on and spoke to them through the gap between the door and the frame.

" 'Ello, 'ello, 'ello, who do we have here then? Well, if it isn't 'Mr. Cheeky Fucker' AKA James Roberts. May I come in?"

"Good morning officer...?"

"Hopkins, DS Hopkins and guess what I've got in my hand Mr. Cheeky Fucker. It's a special bit of paper with your name on it that gives me permission to enter, with Constable Dirker here, to have a good look round your flea pit excuse for a flat."

"Sorry, did you say enter Constable Dirker?"

"No I fucking did not. You are asking for a good hiding my friend."

"Look, if you're looking for Graham, I've not seen him and he isn't here, so if you would kindly..."

"Ah, the elusive Mr. Pilgrimm. All in good time. In the meantime, I have had a little tip off that if I want to purchase tobacco of the more exotic variety, you're the man to see. Now Mr. Roberts, may we come in?" He finished with a broad smile.

There was no way round this. Jim-Bob closed the door, slipped off the chain, opened the door and let them in, his pulse thumping like a hammer inside his hungover head. *Oh Fuck*, he thought as DS Hopkins brushed past him and made his way upstairs.

*

Jacek and Stefan sat nervously in the battered blue transit outside the gates of North Star Electronics on Mill Street, a road giving access to a series of modern industrial units.

"Are you sure this is where he works?" Jacek asked Stefan in Polish.

"That's what Mr. Scud told us. Here, memorise this photo so we get the right one when he comes out."

"I don't feel good about this. Do you?"

"We don't have to do him serious harm. We just need to frighten him, loosen his tongue a bit. Look, we need to find out where this Graham Pillygrimm is or Mr. Scud will not be a happy bunny."

"I hate Mr. Scud's guts. He's a big fat shit with a tiny shrivelled cock who couldn't even satisfy a sparrow. I could quite happily put his balls in a..."

"Yes, you and whose army? Look, we have to do what we're told, you know that. We have no choice if we are going to see any pay this week."

"Wait... look... there, coming out of the door. It's him." Tomo stepped out into the fading light, conscious the nights were drawing in early now. He looked up as it started to rain, then walked towards his car at the far end of the car park. He got in and set off, unaware of a blue transit also starting its engine, the other side of the chain link fence.

The van followed Tomo's Peugeot to a T junction. Tomo slowed down and indicated left. Seeing the exit was clear, he set off along the empty road. As Tomo drove along the road running parallel to the industrial estate, he noticed that the headlights of the transit van behind were flashing at him in his rear view mirror.

Shit, what's wrong now? Tomo wondered, worried he'd a light out or his number plate had dropped off again. The transit was indicating left, telling him to pull over. Worried something was amiss with his car, he obliged. He got out of the car and met one of the two occupants of the van who also got out.

"Hi guys. What's up?"

"This," said a voice from behind. Then everything went black.

Tomo woke up, as if from a dream. Only he wasn't in his bed, or his current girlfriend's. This was somewhere different. His head was hurting and his vision was blurry. He tried to get up, but something was wrong. He couldn't move his arms. Gradually his vision sharpened and he realised he was in the back of a van, *the blue van behind him?* He looked down his body and saw his hands and legs were taped together.

Oh bollocks! This has got to be a dream.

He closed his eyes tight and opened them slowly, hoping the dream would dissolve as he woke up, back in his own bed. When he opened them again, he realised the unfortunate truth, that he had been abducted. *What the hell is going on?* The next thing he heard was a voice, speaking a foreign language... foreign, but strangely familiar.

"Turn right...there. That's it. Now drive into that empty warehouse." The light faded as they went into the derelict building. The engine died and the driver's and passenger's doors opened and closed as their occupants got out.

The temporary silence was interrupted by the rear doors of the van being opened revealing two shadowy figures.

"Get out!" a voice demanded in heavily accented English.

"I can't. You've tied me up."

"Ah, yes. Okay, well... erm... stay there and we'll come in." Stefan climbed in, closely followed by Jacek. Both then squatted at the feet of Tomo. "Listen, if you help us by giving us some information, no harm will come of you. You will be returned to your car in one pieces," Stefan said, trying to sound as intimidating as his nervous body allowed.

"That depends if I know the answer to what you want and if I'm willing to talk."

"Don't be a heroes and no harm will come to you." Jacek, who'd kept quiet so far, added, then turned to Stefan and said in Polish, "if he doesn't talk, what are we going to do?"

"I don't know. I've never done anything like this before have I?" Stefan replied.

A third voice added to the conversation in fluent Polish. "Well, that puts us all in a really difficult position then, doesn't it?"

The two abductors turned at once and stared at their bound captive, then looked at each other.

*

DS Hopkins and PC Dirker left no stone unturned in the flat. As 7am loomed, it was becoming apparent that despite the tip off via earlier enquiries in the Tap, no stash could be found in the limited hiding spaces available in the single bedroomed upstairs flat.

"I am going to kill that fat fucker of a landlord," muttered DS Hopkins.

"Sir, I think we might have to call this one a day. There's nothing here." Hopkins turned to reply to PC Dirker but before he could say anything, a voice interrupted.

"Tea anyone?" a voice piped up behind them. They turned to face a politely smiling Jim-Bob, scratching his crotch, only just concealed under his boxer shorts. He was beginning to enjoy himself now.

"No, we don't want any fucking tea!" barked a purple-faced Hopkins.

"No thank you," PC Dirker replied, more politely.

"I don't want to seem a nuisance, but I'd appreciate it if you tidied up a bit before you went. You've left the flat in a bit of a mess..."

"Now you listen here, if you think you've won, forget it. I'll be watching you, day and night. Remember that... watching you." Hopkins pointed his finger at Jim-Bob, turned and went down the stairs, followed by PC Dirker who turned and left with a polite and somewhat embarrassed smile.

Jim-Bob locked the door behind them, turned and looked up at the ceiling, letting out a long deep breath. "That... was... close," he said to himself. He went back upstairs, into the bathroom and pulled at the corner of a panel behind the toilet, which popped out to reveal several bags of the finest grass in Headingley, neatly piled in a corner of the void around the cistern.

*

"You speak Polish?" a still shocked Stefan enquired.

"I was brought up with it. My parent's came from Poland in the '50's."

"Where from?"

"Krakow."

"Krakow!" Both abductors said in unison, then looked at each other.

"I don't believe it. I grew up in Liszki, just outside Krakow," said Stefan excitedly.

"I came from Skawina," added Jacek, "not too far away either."

"I know Skawina. My parents grew up in Libertow, just down the road."

"What's your name? We just had a photo."

"I was Christened Tomasz, but nobody could spell it at school so ever since I can remember I was known as Tom or Tomo."

The abductors went silent. This wasn't in the plan. They looked at each other again. Jacek opened his mouth to say something, reconsidered, then shut it. They looked at the ground. Stefan drummed his fingers on the side of the van.

"Can we have a moment, please?" Stefan asked Tomo, indicating with a shake of the head he needed to step outside with Jacek.

"Yes, no problem. Don't mind me, I'm not going anywhere," he replied, with a slight hint of sarcasm.

Outside, Jacek pulled out a packet of cigarettes, gave one to Stefan, then lit them both with his lighter, starting with Stefan's.

"This complicates things Stefan. I mean, this guy is one of us."

"Hmm. Yes, yes it does." He coughed and stared at the floor.

"What do you think we should do?"

"Well, erm, I'm not sure," he replied uncertainly. Their pondering was interrupted by Tomo from inside the van.

"Could you hurry up please? I could do with a wee."

"Oh... yes, sorry, won't be long," Stefan called back.

"I think we should let him go," suggested Jacek.

"Hmm. Yes... yes, I think you're right. It's just Mr. Scud, he will not be pleased."

"Well, we could ask Tomasz if he knows where this Pilgrimm is first."

"What if he doesn't tell us?"

"Well... err... I don't know."

"I mean, Mr. Scud said we were supposed to rough him up a bit, put the 'frighteners upon him' I think he said."

"I don't want to do that Stefan. Stefan, I want to go home. What are we doing here? I came to England to get work in the Promised Land, the country of Winston Churchill, William Shakespeare and David Beckham. All we have done is work as slaves Stefan, to Emperor Hyde, who comes over in his big fucking car, then striding around and inspecting like the camp commandants our parents talked about, remember? Then going and leaving the dirty work, the beatings, to the Scuds of the world. Is this the country we dreamed of Stefan? Aren't we better than this?"

Stefan looked down, nodding. "What have we come to Jacek?"

"Stefan, there's only one course of action we can take now with our prisoner." Stefan looked back at his friend and nodded. They returned to the van.

"Well Tomo," said Stefan, "It is really good to meet you. "Jacek, please untie him. We must all go and have a drink together to celebrate this great occasion."

Several hours later, a taxi pulled up outside Tomo's house. Three men staggered out. Tomo embraced Jacek and Stefan, who then both struggled back into the cab, seriously worse for wear after a ridiculous amount of vodka, to be dropped off at their lodging several miles away. Before they set off, Jacek wound the window down.

"I am so sorry for hitting you on the head. It was really rude. Please don't tell my parents when you write home. I feel really bad..." he slurred in Polish.

"And sorry for tying you up too. You are a lovely man. We must do this again... without hitting you first though," Stefan added.

Tomo watched the cab disappear round the corner. He took the keys out of his pocket, opened the door to his house and staggered upstairs to bed. Before he slipped into a vodka induced stupor, he reflected on what had been the most surreal night of his life.

*

"Go on Graham. What are you scared of?" Graham stood on the timber ledge and looked at the ground some 20 feet below him. It might as well have been 200 feet. There was no way he was going to step off the platform.

"I can't," he said in the high, trembling voice of his ten years.

"There's nothing to be scared of silly," laughed his sister. Nothing scared Annie. "You're clipped to a harness. You can't fall. Go on Graham. Just let go."

"I can't." He started crying and the zip wire attendant looked down at him with an expression that said *you are pathetic*. Graham cried even more.

"You'd better unclip him. He's not going to go," said his exasperated sister to the attendant. The attendant obliged without saying a word. What could he say? Graham stood back while Annie was clipped to the wire.

"Are you ready?" the attendant asked.

"You bet!" she yelled and looked down to find her parents looking back up at her, as proud as punch of their fearless daughter.

"Go!" said the attendant and, without a moment's hesitation, she leapt off the platform and was gone, shrieking with excitement. Graham, suddenly anxious, ran to the edge of the platform shouting.

"Annie! Come back, please come back!" His voice changed with each word, becoming deeper, until it sounded like the voice of a man in his mid forties.

He woke with a start, disorientated. The dream still felt real, but then looking at the now familiar surroundings of Shed Heaven, reality dawned. It was just a dream, a distant memory.

He looked at his mobile propped on a bag of fertilizer next to the camp bed and noticed a couple of texts from the lads, reminders they had a planning meeting later that afternoon.

He got up, stretched and looked out at the allotment landscape before him. He had slept in longer than planned, but most of the summer's harvest had been brought in by the plot holders, so the site was still quiet. He went out and breathed the morning air, which had a definite autumn chill about it now.

After a visit to the compost heap he had a cold wash from the tap at the side of the plot and returned to the shed to make his breakfast in preparation for another day in hiding.

*

What on Earth! She looked at the Google News on her iBook, not believing what she was reading.

With her eyes still fixed on the screen, she reached a manicured hand towards her mobile, ringing on the bedside table.

She brushed her long hair back from her face and answered it.

"Yes?"

"Willow?"

"Hunter? Is that you?"

"Yes. It's good to hear your voice. Hong Kong was a bit close for comfort. I was worried..."

"I'm fine, but don't blame me for that fiasco. Your team on the ground were as effective as a chocolate fireguard."

"A what?"

"Just a saying where I come from. We nearly lost Fox. That was no joke."

"I'm sorry and, for what it's worth, so is the Chief. The Fox will pull through."

"If that bullet had gone in an inch lower, he'd be going home in a box. I don't want anything like that happening again or I'm out. This is my last one, you know that, and I want to go home in one piece. I also want the whole team to go back in one piece as well."

"Look... thanks. He owes you his life. That was some rescue." Willow mellowed a little.

"I've still got it, then? Not too slow for an old lady?"

"You're still the best, you know that. Listen, we've had word our target is on the move. It looks like mainland China. You'll be getting documentation through the usual channels."

"Okay. I'll look out for it and Hunter..."

"Yes?"

"No more mistakes, please."

"Point taken. You take care Willow." Throughout the call she hadn't taken her face away from the screen once.

She reached to the bedside table, put the phone back and picked up a packet of Silk Cut. She tapped one out, put it to her lips and lit it with her Givenchy lighter. She took a deep lungful and slowly exhaled, looking at the screen in front of her.

What have you got yourself into boy?

*

"Are you planning to stay there all day?" Viv directed her question to the void under the bed.

"Just a little while longer," a slightly muffled, but still cheerful voice responded.

"Dave, how long is this going to continue? Every time there's a knock at the door... this! I'm getting a bit fed up. It was only the bloody milkman for flip's sake!"

"Look, you never know Viv. Did you tell him anything?"

"Yes, I told him an extra pint of semi-skimmed on Tuesday. I bet he'll be straight back with a SWAT team first thing tomorrow. Tell you what, you stay there. I'm going down to watch Corrie. I'll make a cup of tea at the interval and pass it to you under the bed. Is that okay?"

"Thanks Viv. That sounds great..." Before he could finish, she'd stormed off and slammed the bedroom door.

*

"Right then, if we're all sitting comfortably, let's begin." Tomo started the ball rolling once everyone was finally perched on the varied collection of chairs and crates in a rough semi-circle facing the camp bed on which Graham lay stretched out with his left hand behind his head as he took a long pull from the joint in his right, staring up at the ceiling deep in thought.

"Any apologies to start with?" Tomo continued.

"This isn't the fucking Wheeltappers' and Shunters' Social Club," interjected Jim-Bob. "The only person missing is Dave, who I believe has now phoned in sick at his High School and is currently residing under the spare bed in Viv's house. He is losing it big style. He's had a bit of pressure from the law. Sounds like it's the same copper who came round to Dave's that first night and visited me the other day at 6am, apparently following up a tip from some Judas in the Tap, that I may be storing a bit of herbal in the flat. Could have him for fuckin' slander."

"Slander my arse. You supply most of Leeds University. Okay, so we now have the police on our case. Anyone else had a visit?"

"My folks did early on and so did Kate," said Graham. "Don't think it was the same copper, but they may have given a few names of people I know. Sorry." He looked sheepishly at the gathering.

"It's not your folks' fault. They'd have found out soon enough," added Kevin, reaching towards Graham to relieve him of the joint. "Anyway, for what it's worth, they've not been to see me... yet."

"Okay... Mac? Any visits from the plod squad?"

"No... well... I'm not sure. I think they could be watching me. I've seen a few blokes hanging around at the end of my road lately and, there was a funny clicking noise on the phone line the other day. Like they're tapping me or something like that."

"The blokes hanging around at the top of your road were probably after a quick £20 hand job – it's the new red light area in this part of Leeds in case you hadn't realised. And the clicking on the line is because your phone is shite. Right, anyone else anything to report?" enquired Tomo.

"Use to be a fiver in my day," added Joe wistfully.

"What?" exclaimed Tomo. "Thought Nell Gwyn would have charged more than that. Anyway, back to planet Earth. Anyone else anything to add before I let you know what I've found out?"

"Yes. I've got something," Graham chipped in from the camp bed. "It might not mean much, but Anna called in to see me the other day." He swung his legs round and sat up on the edge of the bed. "It's a long story but she followed Frieda the other day and ended up visiting the country pile of a property developer, just north of Leeds. Some bloke called James Hyde."

"Really? Now that's interesting," added Tomo more enthusiastically. "Go on."

"Well, there's not much more to add, except that Anna shared a car with some reporter from the Post. I'll explain that later. Anyway, this reporter thought she also saw him at the police press conference, that first night I was at Dave's. Might be a coincidence, or they could be friends. Don't know any more at the moment. Anna says she's got some plan of action. God only knows what she's got in the pipeline."

"Well now, are you ready for this?" Tomo asked his audience before rubbing his hands. "I finished work as usual on Thursday, was just leaving the industrial estate when I got pulled over by this blue transit van. Next thing I know I'm unconscious and tied up in the back." He paused for dramatic effect, while his audience gasped and stared wide eyed, suddenly sitting up and alert despite the numbing effect of the weed. "Anyway, we pull into this derelict warehouse. Fuck knows what they were planning to do with me, but the gist of it was they wanted to find out where you were hiding." He looked towards Graham. All were now staring at Tomo open mouthed, except Jim-Bob, who wore a more cynical expression.

"Anyway, they start talking to each other in Polish, so didn't I just scare the shit out of them when I added to the conservation in the old mother tongue. Well, it turns out they came from the Krakow area of Poland and grew up within 20 miles of my folks. Anyway, once they'd apologised for abducting me, we had a few beers and caught up with stories of the old country..."

"Are you pulling my plonker? The old country for you was Huddersfield." Jim-Bob interjected. Tomo pulled an onion off the shed wall and lobbed it at him, which bounced off his head with a dull thud.

"Watch out, you'll bruise it!" yelled Kevin.

"Thanks Kev," Jim-Bob replied, rubbing his crown.

"I meant you'll bruise the onion," he clarified. Jim-Bob mouthed the word 'tosser' at the back of Kevin's head, then Tomo looked at Jim-Bob and continued:

"Listen dip-shit, my parents might have settled in Huddersfield when they first came over, but I'm Polish through and through and I'm telling the truth here about the other night. So if you'll just shut the fuck up and let me continue... thank you. Anyway, as I was saying, we got talking and it turns out these guys were bullied into this by some knucklehead called Scud who works for, wait for it, the one and only James Hyde." Tomo sat back and watched the gathering as this revelation was taken in. "It seems that this James Hyde wants to get hold of you more than PC Plod, Grimy. The question is why?"

"So let me get this right. This James Hyde is some sort of property developer," clarified Mac, "who knows this Frieda and is putting himself out big style to help her get you banged up?"

"Not banged up mate," corrected Tomo. "He wants our friend Graham disposed of before the police get him."

"Disposed of?" queried Kevin, with a slight nervous tremor.

"Terminated," clarified Tomo, with a hint of the dramatic. "According to my new friends from Krakow, this James Hyde is involved in some stuff he wants kept well under wraps.

Graham could feel his bowels churning. As if it wasn't enough being framed and on the run, knowing some wealthy business type is out to do you actual bodily harm was somewhat disconcerting.

"Okay then, if you're not talking bollocks Tomo, then this is getting interesting," said Jim-Bob. "We've got a woman who's put our Graham in the frame for her husband's murder and now some property developer, with some degree of influence and money behind him who knows this Frieda, is out for you as well. What's this other stuff he wants keeping quiet?"

"I don't know. They couldn't tell me that. To be fair, they didn't know. But I do know he's not the whiter than white character he likes people to think he is. Stefan and Jacek are just two from dozens of Poles and other foreign nationals working for next to nothing after deductions for food, lodging and, get this, fines for all sorts of shit from being a few minutes late to having too long a lunch break. They're trapped. They want to go home but have no money and anyway, if they try to leave, this Scud bloke and others like him see to it that something unpleasant happens to them. This James Hyde is a bad man and I wouldn't be surprised if the unfortunate accident that left Frieda's husband with a major headache involved him as well."

"So what do we do now?" Kevin asked Tomo.

"We fish around and find out what we can about this Hyde chappie. We find out what he's been up to and we find out the connection between him and the sexy Frieda. Now who's got what's left of the joint...?"

*

The bus lurched to another stop, throwing the passengers forward. At the wheel an Afro Caribbean in his mid 50's, with a friendly smile and cheery disposition carried on regardless. Owen was popular with friends and colleagues. He was one of those people you just warmed to as soon as you met him. The only problem was he was a truly awful driver.

The Asian youth sitting on his own at the back clutched his chest as he was thrown forward at the next stop. He clutched his chest, conscious of what lay beneath his jacket. He felt the wiring beneath it, the electrical equipment that lay hidden to all around him. But he knew it was there. He knew what it could do. He knew what he was doing was wrong. But there was no turning back, no turning back now. He had to see this through.

Another lurch at another junction. Despite the autumn chill he was sweating, a drop ran into his eye. He wiped it away, looking around to see if any of his fellow passengers had picked up on his fear. *What are you doing?* he said to himself. *This is wrong. If my father ever found out. The shame this would bring.*

*

"So Scud," a seriously pissed off James Hyde addressed the subdued and apologetic figure before him in the Portakabin. "Your team of enforcers let this Tom character go did they?"

"They said they gave him a good hiding, used threats against his family, but said in the end he didn't know anything, so they let him go."

"Is that so? And where do you think he is now? Let me think – yes think – it's something grown up, intelligent people do. Nothing you're obviously that familiar with. Let me think. Ah yes, the police. I wonder if he's gone to the police. You fucking half-wit!" Hyde banged the table and stood up.

"Now just..."

"Don't you dare answer me back you retard. And don't you think about doing anything drastic either." Hyde said as Scud rose up from his seat to face him. "I have some interesting footage of you paying a visit to a certain Leeds residency one evening, not too long ago. What do you think I was doing while you were paying your house-call; listening to the Archers? My dear simple minded Scud. Your amateur attempts at cleaving a man in two were captured for all eternity on my little camera and have been burned onto several discs. Anything happens to me, and you are up for a pleasant 20 year stretch in Armley's finest Victorian hotel for the criminally insane. Now fuck off out of here. I'm going to have to call in the professionals."

Scud left without a word. He was burning with rage. James Hyde had made a serious mistake.

*

The bus lurched to another stop, the one before the university. Umar couldn't stand the tension any longer. Any moment now.

There was no turning back. There could be no turning back. Umar was going to die.

A pair of red Converse trainers got on the bus and walked to the back, finding the empty seat next to Umar. Without a word, he closed his eyes, reached under his jacket and pulled the cable. A small camera sized object attached to a charger fell out onto the seat in the gap between them.

"I am seriously dead when my dad finds out about this."

"Umar, you are a real star. This is fantastic. I owe you big style."

"I'd do anything for you Anna. You know that." Umar blushed as he spoke.

"Oh Umar, you are special to me. You're the brother I never had, although that would look a bit weird, you being Asian and all that." She gave him a hug. Umar blushed even more. He'd had a soft spot for Anna, always had since junior school. Anna was close to Umar too, but sadly for Umar only as a friend for the lovely human being he was. To 'borrow' this piece of kit from father's electrical store was a big deal. Their dads got on well. Sohail Patel had known Graham for years and like all Graham's friends and family, instinctively knew he was innocent. He too would have done all he could do to help. Going along with Anna's idea though might have pushed the loyalty a bit too far, if he had known what Anna had asked his son to smuggle out of the store.

On the seat between them lay a digital voice recorder and charger that could record over 260 hours continuously; slim and easily concealed. Once you got in the house that is.

*

DI Smithson was, he had to admit, completely baffled. How could an ordinary and, if the testimony of friends and colleagues was to be believed, somewhat boring, local government officer evade capture for over two weeks.

He sat at his desk and looked at what they had so far; a man who had escaped from a first floor window of what should have been a secure building, running away with only the clothes on his back and a network of equally inadequate friends who claimed to know nothing of his whereabouts, even when pressure was applied. His more subtle, if somewhat beyond the call of duty, attempts at phone tapping of the one they called 'Mac' yielded nothing other than a liking for those premium lines that take at least five minutes of terms and conditions before the 60 year old granny pretending to be a 30 year frustrated housewife starts stripping and tells you about the colour of her knickers. No, there was nothing. Bugger all.

The one weak link seemed to be the Dave character. Everyone else was at work, getting on with their sad, boring lives, watching dirty Leeds on a Saturday (Smithson was a born and bred Rotherham fan) drinking dirty real ale in that hole of a so called pub, and digging in their dirty allotments on a Sunday. But Dave Butterworth, he was a different case altogether. Phoned in sick a week ago and living at his girlfriend's in Rodley. He got away with it last time. His friends were around. Now he was on his own, well that was different. He was confident that with a bit more pressure from the Rottweiler (as he referred to Hopkins in private) he would crack.

*

As October lurched towards November, Graham became aware of the advantages of this time of year. It was colder on the allotment, particularly at night, but the shorter days meant he could leave the confines of Shed Heaven even earlier in the evening. He kept up with his evening routine. He'd walk around the site and, when he was confident the coast was clear, jog around the site as well, doing that little bit more each week. He steadily increased the number of his evening press ups and pull ups as well. It was all partly to keep fit and sane too it had to be said, but also, well, you never know. He may have to respond quickly in an emergency and being in good shape might not be a bad thing.

He visited his own plot occasionally, sadly neglected now. The September weeds had flourished and smothered the leeks, cabbages and broccoli. One day he hoped everything would go back to the way it was. But then did he really want that? Did he really want things to go back to how they were? However traumatic things were now, perhaps this presented some sort of an opportunity, a chance to change things and make some sort of positive difference to his life. He just had to come through the other side, unscathed and a free man.

He sat down on the fence that bordered one side of his plot and took a drink from the cheap bottle of blended scotch Kevin had brought down for him that day. The alcohol gave him a lift. Perhaps this was all happening for a reason. His father always used to say that to him and Annie, when they were growing up. When things seemed to be going bad, or something unpleasant happened, he'd say things happened for a reason, that it was meant to be. Even if you couldn't always see it at the time, it would lead to something better.

He took another swallow of the scotch and remembered when he'd told his parents that Kate wanted a divorce. He'd been dreading it. When he first brought her home to meet them, all those years ago, they were so happy he'd met someone so beautiful and who cared so much for their son. They welcomed her into the family and when she fell pregnant with Anna, they were over the moon.

When the cracks began to show, they gave their support to both Graham and Kate. They saw the shortcomings in their son, but they also saw them in Kate. Perhaps she wasn't ready to settle down just yet with a baby. She still had career aspirations and these were going to have to be put on hold for months, even years. Perhaps being tied down, when she wasn't really ready built up a frustration and resentment that ultimately drove them apart. Maybe if Graham had been different, showed a bit more ambition earlier on, perhaps that would have given her a belief they were going somewhere as a couple. By then, it was too late though. There was no going back.

So when he finally plucked up the courage to tell his parents that fateful Sunday night (was it really five years ago now?) they weren't shocked. They said all the right things; that they would be there for both Graham and Kate. They said Anna could stay there to give Graham and Kate time to sort out what needed to be done. Above all, Graham remembered his father pouring Graham and himself a large glass of brandy later that evening and saying to him – it may seem bad now, but things happen for a reason. Perhaps the marriage wasn't meant to be, but until you were out of it, you wouldn't know that. It would only become clear later on.

He was right in many ways. Although he hadn't exactly prospered since the divorce, he did realise that there was an unpleasantness to his marriage he didn't see until afterwards. He realised later that Kate was far from perfect and for all his flaws, she was as much to blame for the break up as he was. So maybe, in some strange way, something good could come out of his current situation. What that might be, he had no idea. He just had to survive it first.

He took another drink and was suddenly alerted to a movement to his right. He froze and then relaxed a little as he noticed a tabby, probably from the estate just over the boundary fence to the west of the allotment site. It looked at him, just for a moment, then, head down, it stalked an unseen prey among the long grass. Graham watched, mesmerised, then suddenly it pounced. A field mouse leapt out of the way, just in time. Then it was off, into the long grass and away, free to live another day.

The cat watched it go, probably not hungry enough to exert the necessary energy to pursue it. Graham smiled. He wasn't alone. There were others out there, struggling for survival as well.

He wandered back to Shed Heaven, climbed into bed and a strange feeling of optimism and hope, combined with the scotch, flowed through his veins as he drifted off to sleep.

*

"So how much are you offering for this man's head Mr. Hyde?" The figure wearing a dark Hugo Boss suit and Gucinari shoes, leaned against a black BMW in the Travel Lodge car park, a convenient neutral space that suited both parties. He spoke softly, with an accent betraying his Baltic origins. James Hyde wasn't fooled by this softly spoken well dressed figure before him. He knew this man was a killer, not a mindless thug like Scud, but a professional. He knew this because he'd used him before. He was expensive, but he was good.

"£15,000 up front. You need to find him first. Then £25,000 when he's terminated and I've evidence you've done the job. Make it out like an accident, perhaps a fall from a height while he was on the run."

"What's the story Mr. Hyde?"

"We needed someone to serve a little time, provide a convenient alibi. He wouldn't cooperate so he needs to be removed from the equation."

"Is he dangerous?"

James Hyde laughed out loud. "He's a fucking gardener. He cuts grass and grows flowers. He talks to the animals like Percy the Park Keeper."

"Percy the...?"

"Look, never mind. In here's a photo plus everything we know about him. He cannot be that hard to find." He handed Hugo Boss a large brown envelope.

"Payment?"

"In there as well, used notes. The usual protocol."

"I'll count it later. You have an honest face." Hugo smiled, exposing a gold tooth.

"Just make it quick will you."

"If you want. Quick and painless."

"No. When I say quick I mean soon. I want him out of the way as soon as possible. You can take your time once you have him. Just make it look like an accident in the end."

"Whatever you want Mr. Hyde. You're the man." Hugo Boss smiled and the gold tooth glinted in the fading sunlight."

*

"No way Anna. I am not doing that. You are out of your mind. I've got you the recorder. I've done my bit. I've told you, when my dad finds out about that he's going to kill me."

"Come on Umar. It's a great plan. I know you've still got that old scout's uniform..."

"I haven't been a scout for two years. The trousers will be up to my knees. Anyway, how do you know I've still got a scout uniform?"

"I looked in your wardrobe the last time I was round. It's the kind of thing girls do. You need a serious clear out in there."

"You've no right to do that. There's all sorts of stuff in there. You could have found..." Umar blushed.

"Oh, the educational DVDs under your jumpers? Don't worry, I won't tell a soul, honestly." She smiled. "Go on Umar, for me. Please? She's seen me already and there's no one else I could trust to do this, no one with your courage and resolve."

Umar looked at her. He knew this was crazy, but he also knew he had no chance – he would crack eventually.

"Alright, alright. But if she shows any sign of sussing this, I'm out."

"You are a lovely, brave, wonderful person Umar." She gave him a hug and, that instant, he cracked.

*

Viv opened the door to reveal a tall, grey haired, middle-aged man who stood back from the door slightly.

"Is it Vivien, Vivien Chambers?" He asked politely.

"Yes, that's me. Can I help you?" The man smiled and produced an ID card. "My name is Detective Inspector Smithson. I wonder if I could have a word with David Butterworth please. I understand he's staying with you at the present time?"

"Dave's not well at the moment, he's... er... just not well," she replied anxiously.

"It will only take a few moments - I promise," he added reassuringly.

"Is it about his friend Graham?" Viv wrung her hands slightly.

"Yes, it is." Smithson said with a warm smile, nodding.

"Well, I'm sure David would love to be able to help you, but he doesn't really know anything that can help I'm afraid."

"I'm sure, but it's amazing how much people can remember when they sit down with a cup of tea and just try a little bit you know. May I come in?" Smithson stepped over the threshold with his right foot before she could reply.

"I... I suppose so," Viv said a bit nervously. The police officer was polite, but unnerved her slightly. He smiled and followed her into her modern, imitation Yorkshire stone built town house, directing him into the lounge; furnished almost entirely by IKEA, Smithson observed.

110

He sat down where directed and waited while Viv went upstairs. He heard some discussion, but couldn't make out the words. A male voice sounded a little agitated.

A few moments later Viv reappeared, followed by an unshaven and slightly dishevelled man in his mid forties; greying, but with a full head of thick hair.

"Mr. Butterworth?" Smithson asked.

"Yes... that's me."

"Please sit down." Dave did as he was instructed. "Thank you for agreeing to see me, especially as I understand you aren't too well at the moment. You probably gather we are still looking for Mr. Pilgrimm, who we really need to speak to urgently about the death of Mr. Peter McArthur."

"I... I'm not sure I can help you officer. I've told the police all I know."

"I gather that and thank you for all your help so far, but I would really appreciate it if you could think again of any places he could be staying at the moment. The thing is, Mr. Butterworth, we think he's still in the country." He looked around and behind as if to check if anyone was eavesdropping, then leaned forward towards Dave and Viv opposite him. "All airports and sea crossings have been monitored from the time of his disappearance. And from my experience of similar disappearances in the past, the person in question is often closer to home than you'd imagine." He laughed slightly, shaking his head, as if recalling to himself similar cases he'd investigated. "I don't know," he said. "People can really surprise you."

"There's really no where I could think he could be... he's not here."

"No, I'm sure he's not," and he was. He'd had the house closely watched for some time and observed nothing more suspicious than appearances at the window of a somewhat agitated Dave while Viv was out at work. "By the way, you appear to have some fluff on your top Mr. Butterworth." Dave looked down and realised his black sweat shirt had picked up a selection of dust, fluff and other fabric from underneath the bed.

"Oh, right. Thanks." Dave made a half hearted attempt to brush it off.

"Now then, let's start at the beginning again with a list of all his known friends and acquaintances shall we?" He looked over to Viv. "A cup of tea would go down wonderfully thank you."

*

Becky surveyed the artist impression of Riverside on the exhibition panels. It looked good. There was a buzz around the room. Local councillors, senior council officers, together with the movers and shakers of the Leeds business community, all mixing together to see how they could further their own individual agendas over a glass of chilled white and a canapé. At the heart of it all the smiling figure of James Hyde, always close at hand.

At the designated time, all were gathered together by the Town Hall stewards, and encouraged to take their seats to face the platform in front of them.

Two figures took to the platform; the beaming figure of James Hyde, who sat on one of the three seats, followed by a smartly dressed greying figure who approached the podium and also smiled at the gathering, a little nervously Becky noted.

"Ladies, gentlemen and colleagues, I am delighted to be able to welcome you here to the unveiling of our agency's vision for the Riverside Project. I am Councillor David Neil, chair of the development agency, and also have the honour of chairing the project team who selected the company to turn our vision into a reality. At the heart of this company, I am delighted to introduce a man I'm sure familiar to many of us in the business community of Leeds, not only for helping to transform our once derelict skyline, but also for his generous support of numerous community and arts projects in our city. Please welcome a man who has transformed the lives of thousands, Mr. James Hyde of Hyde Constructions."

A spontaneous round of applause was greeted with a smile and a nod from Hyde in his chair next to the podium.

"Before we go any further though, I'd like you all to welcome the mayor to the stage to say a few words about how this scheme will play such a key role in the regeneration of our city. Ladies and gentlemen, the mayor of Leeds Cllr..."

*

"Saw your photo in the paper James. You looked better at the launch than the last time I saw you."

"Thanks Fri. I'm feeling better because I have a feeling our problem is going to be resolved in the not too distant future, and then..."

"We'll see my friend. I told you before, nothing until I know he's out of the way... hang on, I'll ring you back. There's someone at the door." She put her mobile down on the dining room table and went to the back door. She opened it to reveal a sorry looking, and slightly oversized, Asian youth in a scout uniform.

"Yes?" Frieda asked, looking at him with contempt.

"Hello Miss I'm wondering if you'd like to make a small donation to our scout group please? We're trying to raise some money for urgent repairs to our scout hut."

"No, I would not like to make a donation to your scout hut thank you. Now please leave my property."

"That's fine Miss. Thanks for your time... oh, what's that noise?"

"What noise?"

"It sounds like there's someone at your front door."

"I didn't hear anything."

"I think there is. I definitely heard a knock."

"Well I didn't hear anything. Now will you please..." Suddenly there was a loud knocking at the front door. Frieda, with a puzzled look, scrutinised the youth. "Don't move until I answer this."

She began to walk the length of the house to the front door. The moment she turned, Umar sprinted noiselessly into the kitchen and put the device he'd been hiding under his rolled up coat on top of the closest kitchen unit, well out of view behind the pelmet. With a quick glance to check the coast was clear, he sped back outside and waited for Frieda's return.

He greeted her with a smile when she came back a moment later. "There was nobody there," she said as she looked at him somewhat suspiciously.

"No? Perhaps it was another scout and they realised I was already here. Anyway... er... I'd better be going. Thanks Miss and... er... thanks."

Without another word he was gone, leaving Frieda speechless and slightly confused. *What the fuck was that about?* She did a quick check around the kitchen to see if anything obvious was missing. When she saw nothing was, she looked quizzically at the back door again, locked it and went upstairs to run a bath.

"Could you have waited until I knocked before you told her you heard something," Anna asked crossly. "I heard you through the front door."

"I started panicking. I couldn't help it. Anyway, I did it. I thought you might at least be pleased about that. Don't forget, you're talking to a dead man. When my dad finds out..."

"Oh man up Umar. Anyway, you look quite hot when you get cross..."

"Do I? Oh Anna, you're always taking the piss." They both laughed as they took the long walk back home, the tension and stress of the evening eased as they walked back to the bus stop.

*

Hugo Boss studied the overweight figure behind the bar as he stood near the freshly lit open fire, the smoke rising through the piled up coals in anticipation of the growing flames soon to burst forth and bathe the dark interior of the Tap with the warm red light that went well with the consumption of real ale and good conversation.

This was not his kind of place though. He peered around the room looking for any signs of CCTV cameras - he didn't want any evidence of his visit here. His eyes wandered over the stained tables, grubby wallpaper and even worse wooden floor. *What a shit-hole* he thought as he lifted his Gucinari shoes in turn, to see if any stains from the boards had corrupted the expensive leather soles. He looked around again, confirmed they were alone, and moved towards the bar.

"Are you the landlord?"

"No, I'm..." George reconsidered his response when he looked up and met the gaze of the immaculately attired figure before him. Well dressed he might have been, but there was something deeply unpleasant about him. Even with his thick skin, George quickly realised that. "Yes... yes, I'm the landlord. Can I be of assistance?"

"I'm looking for someone you may know."

"Oh? Who would that be?" George tried to sound matter of fact, but the fear he felt in the pit of his ample stomach crept up to his throat, raising the pitch of his voice a few tones and adding a little waver. He knew the answer before it came.

"Graham Pilgrimm." Hugo Boss fixed an unwavering stare at George.

"I haven't seen him for a while." George averted his eyes from the piercing gaze and decided honesty was the best policy. There was no point denying he knew who Graham was, this man would suss that out. Luckily though, he hadn't seen him since that fateful night when Graham first me Frieda. "Is he a friend of yours?"

"No. I don't really think Mr. Pilgrimm would really like to meet me. The problem for him though is that I want to see him. We have some business to conclude." He smiled at George showing a hint of gold tooth, which sent a chill through him, despite the roaring fire that had now sparked into life across the room.

"Well, if I see him I'll..."

"If you see him? Are you likely to be seeing him?" He stared at George.

"I mean... it's a figure of speech. I don't know where he is, really. I've told the police everything I know." He didn't mention the earlier visit from Scud though. He would never have guessed there could be any connection between the two of them; poles apart in appearance and background, but linked together by a most unpleasant Leeds based property developer. George was terrified.

"What do you want of me?" George asked with a shaky voice.

"Mr. Pilgrimm has friends, does he not, that drink in this... er... establishment?" He cast another disdainful look around the Tap.

"Yes, I know who they are."

"So do I. That makes two of us." He suddenly laughed a menacing laugh at the irony of it. Then, suddenly serious again, "I understand they've still been coming in here since their friend went on the run?"

"Yes, usually after every Leeds home match."

"After what? Look, I don't need to know details, but the point is they still come here?"

"Yes... yes, they do."

"Well then. I have a proposition for you my friend."

"Oh?" George did not really want to hear any proposition from the immaculately dressed figure before him.

"When Mr. Pilgrimm's friends next come to enjoy your hospitality, I want you to watch them and, most importantly listen. I want you to listen very carefully for any clues as to his whereabouts." He lowered his voice as several figures wandered in chatting away to each other, oblivious to the drama happening at the bar. "I want you to be my eyes and ears and to learn anything you can that that will help lead me to him. If, and when, I find Mr. Pilgrimm and our business is concluded, you will be rewarded. You will of course never have met me. That goes without saying. The consequences otherwise will be most unpleasant. Likewise, I will be most disappointed if the next time I visit, you have not learned anything of Mr. Pilgrimm's whereabouts. I don't like to be disappointed. But I'm sure I won't be." He laughed out loud again making George jump, then stopped as quickly as he started, fixing George with that stare again. "I will be back soon." He backed away, turned and walked to the door as the group who'd arrived a few moments ago wandered over to the bar.

As soon as the figure of Hugo Boss disappeared through the doorway, George, though still a little unnerved, felt the warmth returning back to his body. *Who the bloody hell was that? And was that a gold tooth? What a wanker!*

*

"No way Anna!" Graham blurted out to his daughter down the mobile, nearly dropping it on the wooden floor of Shed Heaven, shocked that she'd even suggested the idea. He thought she had more sense than that. "Have you lost the plot? All she wants is to expose me, sell the story and probably add a few touches;

perhaps I'll kidnap her, threaten her with murder as well. No way. What in the name of God possessed you?"

"Dad, she's not like that. She believes you're innocent. She wants to help you. Don't forget it was Becky that found out where James Hyde lives. I believe her. She wants to meet you, find out what really happened and expose him and this Frieda as the people behind this. Maybe she might want to write about it afterwards, but not until you're free!"

Graham took a deep breath, about to chastise his daughter for her naivety and then paused. He slowly exhaled and rubbed his forehead. What had he got to lose? He'd been trapped here for weeks, seen summer drift into autumn. As the days merged into one long blur, he was constantly fluctuating between hope and despair. Unfortunately, though, the hope was beginning to fade with each day. His increasingly rare moments of optimism, that all this would be resolved and he would emerge a hero from his shed, the all conquering hero, seemed as unlikely as Leeds topping the table. And what were the chances of that?

It was all quiet on the news front, but the Compost Killer was still on the loose. The police (especially that psycho Hopkins) were still pursuing him with the tenacity of a bulldog on heat, terrifying his friends and family. Someone would crack. And Graham and his supporters were no closer to finding the truth. What, in the end, had he really got to lose?

"Okay... okay Anna. What the Hell. Yes... yes, I'll meet her." He felt this was a mistake. But he was beginning to feel so negatively about everything now that even prison could be no worse than this. No, there was really nothing to lose.

"Dad, she can help you, I really believe she can." Graham heard his sister in Anna. Thank God she at least had the genes with bottle, the genes that wouldn't take no for an answer, that wouldn't compromise.

*

James Hyde wound the window down with a slow and steady determination and watched the team of labourers preparing the ground at the Riverside site. The old warehouses and 19th century industrial shells, far beyond the skills of even the most skilled restorers and miracle workers, had finally been levelled. The bricks and anything else salvageable were being sorted, graded and made ready for the new miracle, the phoenix that would ultimately rise from the ashes. The new Jerusalem, the second coming - Riverside. And the Grand Architect of all this? Why, James Hyde, of course.

He smiled to himself. At least this part of his world was going well. He thought of Frieda and his smile faded. If only he hadn't agreed to that stupid idea of framing that fucking council gardener. How did he escape? How the fuck is he still on the loose? Hyde was seriously, most seriously, pissed off with this man whom he had never met, but he had decided, when he found him, he was going to cause him the most serious grievous bodily harm. He was personally going to provide this Graham Pilgrimm with the slowest and most unpleasant death, and he was going to relish every moment. He was just about to get on the phone to Hugo Boss to inform him of this subtle change of plan, when the bulky form of Scud stumbled into view.

He studied him from inside the Range Rover. Scud had had his uses in the past but was now becoming a liability. He was too unstable and once or twice as Hyde had bollocked him for his clumsiness and stupidity, Hyde had caught a look, a glance back from those thuggish eyes suggesting a menace that could be unleashed in the direction of his master, like the dog that takes so many beatings and one day turns and bites back.

Hyde stroked his mouth and chin with his left hand as his thoughts wandered into a dark place. Perhaps Scud had finally outlived his use. He was, after all, the ultimate witness that could implicate Hyde in the murder of McArthur as it was the fair hand of Scud that had delivered the killer blow, under the orders of Hyde himself. Perhaps now was the time.

He took out a mobile from the glove compartment, one he normally kept locked away back home, and spoke slowly and clearly into it as his eyes remained fixed on the bulky form of Scud before him.

*

"Is that Graham... Graham Pilgrimm?" Graham had been expecting the call, but felt a sudden rush of nerves, a churning of the stomach and urge to break wind.

"Who is it?" Graham asked, trying to sound more confident than he was.

"It's Becky... Becky Andrews and it's really good to speak to you at last."

"Well, you have my daughter to thank for that. How do I know I can trust you?"

"I suppose the answer is you don't. All I can say is the same as I said to Anna. I don't believe you are guilty. I doubted your guilt at that first press conference and as the weeks have gone by, I'm even more convinced of your innocence. Graham, I want to help you. I want to find out who really did this and why."

"That makes two of us, though I've a pretty good idea who's behind this."

"So have I Graham. What we need to find out is why. Graham, can I meet you?"

"I'm... I'm not sure. I don't know. Look, why are you doing this? Are you after a story, an exclusive interview with the Compost Killer? Forgive me Becky, but I'm a bit cynical when it comes to the motives of the press."

"No Graham. Yes of course I'd love to tell the real story. But that would come later and would only come with your permission and approval. Why am I doing this? I want to solve an injustice. That's what motivates me and why I do this job. The trouble is... the trouble is Graham I'm losing it. I don't get the jobs that drive me. I get the crap, the leftovers. I want to find the reason I did this job to start with, to expose the corruption, the shit. To fight injustice." She paused. "I'm sorry I must sound like the Lone Ranger's daughter. Look, it's okay. If this is going to be difficult for you..."

"It's fine. Yes, yes, I'll meet you. I don't know for sure if I can trust you, but I trust my daughter. There's one condition, though."

"What?"

"I haven't had a curry in over a month and could really murder one; excuse the bad pun. If you bring a chicken Madras with you, I'm all yours. My daughter will sort you out a key... don't ask, Anna will explain. And this is my address, if address is the right word for it..."

*

Monday nights were usually quiet nights in the Tap and this particular November night was no exception. George was unusually edgy. The reason? The well heeled customer sitting quietly at the table by the fireplace, watching every move that he made. He'd been there since before 10pm, sitting in the same seat, nursing the same large vodka he had been slowly sipping at for over an hour. Around 11.35pm, as the last customers drifted away, Hugo Boss gestured to George to join him, with a subtle wave of his left hand.

"Good evening, my friend. How are you tonight?" he smiled at George, exposing the gold tooth.

"Fine... fine, thanks." George shuffled nervously, looking around to see if there were any staff members around to call upon if needed. Sandra, the only barmaid still on duty that night, was round the back, clearing up. He was pretty well alone.

"You know why I'm here, don't you big man. I set you a little task and I want to know what you've found out." He reached into his jacket. George's ample buttocks clenched, wondering what was about to come out. With a sense of relief, it turned out to be a silver cigarette case. Hugo Boss opened it and put a cigarette in his mouth, pulled out a silver lighter from his pocket, and deftly lit it.

"Hang on, you can't smoke that here. I could lose my licence." George suddenly found his courage. That dissipated somewhat when the reply came back.

"My fat friend, if you don't give me what I need, it won't be your licence you will be losing, it will be your miserable and insignificant life. My friend, I have been given a task and if you don't give me a little assistance tonight, I will have to give serious consideration to removing your rather ample liver, cooking it slowly before you, and serving it back to you, one forkful at a time."

Hugo Boss smiled as George began to talk.

*

Graham fidgeted on his bunk, checked the time on his mobile for the umpteenth time that evening and, realising it was now 8.10pm, began to fear something had gone wrong. They were supposed to be there at 8pm, bang on. What if this was a trap? Any moment now, would he hear a loud hailer to tell him he was surrounded by armed police and to come out with his hands up? Perhaps there wouldn't even be a warning. Perhaps a canister of tear gas would come smashing in through the window. Would the door then be kicked in and, before he knew what was going on, would he be tied, hooded and on his way to Guantanamo Bay? Actually, that was probably unlikely.

Suddenly Graham was brought back to the real world with a start as he heard a short, sharp rap on the door. He knew from the rhythm who that was though. He took a deep breath, composed himself and, after a slight pause, opened the shed door.

Outside in the gloom, Graham perceived two figures. The first was the tall, slim figure of his daughter in her green combat jacket. The second, a step behind, a woman of medium build with shoulder length dark hair, wearing jeans, a black coat and carrying a shoulder bag.

"Hi, come in." Graham stepped back to allow them into Shed Heaven, somewhat tidier than earlier that morning. The only guests he'd had to date, with the exception of his daughter, had been male and who frankly didn't give a toss about the state of his refuge. As long as they had somewhere to sit and smoke, they were happy.

"Hi dad." Anna rushed in and gave him a hug. Graham responded and hugged her tight. "This is Becky." She turned and introduced the figure behind her. Becky put out her hand and Graham responded.

"It's really good to meet you at last Graham."

"It's good to meet you as well... Becky." He smiled. She wasn't what he'd expected from a representative of her profession. She exuded a warmth and friendliness, and she had the most attractive large brown eyes that transfixed him. Momentarily lost there, he held onto her hand longer than expected. "Oh... sorry." He let go and gestured for her to sit down on the cleanest of the eccentric assortment of furniture. "Welcome to Shed Heaven," he smiled.

"Shed Heaven?"

"It was named after the band Shed Seven by one of my dad's embarrassing middle aged friends," Anna added helpfully.

Suddenly aware she was there, Becky turned to face her. "Anna, thank you for all your help and trust in me, and for introducing me to your dad."

"You are going to help him aren't you?" Anna fixed her with an assertive look that immediately reminded Graham of his sister.

"I'm going to try, Anna. I'm going to try."

Anna relaxed her gaze and nodded at her. She turned to her father, now sitting back on his bunk.

"Dad, I'm going now. Mum doesn't know I'm here. I'll... I'll see you soon?"

Graham stood up and gave her a tight hug. "I'll see you soon, love, and thank you. You've been amazing."

"I suppose I've just inherited those Pilgrimm genes, eh?" Graham laughed. Inside, he wished he had.

After Graham had closed the door behind Anna, he turned to face Becky.

"So what happens now?"

"Now, we have an Indian." Becky smiled a warm smile and Graham laughed as she reached down towards her shoulder bag.

*

Anna locked the gates to the allotment site and turned round to begin the 20 minute walk that would take her to her mum's house, only vaguely aware of a BMW parked less than 100 metres down the lane to her left with a solitary figure behind the wheel, dimly illuminated by the glow of the cigarette he was smoking. *Drug dealer* she thought, and carried on.

*

Graham was amazed how quickly Becky rearranged the ramshackle collection of furniture and clutter to create an attractive, central space in Shed Heaven, with a table, cloth and even candles, for their meal.

"I've taken the liberty of bringing wine as well Graham, if that's okay with you?"

"Yes... yes that's fine, great. Thanks." He turned round after moving a few random tools out of the way into the furthest corner to create more space.

"Four candles?"

"No, three," replied Becky, puzzled.

"No, fork handles." Graham grinned at her holding the broken shaft of a garden fork he was tidying away. "Sorry, old Two Ronnies joke."

Becky laughed. "I remember that. Very funny." They looked at each other for a moment, Graham transfixed by her beautiful brown eyes. Becky gestured for him to sit down.

"I promised you a chicken Madras and that is exactly what I present before you. We should really be drinking white, but I thought it wouldn't be chilled enough. Are you ok with a Merlot?"

"Yes, yes of course. Thank you Becky." They sat down and ate. Becky had even brought plates, cutlery and wine glasses.

"So tell me about yourself Graham. How does a humble local government officer manage to evade the law for so long, hiding right under their noses here in Leeds?"

"Hey, this isn't being recorded is it?"

"You can frisk me for a wire if you want," she replied with a fake American accent, holding up her arms. Then, suddenly aware of what she was doing she looked down, embarrassed. "Hey, sorry, I wasn't meaning anything, or coming on to you. I... er..."

"Hey, it's okay." Graham laughed. "I believe you. How have I escaped so far? Good friends, I suppose, and family," he added, thinking of Anna. "Tell me about you though. You sounded somewhat frustrated on the phone the other day."

"Are you turning the tables on this interview? Alright Mr. Pilgrimm, I'm 35, been a reporter for nearly 15 years, mostly with the Post, and am getting nowhere fast. My greatest achievement was the exposure of the Golding brothers in the Enterprise North banking scandal when I was 26, shortly after joining the paper; since then, nothing."

"I remember that. That was a really big deal, national news. Didn't that open doors?"

"No, not at all. Part of me thinks *conspiracy theory*, jealous male colleagues. I'm ambitious. I work hard, but my editor and colleagues seemed to stop giving me the sexy stories, the leads that I could really get my teeth into. But then maybe I'm being paranoid. Maybe it's me. Maybe I was lucky, in the right place at the right time then. Oh, I don't know, maybe I'm not really reporter material."

"I think you are. I mean you're here after all."

"Thank you. Well, a little bit of luck again to start with. I ended up attending the police press conference after you escaped from custody."

"Don't tell me, it should have been one of your male colleagues attending?"

Becky laughed. "Bang on – hey, maybe there is something in this conspiracy theory after all? Anyway, I remember watching Frieda and watching her closely, and I had an instinctive feeling that this didn't add up. It seemed straight forward enough. A beautiful woman, an obsessed and jealous stalker driven mad with desire, who also happen to own the murder weapon, and then to cap it off, escaping police custody instead of fighting his case in court."

"I escaped because I'd been set up and knew I had no chance of finding out what was going on while I was locked up."

"I know. I realised that pretty quickly."

"How?"

"Call it female intuition. There were glimpses of something behind the mask of the poor victim she portrayed that day. And then there was the figure at the back of the hall, in the shadows, watching."

"Oh?"

"Yes. I just caught a glimpse, but it was enough. I found out later it was none other than a property developer James Hyde, who's rather interestingly just secured the lucrative Riverside development." Becky didn't notice an almost imperceptible nod and smile of recognition on the face of Graham in the subdued lighting in Shed Heaven.

"You think all this may be connected?"

"I don't know... not for sure anyway. But it's funny how it's all happening at once. Trouble is, this James Hyde seems like a real pillar of the community. He's a respected philanthropist. He supports numerous local charities around young people and the arts, but there's just something... something..."

"Maybe I can help you out here. One of my support team, Tomo, who I've known since junior school, was taken for what could have been a life threatening ride in the back of a van by two Polish construction workers, with the idea of ascertaining my whereabouts. In theory, by force."

"In theory?"

"Yes, they turned out to be about as dangerous as Pinky and Perky. Anyway, after realising that Tomo's parents came from the same part of Poland as they did, a large quantity of vodka and male bonding loosened their tongues to reveal they work for non-other than James Hyde and had been intimidated themselves into kidnapping Tomo with the idea of Hyde finding me, before the police did, and removing me from the equation. The ironic thing in all this is I've no idea why. Everyone is after me for different reasons and I haven't a fucking clue what is going on!" "Sorry..." Graham added, after realising he's sworn in front of Becky.

"Oh Graham. You poor thing. This is worse than I thought."

"Thanks," said Graham, rather flatly.

"Oh, sorry Graham, but perhaps this gives us a lead. Why would he want to get to you before you are arrested, unless he thinks you could reveal something to them that would prove your innocence? In which case, the only logical conclusion is that our friend Mr. Hyde was involved in the murder, but why though? What could the motive be? One other thing is for sure, there's something going on between him and Frieda." Becky wrinkled her nose and stroked her chin as she thought.

"Just good friends? Perhaps he was a friend of her husband and wanted revenge for his murder?"

"No. That doesn't add up. He'd help the police, pass any evidence or information on to them. He wouldn't compromise his position, he's too much to lose. Besides, if he's getting his workers to abduct your friends, he's not exactly doing his Santa Claus image much good is he? No I think he and Frieda have a special friendship of their own, so to speak."

"So he had her husband murdered so they could be together?"

"Possibly, perhaps keep his wholesome image intact. Instead of home wrecker, after an appropriate period of time for mourning, he gallantly steps in and rescues the heartbroken widow for a new life of luxury in North Yorkshire? We might have something, but there's a lot more work to do."

They finished their meal and Becky packed away the plates and cutlery to wash at home later. Graham refilled their glasses and they sat back at the table.

"So, back to you Graham. I don't really know anything about you."

"There's no much to tell really. I'm nearly 45 - it's my birthday in December. I was born in Leeds and will probably die here... possibly sooner than I would have hoped. Sorry." He smiled and raised his palms apologetically. "Excuse the gallows humour. Anyway, back to my story. My parents are still alive and obviously worried sick. I daren't tell them where I am, but they know I'm alright, for the moment at least. I went to Askham Bryan College straight from school and studied Horticulture. I wasn't sure when I qualified what I really wanted to do. I thought about getting into conservation for a while. It was a big passion for my twin sister Annie. We both did a bit of voluntary conservation work, but, after a while, I saw there were some vacancies in the Parks Department here in Leeds so I applied for a job and have been here ever since."

"Do you mind if I ask you about your sister?" Becky asked, aware of her recent death. Graham paused and took a mouthful of wine.

"Annie was beautiful. She was my twin sister, believe it or not." Graham laughed in a self deprecating way, pointing at his own face. Becky smiled back. Despite wanting to keep her professional head on, she actually found him really attractive, even more so than from the photos and footage she had seen earlier. Living rough all these weeks seemed to give him even more of a rugged appeal. "She was always confident, even as a little girl, brave – afraid of nothing. And she was focussed. Whatever she wanted in life, she worked hard for, and usually achieved it. There was never any stopping her. Even though she was my twin, I supposed I always saw her as an older sister. She was always the leader in our games as kids, and that's how it seemed to pan out when we grew up, though I saw less and less of her as her career in environmental research took off and she travelled all over the world. She never married. Her career seemed to be her life."

"Did you name Anna after her?"

"Yes. Kate, my ex wife, wasn't keen on the idea. So instead of Annie it was Anna, a compromise in the end."

"Tell me about your wife."

"Kate? Well, she's a couple of years younger than me. We met at work, nearly 20 years ago to the day funnily enough. She worked in the finance team for our part of the service, managing our grounds maintenance budgets. A few weeks later we got together at our work's Christmas party and then were together ever since, until the divorce a couple of years ago."

"What was she like?"

"Oh, she was a looker." Graham nodded and smiled to himself as he spoke and Becky, despite herself, felt a heavy twinge of jealousy. "We had a lot in common at first, got on really well, and one day after we'd been going out together for a few years, she broke the news she was pregnant. Everything changed really after that. At first it was great. We got married, got our house, where Kate still lives, and had Anna. Then we seemed to get stuck in a rut. Work and other routine got in the way of the spontaneity, and we slowly just seemed to drift apart until one day, Kate said she'd had enough."

"I'm sorry," said Becky and, despite her jealousy, she was.

"I think a big factor, if I'm honest, is I didn't always help myself. I lacked the drive Annie had. There were a couple of opportunities at work where I could have pushed myself, got promoted and climbed the career ladder. The money would have helped. But worse than that, I think after a while Kate saw me as a bit of a loser. We had some big arguments..." Graham looked down, embarrassed.

"I'm sorry I'm dragging this up Graham. For what it's worth, to have survived the last few weeks and kept it together like you have done shows a strength of spirit that I think most other people wouldn't have. I think there's more to you than you realise." Graham looked up and smiled.

"Thanks Becky."

"So what makes you tick Graham? What is your passion?"

"Well, footy for one thing."

"Footy?"

"I follow the mighty whites, Leeds. Always have done. It's in the blood. I was a bit too young to enjoy the glory years in the 70's. But hey ho, good times and bad, you still follow your team.

They're kind of this big dysfunctional family that, love 'em - even hate 'em at times, they're still family. Sorry. I'm going on."

"No, don't worry. My last boyfriend was a big Leeds fan."

"Oh? You're not together?"

"No. We split up months ago. I found out he'd been seeing his secretary at work. What a cliché." Graham resisted the idea for one of those *can I take your particulars down sir?* Carry On type quips.

"I'm sorry Becky." Are you okay now?"

"Yes. It took a while. You know he blamed me? Said I was too focussed on my career. Maybe he was right."

"Hey, if he really loved you, he would have supported you and got behind you. He may be a United fan, but he was a fool to lose you."

Becky smiled. "Thanks Graham. You're a real gent." They talked for the better part of another hour, then downed what was left in their glasses and Becky stood up.

"I guess I'd better be making tracks." Graham reluctantly stood up too. He was deeply aware that he didn't want her to leave.

He opened the door for her as she reached for her bag. They were then both greeted by the sight of torrential rain outside.

"Oh!" Becky exclaimed. "What now?" They both looked at each other and, after a moment's hesitation, Graham put his arms around her and kissed her.

Becky accepted his kiss and responded, with a deep and passionate kiss back that took them both by surprise. His heart beat like a drum as he began to undress her. He guided her to the bunk then gently, very gently, they made love.

Afterwards, as they lay together tucked up in his sleeping bag, his arms around her and her head on his chest, he stared up at the timbers above, illuminated by the subtle orange glow of the dying candles. Outside, the falling rain lightly drummed on the roof. He reflected on their lovemaking. It had been

131

passionate but gentle, a contrast to the fast, furious and urgent sex with Frieda. Becky shuffled and woke from her doze.

"Hi big boy," she croaked sleepily. Graham's ego, and manhood, immediately rose a couple of notches.

"You've noticed then?" he replied with mock arrogance. Becky laughed and gave him a gentle squeeze between the legs.

"You never finished telling me."

"Telling you what?"

"Telling me what makes you tick, what you're passionate about. There's got to be more to you than football and allotments."

"Oh, I don't know. I had dreams when I was younger, like everyone has I suppose, but life gets in the way."

"What sort of dreams?"

"Well, don't laugh, but I always fancied being a writer."

"Really?"

"Now you're mocking me."

"No I'm not."

"You are. You're laughing." He climbed on top of her, pinned her down and started tickling her. "Say you're sorry."

"No, never," she laughed. He tickled her more. Then he felt a much firmer grip than before down below.

"Oh, that's cheating!"

"All's fair in love and war. Now you say you're sorry," Becky laughed.

"Ow! Okay, okay I'm sorry!" he exclaimed, laughing.

"So? What's this about being a writer?"

"You reporters never give up, do you? Anyway, promise you won't laugh?" Becky smiled an over the top angelic smile, then crossed her heart dramatically. "When I was younger, at school, I wrote short stories. Some got published, the school magazine and even a couple in the local paper. I dreamt of being a real writer when I got older, but, well... as I say, real life got in the way."

"But you are a writer. 'Graham's Garden' in the Post, remember?"

"No, I mean crime novels, mysteries, that sort of thing. 'Graham's Garden' hardly ranks alongside 'To Kill a Mocking Bird' does it?"

"Well give it a go. The only thing stopping you is you Big G."

"Yeah. Yeah, you're right. Maybe if I survive this. Well, maybe." Becky smiled at him and snuggled close to keep warm in the autumn chill.

"You know what?" she added sleepily, "if this ends happily, it's going to make one heck of a story."

Graham smiled and held her close. As the light from the dying candles began to fade, they both fell fast asleep."

*

The figure dressed in the expensive overcoat peered over the railings from his vantage point, where the road rose to its highest point near the canal bridge. His gaze wandered across the allotment site as the rain began to fall around him. *Well, my fat friend*, he said to himself, *maybe you did hear right after all.*

There was no mistaking the faint glow from the shed window, some 300 metres across the site. *Now why on earth would any of those sad old men be out working in their shitty little plots at this hour?* He smiled to himself and instinctively reached under his coat to touch the handle of his Beretta, his choice weapon of termination. Except that this wouldn't be used to kill the gardener. No, it had to be an accident, or suicide. The canal, being so close, presented an opportunity. He was mindful of Hyde's instructions though. He personally wanted to supervise this. It would make things a little more complicated, but hey, Hyde was paying the bill. He'd have to get him down here.

The rain fell harder. He pulled his lapels up and returned to his car. *No rush my gardener friend. You've been there a long time. One more day won't make a difference.*

*

Willow lit another Silk Cut and watched from the café on the platform as the Moscow - Beijing express pulled in, bang on time. She took another sip of coffee and lifted the newspaper higher to obscure her western face from the passengers alighting from the express, then noticed her quarry among the multitude. *Got you, you piece of shit.*

She waited until he'd passed, then she rose and followed at a discrete distance, leaving Beijing Central for a run down part of the city. Although Vidic wasn't aware of the tall, attractive figure following him, Molokov was. He rang Vidic on his mobile and suggested an alteration to their planned route.

Willow kept a healthy distance, but kept Vidic in her sight. Her orders were clear, to bring him in alive. There would be no problem with the Chinese. He was an embarrassment being in their country in the first place. He dealt in people, hard drugs, weaponry and anything than else that could make him money. He was also a key player in the lucrative trade in young girls for the sex industry, many of the victims barely ten years old. This, more than anything else in his business portfolio, particularly bothered her.

He turned down a narrow alley. Willow instinctively felt a twinge of anxiety. Nevertheless, she was close now, almost there. She got her phone out to call for backup then paused. At the bottom of the alley Vidic stopped abruptly, then turned slowly to face her, a big smile on his face. Momentarily surprised, Willow froze and stared back, as Vidic lifted his arms in mock surrender.

Instinctively she turned around, just in time to avoid a knife that was inches from her jugular. She took the measure of the three assailants; one, the leader, slightly back from the other two who moved towards her, both armed with knives.

"You are a very careless lady. These streets can be dangerous to the unwary traveller," Molokov mocked from the rear. His two henchmen closed in on Willow.

In a split second, the first dropped like a stone from a well placed kick to the genitals. The second paused for an instant in surprise – a fatal mistake. Willow leapt up from the ground and turned, placing a kick to the side of his head that knocked him unconscious instantly. It would be 24 hours before he would fully regain his senses.

Molokov, momentarily distracted, wasn't going to make the same mistake. He drew an automatic and beckoned Willow back down the alley towards Vidic. The henchman with the traumatised testicles moaned pitifully as Willow stepped over him and moved down the alley towards Vidic. She stopped, turned and faced Molokov.

"Now what?" she asked Molokov.

He shrugged mockingly. "Now you die." He raised the pistol and then paused as he saw a smile and knowing glance from Willow, not at him but over his shoulder, behind him. "What...?" he turned to look, then, realising he'd been tricked, he turned back.

Too late.

With a kick to his wrist, he dropped the weapon. Bending to pick it up, Willow's long right leg struck him under the jaw. The single blow was all that was needed. This would require a longer spell in hospital, some surgery, followed by a sentence that wouldn't see him back on the streets for 20 plus years.

She turned to Vidic who came at her with an iron bar. She deftly avoided it then struck a blow to his back that sent him sprawling across the alley. She moved towards him, but before she could immobilise him, he spun round and pointed an old fashioned Saturday Night Special at her. She saw him squeeze the trigger and leapt to one side as the bullet missed her by inches. He altered his position and aimed again. This time she jumped up, grabbed onto an iron fire escape and pulled herself onto it as the bullet hit the stonework below her.

He stood up and anxiously moved back to get a better view of the fire escape, but there was no sign of anyone. She'd disappeared. He looked all around him. Then, without any further hesitation, he ran out of the alley and disappeared into the Beijing afternoon.

Chapter Four – Out of the frying pan and onto the plate

One of my favourite vegetables is another member of the onion family, the leek. Don't be afraid to give these a go. They're easy and will give you a fresh vegetable crop right through the winter. There's nothing tastier than homemade leek and potato soup made with your own leeks and spuds!

Sow the seeds thinly in trays and grow on in the greenhouse or windowsill.

You could stagger the sowing, starting in early spring, to ensure a continuous crop that will give you a harvest all through the season and even into spring the following year. Now comes the clever bit. When the leeks are around the thickness of a pencil, carefully separate them, teasing the roots apart, and pop each plant into a hole around 6 inches deep by an inch or so across. Use something like an old tool handle to make the row of holes, each around 4 inches apart. Instead of backfilling with soil, fill each hole with water to settle the soil around the roots. Planting the leeks so deep encourages the development of the characteristic long white stems, as does earthing them up through the growing season.

"What are you doing here?" Frieda hissed at him through the gap in her kitchen door. "You were supposed to stay away until all this is sorted."

"It nearly is my love. It nearly is!" Hyde could barely contain his excitement. He'd clearly been drinking and was carrying a bottle of something, waving it around with his left hand in a reckless fashion and almost dropping it once or twice.

"Oh really? This time?" Frieda enquired cynically, peering behind him to ensure there were no neighbours in earshot. "How did you get here?"

"I drove. The car's down the road. I was very discreet." He wobbled slightly as he tapped the side of his nose with his right hand. Frieda eyed him and his crumpled suit with equal disdain, then invited him in, looking around once more to ensure there was nobody in the vicinity.

"It seems like a lifetime since I was here Fri. Do you remember? Your husband was away in Birmingham on business and you were blowing me there in the lounge, on the sofa. God Frieda, I need you. Just a quick one, please. I need to feel that sexy mouth around my..."

"So what's this development then?" Frieda interrupted, ignoring his pleas. Hyde, by this time had got on his knees. He looked up her, perched on the kitchen stool. Her face was impassive.

"Just give me something and I'll tell you everything." He grabbed her bare foot and started kissing it. She pulled away and stood up.

"I told you Mr. Hyde, nothing until this is concluded. You've been drinking as well."

"I know," he smiled, recovering quickly from Frieda's rebuff. "I'm celebrating. Are you going to ask me why?"

"Okay. Why are you celebrating?"

"We've found him!"

"Pilgrimm? You've got him?" Frieda asked, suddenly interested.

"Nearly."

"Nearly?"

"Yes. We know where he's hiding and tomorrow..."

"Tomorrow what?"

"Tomorrow, he'll be found floating down the canal. A suicide note will say he couldn't take any more. The guilt was too much. He had to end it." A smile slowly spread over Frieda's face.

"Where is he?"

"He's in an allotment shed." Hyde could barely contain himself. He started clapping his hands for joy. "He's been living with the other vegetables on a council allotment plot here in Leeds all the time." He burst out laughing. "Can you believe it?"

"Does he know you know?"

"What?" Hyde wobbled, still perched on his knees, definitely too much the worse for drink."

"I said does he know you know where he is?"

"Oh. No, hasn't a fucking clue."

"Well, that is interesting. What's in the bottle?"

"A little of your favourite tipple." Hyde reached up for the vodka he'd placed on a worktop and showed her the label.

"Ah, how thoughtful," she smiled a little warmer. "Well, you don't look like you're in any condition to drive Mr. Hyde and I certainly don't want you bringing any attention to yourself by causing an accident in my neighbourhood. I suppose you'd better stay here."

"Thanks Frieda." Hyde could barely contain his excitement. Age was no barrier to an erection when in the company of Frieda Olin.

"My rules, though." She looked down at him from her stool. "First, I want you to start with my toes." She probed around the fringes of his mouth with her right foot.

"Yes, yes," replied Hyde rather weakly.

"Then I want you to work your way up my legs to here." She stroked her crotch. "I want you to take your time though, and really please me. Is that okay?"

"Yes. Yes, anything you want."

"I'm glad we understand each other Mr. Hyde. Well then, what are you waiting for?"

*

"Sorry to bother you Miss, but we wondered if Mr. Butterworth was in?" Constable Dirker enquired politely when Viv opened the door.

"Oh. Yes, yes, he's in, but not feeling himself at the moment. Can this wait?"

"No Miss Chambers. I'm afraid it can't," barked the now familiar voice of DS Hopkins behind Constable Dirker; familiar, because barely a day seemed to go by now without a call from him. Viv was at the end of her tether. Dave was losing it, big style. She knew Dave knew where Graham was hiding and she knew Hopkins knew Dave knew. Dave was going to crack. His behaviour was becoming increasingly erratic. He was convinced the house was bugged and would only speak to her of confidential matters from the safety of the airing cupboard. He didn't even consider the space under the bed safe anymore. *What the heck* she thought.

"Come in officers... Dave!" she shouted up the stairs in the same breath. "Dave! You've got visitors." She turned to the officers and said with the sweetest of smiles, "tea?"

*

It wasn't quite daylight yet when Becky opened the door to leave Shed Heaven.

"I'll call you later. Are you going to be alright today? Do you need anything?" she asked Graham.

"Well, I can think of a couple of things." He put his arms around her and gently squeezed her breasts.

"I'll see what I can do Big G." Becky turned and kissed him deeply. "Would you be up for a visit from the press later this evening?"

"I'm up for the press now Miss B." He placed her left hand on his crotch while they kissed again.

"Mmm. Well, we can't leave it like that, can we." She closed the door and knelt down. Graham gulped with anticipation as she unzipped his fly.

Dave looked horrific. His clothes were dishevelled, he was unshaven and his hair clearly hadn't been combed in days.

"How are you today Mr. Butterworth?" Hopkins enquired.

"Fine, thanks," he mumbled, looking nervously at the officers.

"You look tired, like you've not slept for a while. Is there anything on your mind, any particular burden you'd like to offload that might help?" Hopkins probed.

"About...?" replied Dave vaguely.

"About the whereabouts of a dangerous and sick fugitive, Mr. Butterworth."

"Tell him!" demanded Viv.

"Viv... no!"

"Tell him, or I'm leaving you!"

"What would you like to tell me Mr. Butterworth?" asked Hopkins, quietly, but firmly.

Dave paused and stared straight ahead into space.

"The allotment."

"What?"

"He's hiding down at the allotment, in a shed."

"He's hiding in a fucking shed?" Barked Hopkins. "If you are taking the piss out of me, I am going to seriously kick the seven colours of shit out of you!"

"He's there. I swear." Dave held his head in his hands. He'd betrayed his friend, but he knew he couldn't take anymore.

"Give me an exact location now Mr. Butterworth, and you might just avoid a long prison sentence!"

*

Graham lay back on his bunk. That had been a fantastic night. He was on the run, the odds were against him, but he felt on top of the world. He'd known Becky less than 12 hours, but felt he'd known her all his life and, crazy as it seemed, he was in love. There was no doubt Frieda had turned him on. The sex was like nothing he's ever had before. Frieda was a looker and knew all the tricks, but even if you put her psychopathic personality to one side, there was something more with Becky, much more. He was in love.

As the sun rose and illuminated the inside of the shed he began to plan his next move. He was aware he'd changed over the last few weeks. He was different. Yes, he was still a long way from finding out the truth and clearing his name. He still had the police after him and now various goons from James Hyde. But strangely, he was now beginning to feel more in control of his own destiny, perhaps for the first time in his life. Becky's belief in him also gave him an inner strength. Perhaps now, his luck might be on the turn.

He got up and stretched, conscious he'd better get a wash before the allotment holders came down to tend their plots in the autumn sunshine. He was reaching for his towel when there was an almighty crash and the shed door literally flew off its hinges.

The first thing that struck Graham was that the figure standing in the doorway was immaculately dressed. The second was that he was holding a firearm in his right hand. The third was that he was smiling, displaying a gold tooth.

Graham stood frozen to the spot. Oddly, once the initial shock had passed, he felt a strange sense of calm. He wasn't afraid. *That's not logical*, he thought. *Maybe the fear hasn't had a chance to kick in yet.*

He was brought out of his reverie by a cold, calm voice, with a tinge of an accent.

"Graham Pilgrimm?"

"Yes." Why deny it?

"We've been looking for you."

"We?"

"Yes. That's not important to you though. What is important is that you will die this morning? Does that bother you?" he asked nonchalantly as he attached a silencer to his weapon.

"No." Something told Graham he wasn't going to die this morning. He didn't know what. Perhaps it wasn't his time yet? He glanced around. There was no weapon to hand, nowhere to run either. He stood and faced his executioner.

Hugo Boss was unnerved. Why wasn't this gardener on his knees begging for mercy like the others had over the years? After a brief pause, he continued.

"We are going to make this out to be a suicide Mr. Pilgrimm. I've already prepared a note. It would be helpful if you'd just sign it first, if that's not too inconvenient?"

"May I read it first?" Graham enquired politely. "It would be nice to know why I have decided to depart this Earth."

"That would be wasting time Mr. Pilgrimm. I really want to be away before it gets too light. I have another visit to make for my employer today, another inconvenience that will also need to be removed from the equation, so to speak. So if you don't mind signing this?" He reached into his expensive jacket with his left hand and pulled out an envelope and a pen. He was about to open the envelope and produce the letter within, when a startled expression suddenly spread across his face. It coincided with a loud clang from behind. He looked at Graham with a puzzled expression, then fell forward onto the floor, unconscious.

Graham looked behind where Hugo Boss had stood and, in the doorway, there stood the unmistakable figure of Joe holding a garden spade.

"Well, Joe, am I pleased to see you!"

"I hope you don't mind me interrupting. Only that feller had a bit of an ill look about him, so I followed him here to your shed. Looks like he wasn't here to deliver the milk." He added after seeing the pistol on the floor.

"No Joe. I think you just saved my life. Thank you."

"No problem, lad. I thought I'd hit him with the flat end though. I didn't want to make a mess. Who is he?"

"I don't know, but I can guess who he's working for."

"That James Hyde scum bag?"

"I think so."

"Well then. I think we ought to find out Graham don't you? And if he doesn't want to talk, maybe we ought to get a bit medieval with my secateurs?"

"You've been watching too much Quentin Tarantino Joe. I thought 'Last of the Summer Wine' was more your scene."

"Cheeky sod. Either way, he's going to come round soon. So, for what it's worth, I suggest we tie him up and then decide."

"Sounds good. Got any of that string you've been using for your onions?"

Five minutes later they had the unconscious figure tied up and the pistol carefully placed onto a higher shelf with the help of a couple of pea sticks, to avoid leaving prints. They'd no sooner perched on a couple of chairs when the bound figure began groaning and shuffling on the floor.

"Wakey, wakey, you pile of shit," growled Joe, prodding the figure with the toe of his wellie.

Hugo Boss mumbled something in an unfamiliar language before opening his eyes and looking up at Graham and Joe.

"Welcome back to the land of the living," grunted Joe. "Now to avoid any unnecessary unpleasantness, I think you ought to start talking. Who are you?"

"Fuck off old man. What are you going to do?" Hugo Boss looked up at Joe's ancient face with contempt.

Joe knelt down and put his face close to the would be assassin's and whispered, "I'm going to get my old, wizened cock out and..." Hugo Boss's eyes opened with alarm and his lips moved silently as Joe continued out of Graham's earshot. The quiet was interrupted by Graham's mobile. It was Tomo.

"Hi Tomo. What's happening?"

"Listen, you've not got much time. I'm just down from the allotment gates and two pandas and a police van have just pulled up. Grimy, I think they're on to you."

"Shite!" Graham exclaimed. Joe looked up and Graham filled him in with the news.

"There's only one thing for it, you'll have to get off the site, and now," said Joe.

"How? They're at the gate."

"There's a way out along the canal bank. Look, grab your essential stuff and follow me."

"What about him?"

"Well, kid, looks like he'll have to explain himself to the law. That could be interesting." Hugo Boss wriggled unsuccessfully against his bonds and gazed up at them with venom in his eyes. "A pretty boy like you should have a fun time in those prison showers," Joe smiled down to him. "Come on kid. Follow me. Quick!"

For an old man, Joe moved with some pace. They went to the fenced boundary at the back of the allotment site and found a gap, just wide enough for Graham to squeeze through.

"Just follow the fence. It's a bit overgrown, but there's an old path that will take you to Bridge Street. Good luck lad."

"Thanks Joe. I hope to see you soon." Joe looked at him and nodded. "Go on. Get out of here". *I've just to figure out what I'm going to say to the boys in blue,* he thought to himself as he walked back.

As it was, Joe didn't have to worry about that. A crowd of the early plot holders was already gathered around Shed Heaven as the handcuffed figure of Hugo Boss was brought out.

Hopkins stood a little back from the uniformed officers making the arrest. Possession of a firearm, knife, and small quantity of cocaine. That should be enough to be going on with. *But,* he thought as he watched the figure being led away, *who the bloody hell is he and what in the name of God is going on?*

*

Hyde woke up next to Frieda as the Saturday morning sunshine poured into the bedroom window. *Good morning world, he thought to himself.* He felt great.

The gardener would soon be dead and he'd just had the best night's sex he'd had in weeks. He looked over at the sleeping figure of Frieda. *You are a very dirty lady.* Feeling himself getting aroused again, he reached between her legs and started probing her mound. She woke up groaning. *I'm in here,* he thought.

"Get your hands off. I'm tired."

"Come on woman. You know you want it."

"Fuck off! I decide when I want sex. What time is it?" Seeing the time on her mobile she added, "get out of my bed and get out of here. You should have left hours ago."

"What's the problem?"

"The problem is you pushed the boundaries last night. You shouldn't have come round. What if one of the neighbours sees you?"

"I've waited long enough Frieda. It's been over a month since we got rid of your husband and soon the gardener will be dead as well, there's nothing to stop us moving forward.

"Have you heard?"

"What?"

"Have you heard from your man? Wasn't he supposed to be calling you first thing this morning?"

"No. Not yet, but..." Hyde paused. Actually, he hadn't heard. He felt for the alternative mobile phone he used for those sorts of business transactions by the side of the bed. No message or missed call.

Frieda interrupted his thoughts. "Well?"

"Nothing... yet."

"Look, I told you already, you need to be out of here now!"

"Alright, I'm on my way." He flung back the sheets and started dressing. "I'll call you later."

"Only when you've something to tell me. Until then, I don't want any more contact with you."

"Fri..."

"You heard. When you know the gardener is dead, then you can call."

*

Unaware that her dad was on the run again, Anna had already made her plans for that Saturday morning. She'd met a reluctant Umar at the bus stop and they began walking towards the affluent residential area where Frieda lived.

"This is not going to work Anna," said Umar nervously. "She is going to see right through this."

"Have faith Umar. No one is going to be suspicious of a panda."

Umar wasn't convinced. The bus ride had been stressful enough, with sniggers from the older kids and anxious looks from the under 5's at the 6' 5" sweating panda sat on the back seat of the bus, but the idea of facing this woman he'd met before as a boy scout was different. He had a bad feeling about this. They were both taking a serious risk.

"Just do what I told you and everything will be fine. Trust me." She fixed him with a look that both reassured him that she knew what she was doing and that he didn't really have a choice in the matter.

"Okay," he said, without much conviction. "Where did you get this from anyway?"

"My dad used to raise money for the World Wildlife Fund when he was younger. He used to dress up in this to save tigers and, err... hedgehogs, that kind of stuff."

The panda walked down Frieda's drive and knocked on the back door. After what seemed like an eternity to Umar, the door opened.

"What the...?" blurted Frieda, surprised to see a panda stood on the doorstep. "Who the hell are you?"

"Oh, hello Miss. I'm collecting in the neighbourhood for the World Wild things Fund."

"What are you specifically collecting for?" enquired a clearly unimpressed Frieda.

"Err, pandas and... hedgehogs."

"Just piss off now or I'm phoning the..." Before she could say 'police' there was a hammering on the front door. "Who the hell is that?" She turned and walked to the front door.

As quick as he could, within the constraints of his panda outfit, he leapt into the kitchen and reached up for the concealed recording equipment. Mercifully, it was still where he'd deposited it a week ago. In an instant, he was out of the back door, just before a furious Frieda returned to the kitchen after seeing the figure of a teenage girl running away from the front door. She ran back to the front of the house and watched the panda and the girl as they headed out of the cul-de-sac. They had something, some sort of device? And that girl, she'd seen her before. She put 2 and 2 together and came up with a big fat 4.

*

Graham lay concealed in the vegetation at the side of the road considering his next move. He needed somewhere to stay. Friends and family were out of the question. He knew they would all be watched closely, especially now the police knew he was on the run again. The Shed Heaven incident would probably raise his profile in the media again after things seemed to have quietened down. He'd become old news, and once the press and TV realised that he probably wasn't a serial killer after all, they quickly bored of him. Things would be different now, though. The arrest of the sharp dressed assassin would, without doubt, raise his profile again.

There was really only one place he could go. He retrieved his mobile from his pack and phoned Becky. Just when he thought she wasn't going to answer, he heard her voice.

"Hello Big G. I didn't expect to hear from you until this afternoon."

"Hi Becky. Can you talk?"

"Well, not for long. I'm still at work. I'll be knocking off at one..."

"Becky, I've a major problem!"

"What is it? What's wrong?" Becky asked, clearly concerned.

"I had a visitor after you left. I think he was one of Hyde's stooges. Anyway, he dropped by with the intention of delivering some major trauma to my anatomy. To cut a long story short, one of my neighbouring plot holders came to my assistance, and we left him trussed up in the shed."

"Left him?"

"Yes. Before we could get to know him better the police turned up in force. They must have had a tip off where I was. Anyway, I got away and, well..." He didn't have to ask any more. Becky responded immediately.

"Stay where you are. I'll come and fetch you. You're coming home with me."

*

Once they were a safe distance from Frieda's house, they found a quiet spot in a park where Umar could strip out of the panda costume.

"Sexy," mocked Anna. Then she looked down at the recorder.

"Very funny. It was boiling in there. What do we do now?"

"Now I take our little friend here back home, and find out what little secrets it has to reveal. This is going to be interesting."

*

By the time Hyde got back to The Beeches, he was seriously concerned. He parked up and went in, picking up the decanter of scotch in the hall, taking it into the lounge while he examined the mobile in his left hand, as he had every five minutes since he'd left Frieda's house in Leeds. *Why hasn't he called?* He should have called hours ago, but there was no missed call, text or anything. Hyde looked at his watch. He should have been on with his next job, tidying another loose end up. Perhaps he was? Maybe he's on with that now and he'll ring when both are finished. Yes. That's it, that's what he'll be doing. *Stop panicking,* he told himself. This guy is a professional. He doesn't make mistakes. Part of him was annoyed at the thought though. Hyde wanted to be there when Graham was to be killed. He didn't just want to watch, he wanted to take part.

He settled back into his chair, poured a large measure of scotch into a tumbler and took an equally large swallow while he relived the memory of his night with Frieda. After a few more glasses, and with a smile on his face, he fell asleep in front of his plasma screen, balanced on the 17th century chest in the corner of the room.

*

"You've got a lovely pad Miss B." Graham looked round the converted warehouse flat next to the canal. It was modern, but tastefully furnished. Minimalist and uncluttered, the glass, chrome and black leather furniture worked in the subtly lit, brick walled apartment.

"Thanks, Big G. I'm glad you're here." She gave him a hug, then added after sniffing at him, "if you want to take a bath, it's through there."

"Subtle Miss B, but no denying it, I could kill for a hot bath... sorry. I keep doing that."

Becky laughed. "Just get yourself in that bath and I'll bring you a glass of wine through."

Oh, did it feel good to get in a hot bath. He'd washed the best he could in the cold water of the tap next to the plot. But this was pure bloody luxury.

Five minutes later Becky came into the bathroom with two glasses of chilled white. She placed them on the side of the bath and began to undress, starting with her top.

"Oh ambassador you do spoil us with your hospitality, fine wines and magnificent tits."

"You are a very cheeky man," she replied, slipping into the bath facing him.

"So what do we do now?" Graham asked with a heavy dose of sleaze in his voice.

"We aren't going to do anything. You are going to thoroughly remove all traces of that allotment from you. Then... well... we'll see."

Half an hour later they were making love on Becky's cast iron frame bed. Graham, on top, arched his back as he gently pushed himself as deep as he could inside Becky. He held there for a moment, conscious that the weeks down at the allotment had honed his body so he looked lean and fit again, in a way he hadn't for more than a decade. Becky moaned with pleasure and gasped as he started gently moving in and out. When the final release came, he felt all strength leave him and he collapsed next her on the bed. It was only then he realised just how tired he was. They held each other as Graham drifted off to sleep. The next thing he was aware of was Becky gently waking him. He opened his eyes to see her beautiful face smiling at him.

"Come on sleepy head. I've made you some dinner." He pulled a rather ill fitting robe on and followed her into the open plan living area. She'd set the table with four candles. "Fork 'andles." She said with a smirk and he laughed as he sat down at the table.

"Something smells good."

"It's pasta with leeks and ham, in a cream sauce, based on a recipe from my Italian grandmother. I hope you like it." She divided the contents of the pan between two plates and brought them to the table.

"This is amazing!" Graham had not had that many hot meals over the last few weeks and so with the added bonus of Becky's excellent culinary skills, he was in food heaven. They finished the rest of the bottle of wine and as Becky went to the fridge to open a fresh, she suggested they move to the sofa. He made himself comfortable on the leather sofa and Becky returned with the wine.

"Shall I put the TV on?"

"Yes, if that's alright. I've not seen a TV since early September."

"Well don't be scared by this. When you see the people, they aren't in the box really. They're pictures brought here from miles away, through the air as if by magic. It must seem so alien to you and your tribe."

"Bollocks!" said Graham, and he threw a cushion at her as she switched it on.

There wasn't much on but Graham didn't care. Curled up with Becky on the sofa, in front of the TV, he truly was in heaven. He did feel though like he'd just returned from some expedition to a far corner of the planet. To be back in a world of comfortable furniture, light, hot food and hot baths, felt bloody great. He was brought down to earth with a rather large bump though when the early evening news came on.

"The search for Graham Pilgrimm, the missing Leeds Council officer wanted for the murder of the builder Peter McArthur, who has been on the run since early September, took a dramatic turn this morning when police, acting on a tip off, raided an allotment site in South Leeds. Instead of finding Mr. Pilgrimm as they expected, they apprehended a man of Eastern European origins found tied up in a shed believed to be the hideout used by Mr. Pilgrimm. It's believed this man has connections to the Eastern European underworld and is also suspected to be connected to a number of gangland killings. Let's turn to our reporter on the scene, Danny Webster, to give us the latest on this case. Danny, are you there?"

"Yes, good evening. I'm down here at the gates to the allotment site and here to report on the latest twist in this extraordinary story of a council employee who seemed just like any other council employee, implicated in a crime of passion after being rejected by the wife of a Leeds builder, and now it seems having some connection with the Eastern European mafia as well. There appears to have been some sort of dispute between them down at the allotment site, which it looks like Graham Pilgrimm had been using as a refuge, resulting in a struggle and the as yet unnamed gentleman being found tied up in the shed, together with a weapon and small quantity of drugs."

"Was this man believed to be selling Graham Pilgrimm drugs or perhaps even working for him?"

"The police simply don't know. The suspect is in custody now, but to date, nothing further has been forthcoming. What I can say after speaking to Detective Inspector Smithson, in charge of the case, is that this backs up his original assertion, providing further evidence that Graham Pilgrimm is likely to be a highly dangerous man and not to be approached by the public. When you have associations with people like the unnamed gentleman arrested earlier this morning, you are moving in serious criminal circles."

"Thank you Danny and (looking at the camera) when we hear of further developments in this case, we'll keep you updated. Now in other news..."

"Oh... shit," said Graham, momentarily lost for words. Becky said nothing. She lowered the sound and stared at the TV, wrinkling her nose deep in thought.

"We are going to have to move really carefully from now on. It looks like James Hyde has connections with dangerous people and organisations. More worrying Graham, someone who knew you were there tipped off the police."

*

While the early evening news revealed the latest twist in the saga to the people of Yorkshire, James Hyde snored in his chair, oblivious.

*

Dave stared at the TV in Viv's bedroom, gutted that he'd betrayed his friend.

He had to do something about this, to make it right.

"Shouldn't you be under the bed or perhaps in a cupboard?" Viv enquired as she entered the bedroom.

"No," said Dave, with a new look of determination on his face. "The time for running is over. It's time to make a stand for truth and justice."

"Well, Captain America, I'm glad to hear it and, in the meantime, I'd be grateful if you could please pack your bags and piss off. I've had enough. Believe it or not Dave, I just want a normal life."

"But Viv...?"

"No buts. You've got 10 minutes to pack up your stuff. We're finished. Go and join the rest of your middle-aged, pot smoking, waste-of-space friends still stuck in your playground days. Go and help your axe-murdering friend. I... have... had... enough!"

She slammed the door as she went out into the garden, while Dave contemplated his next move.

*

"Now, Mr... Ruka. Aleksis Ruka? Would you mind explaining what you were doing down at the allotment site on the morning of your arrest."

Hugo Boss eyed DI Smithson with contempt. "I was just having a look around thinking how nice it would be to have a plot on the site, to grow a few vegetables, so much healthier than the ones in supermarket, when I was jumped from behind and the next thing I wake, tied up..." he raised his hands to emphasise his surprise at the attack down on plot 29. "Leeds is a very dangerous city." He shook his head as he spoke to confirm his disappointment in the breakdown of law and order in this once respected city.

"You were found in possession of Class A drugs and a weapon was also found in the shed, with your prints all over it."

"Officer. I do not know what is going on here. Yes, the drugs are mine. I admit that." He looked down, ashamed. "It is a bad habit, but I am working to free myself of it. I fell into bad company when I was younger. The weapon...?" He shrugged his shoulders, then looked serious. "I wonder if somehow this Graham Pilgrimm was trying to frame me for this murder. Do you think that could be possible? You see, while I was unconscious how easy it would be to put my fingerprints all over this weapon. Yes, the more I think about it, the more I see what happened. " He nodded to himself as if realising what must have happened in the shed. "This Graham Pilgrimm is clearly a very bad man."

*

Text to Kev, Tomo, Mac and Jim-Bob:-
Guys. Need to see you ASAP re G. Can you come round to mine this eve at 8? D.

*

Around 8pm, Hyde was awoken by his mobile. Confused, he picked up the one reserved for the assassin. No call, or text. He looked around the room and saw his other phone on the sideboard, moving with the vibrations accompanying the sampled popular classic used for the ringtone. He stumbled out of his chair and picked it up, not checking to see who the caller was.

"Hello? Hyde here."

"Oh, hello lover boy. I thought you weren't going to answer."

"Fri? Sorry I drifted off. What time is it?"

"That doesn't really matter right now Mr. Hyde. Have you seen the news by any chance?"

"What? No. Why?"

"Well. Now this is really funny, you are going to love this. The police made an arrest down at Pilgrimm's allotment."

"An arrest? Pilgrimm?"

"No. This is the really funny part. No, it wasn't Pilgrimm, it was that Baltic buffoon you hired to kill him. Pilgrimm was nowhere to be seen."

"What? How? He's the best in the business."

"Clearly."

"But..."

"Please. I don't want to hear excuses. There's something else that's worrying me and I want this sorting quickly."

"What is it?"

"I've been stalked by a girl, 15 or 16? Don't know for sure, but she's been making it obvious; someone with a grudge. She's been to the house, twice now, with a stupid looking Asian boy in tow. Earlier today they took something from the house. I don't know what it is, but it could be important."

"Wait a minute," said Hyde, as his head began to clear. "Pilgrimm has a daughter that age."

"Well, that's interesting. If that's the case, she's going to be looking for evidence to clear her father's name. I don't know what she's got but she's got something. Find her and find what she's got and what she knows."

"I... I don't know. Pilgrimm, your husband, fine. A 15 year old girl. I don't know."

"Well I do! You find her. NOW!" Hyde continued to hold the receiver for a full minute after the call abruptly ended.

*

Willow lay on her bed and studied the latest news from England. Her brow furrowed and she tapped her front teeth with the manicured forefinger on her right hand. Her mobile rang and she picked it up with her left hand.

"Yes?"

"Willow? It's Hunter. We've got a positive location. We need to act fast though. He's chartered a private plane – we think he's heading to Russia."

She got off the bed as she spoke.

"That suits me. I need to get back to England soon. I've got work to do there. Listen, can you rustle up a pilot at short notice?" She continued the conversation as she got her clothes together, with the occasional glance back to the TV screen.

*

"What do you make of this?" Smithson's colleague passed him the paper, sealed in the plastic wallet to prevent contamination of potentially important forensic evidence.

"What is it?"

"Believe it or not, it's a suicide note."

"A suicide note from our friend Aleksis?"

"No. Found on Aleksis, but appearing to come from Graham Pilgrimm. It's been typed, but looks like a space at the bottom conveniently left for his signature." Smithson carefully examined the note.

"Well now, this gets more puzzling by the hour. I'm guessing that our friends in the lab found no trace of Mr. Pilgrimm on this?"

"Correct."

"So looks like our friend Aleksis was here to remove Mr. Pilgrimm from the equation with a rather convenient suicide. Now why on earth would he want to do that?"

"Like you suggested earlier, perhaps Mr. Pilgrimm has been a bit of a Walter Mitty character, gardener by day and gangster by night."

"Hmm. Perhaps you are right." Smithson picked up an old copy of the Post and glanced at one of Graham's articles. "Mrs. Smithson's an avid reader of Pilgrimm. Since she started reading his column, her onions have never looked more impressive." Oblivious to the smirk from his colleague, Smithson continued. "I think because of where he was hiding, we've got strong grounds to round up his peculiar associates, particularly the ones that have allotments there, to find out what they know."

"Guys. I don't know what to say." Dave looked nervously down at his hands.

"What do you mean? What do you know Dave?" probed Tomo.

"It's about Graham, what happened earlier today down at the allotment."

"Go on."

"I told the police where he was." Dave shut his eyes in preparation for a beating. What came next though was far worse.

"Dave, I don't believe it. You cock. You've let us and Graham down," said Tomo.

"I'm sorry." Dave held his head in his hands. "They just kept coming back and..."

"It's alright Dave," said a slightly more sympathetic Mac. "Hey, come on guys we all knew they were putting the squeeze on Dave, especially that copper Hopkins."

"I suppose. He's a right twat that bloke. He's got a substantial attitude problem," added Jim-Bob in support, scratching his behind.

"You are not off the hook yet!" Tomo pointed his finger at Dave. Then, turning to the others, "it's a case of what do we do now. Grimy's on the run again and we don't know where he his. For all we know he's lying in a ditch somewhere, freezing to death, or worse! We've not time to lose. Dave, put the fucking kettle on will you? Have you got any biscuits?"

*

"Oh yes. OMG yes. Yes!" Anna exclaimed, and started jumping up and down on her bed. "I've got you, you murdering munter. Ho, ho, ho you ho!" The hours of searching what seemed like endless emptiness occasionally punctuated with the sounds of cooking, washing up and at one point a rather impressive fart (even you Princess Perfect, even you fart) finally paid off big time. Right at the end of the recording, as the machine was running out of memory, there was the knock at the door, followed by Frieda, clear as bell, demanding to know what he was doing there at her house. It was all there, the confession. It was Hyde, the old man who lived at The Beeches. She listened carefully, a mixture of fury, joy and relief careering around her brain. *I've got you. I've got you both.*

Then the expression on her face changed. She screwed up her face, but still couldn't resist a smile. *Ugh, you dirty old...*

*

It was while they were on their second cup of tea and Jim-Bob had just started rolling the first joint, that Mac made the breakthrough. "Why don't we try ringing him?"

"Oh, aye. That's not a bad idea," said Tomo. "Kev. Can you give him a call?" Kevin dutifully obliged. Just after the fifth ring, a voice answered.

"Kev? Kev? Is that you?"

"Graham, are you okay mate? Where are you?"

"I'm fine. Can't say where I am at the moment though. Someone gave me away before and I can't take the risk again. More importantly, it would get someone else into serious trouble and she's put herself out on a limb for me."

"She?"

"I've said too much."

"Are you... err, you know?"

"That would be telling Kev and not very discreet, but I'm safe and the hospitality is...," Graham looked at the naked body of Becky as she wandered into the living room after hearing him on the phone, "...excellent."

"Is he okay?" Tomo pressed.

"Yes, reading between the lines, sounds like he's landed on his feet."

"What?" Graham's voice came through the phone.

"Sorry Grimy, I was just talking to Tomo. He was just asking after you. Listen, we know who told the police. Promise you won't go mad?"

"Why? Who was it?"

Dave took the phone off Kevin and spoke into it.

"Hi Graham. I'm really sorry. It was me."

"You fucking...!" Dave held the phone away from his ear and grimaced.

"Sorry mate. It was the police, they drove me to it. They were coming to the house every day. I was going mad. I'm fine now, though."

"I'm really glad you are Dave because when I get out of here I'm going to..." Dave held the phone away again with another grimace. "Now hand me back to Kev."

"How did he take it?" Tomo asked Dave, after he'd handed the phone to Kevin.

"Not bad. Better than I thought."

"Well at least it's out in the open now." Tomo leaned in to listen in as Kevin talked to Graham.

"Right. Right. Okay. What? Really? Fuck. Do you think that's what he was...? Shit? Okay. Yes. Yes. Did he? Bloody hell! Yes, of course. Well take care mate and we'll speak tomorrow." Kevin ended the call and turned to the others. "Right, there's more. That guy they found in my shed after Grimy got out was there to kill him." There was a stunned silence around the room.

"What? Who was he?" asked Tomo.

"He doesn't know, but he thinks he was working for this James Hyde. He was going to make it look like suicide."

"The sick fucker." Jim-Bob added with disgust in his voice.

"We need a plan of action," said Tomo.

"Well, we know we can't go to the police," Jim-Bob continued after a brief pull on the joint. "Even if they believed us about the suicide plan, they'd still say it was all connected with a gangland dispute."

"We need evidence," said Kevin. "I think we need to draw up a rota between us and watch both this man Hyde and Frieda, 24/7."

"We can't do that. Evenings and weekends are fine, but we all work," said Tomo, then thought for a moment. "Except you Dave. You're still off aren't you?"

"Well, I was thinking about phoning the school with a view to going back..." realising that after what he had done, he'd quit there. "Yes, yes. I could, I suppose."

"What are you up to at the moment Jim-Bob?" Mac asked. Momentarily caught off his guard while inhaling the lion's share of the joint, Jim-Bob coughed loudly.

"Err, one or two business dealings, but, erm, I could find some windows in my diary I suppose?"

"Right, then let's draw up a rota tonight. Dave, have you any paper in this place?"

Before Tomo could get an answer there was a loud and persistent knock at the door. They all looked at each other. They'd heard that knock before.

"Dave, can you fob them off?" Tomo asked. "Tell them you're having an early night and you'll see them down the station tomorrow.

An anxious Dave walked to the front door and, after a pause and a deep breath, he opened it to reveal the smiling figure of DS Hopkins on the doorstep, with several uniformed officers behind him.

"Evening officers, can I help you?"

"You certainly can Mr. Butterworth, by opening the door and allowing my good self and my colleagues into your house."

162

"Well, I was wondering if I could possibly come down to the station tomorrow. It's been a very stressful day couple of days and I was hoping..."

"Nope. Sorry. We're coming in I'm afraid." He barged in and went into the living room, followed by the uniformed officers. "Hello everyone. It's lovely to make your acquaintance again, especially you my old friend Cheeky Fucker," he looked and smiled at Jim-Bob. "And what is that delightful smell? Oh, this gets even better." Hopkins could hardly contain himself realising he could also add possession of Class B drugs to his list. Tomo stood up to challenge the intrusion when Hopkins held up his hand to stop him. "Before you say anything my friend that may be used in a court of law against you, I have the necessary paperwork and authority to take you all down to the station for a cosy chat to discuss matters such as harbouring a criminal, perverting the course of justice and, well where do we stop, possession of Class B drugs? This evening is just getting better and better."

*

"Umar, Umar!. Get your arse over here now! This stuff is dynamite. I'm going to ring my dad and get it to the police, but you've got to hear it first."

"I'm not sure. I've homework and you know what my dad's like."

"Just get here now. My mum's out for the evening, so you can enjoy this stuff in all its wonderful sordid glory."

"Um... oh... okay, but I can't be out too late. I'll be over in half an hour."

*

"Yeah, who is it?" The unmistakable, gruff, Barnsley accent came out of the earpiece, conclusive proof that part-two of his plan for the assassin had failed as badly as part-one. At least alive, he could still have his uses, as long as he didn't cock this one up.

"It's me, your long suffering employer."

"Oh, hello." Hyde could hear the sudden tension in his voice.

"I've a job for you and some of your, erm, acquaintances, but not the Poles. I want people who know what they are doing this time."

"What is it?" Scud asked, suddenly curious.

"I want you to kidnap a girl, Pilgrimm's daughter." As he said the words, Hyde broke out into a sweat. He was out of his comfort zone, but saw no other option. It was what Frieda wanted.

"Why?" asked Scud, cautiously. He was aware his employer had a sleazy reputation and age hadn't always been a barrier to his advances.

"It's not what you think. She has something, some information. I need you to get her without anyone else seeing or suspecting anything. This can't go wrong."

"Where do you want me to take her?"

"Take her to Riverside, the new office extension we're building behind the old brick warehouse. Ring me when you're there."

"This will cost." Scud had him, and was enjoying this. He knew Hyde had his back to the wall and was desperate.

"How much?" Hyde clenched his fists hating the fact that he was, temporarily at least, in Scud's power.

"10k."

"No chance, 5k."

"10k or no deal, and you find someone else."

"Alright 10 and no fucking cock ups!"

*

Vidic and his minder pulled up in the black Merc next to the hangar housing the twin engined Cessna that was going to take him over the border. They got out of the car and entered the hanger, looking for the pilot they'd hired to fly them to the next stage in their journey. Vidic called out into the dark.

"Chan? Are you here?" Silence greeted them. Then after he called out again a noise distracted them from behind. A solitary figure stood in the hangar entrance, a silhouette framed by the bright sunshine behind.

"Chan?" asked a nervous Vidic. The figure moved towards them and as they adjusted their eyes, they began to make out a tall female figure brandishing a weapon.

"Hello Vidic. I think it's time to conclude our business. I've a flight to catch and I really don't want to be held up any more than necessary. The minder began to reach for a concealed weapon. "Don't even think about it friend. Reach your hands high into the air..." Vidic suddenly bolted to his left. Willow, with barely a noticeable movement, shot him in the thigh. He collapsed and reached under his jacket, but before he could make a further move, the lights were switched on, illuminating the hanger and at least a dozen members of the Chinese security forces, all noticeably armed to the teeth. Vidic looked around in panic.

"Don't worry my old friend. Much as I'm sure you'd rather enjoy the hospitality of the Chinese authorities, you'll be coming back to England to join us later. Now if you don't mind, I have a plane to catch..." She blew Vidic a kiss, winked and put on her Gucci sunglasses, then turned and walked out into the sunshine.

*

The large white van pulled up opposite the semi-detached that Anna shared with her mum half the week. The van was grubby on the outside and worse on the inside; screwed up cigarette packets, invoices, fish and chip papers fought for space on the dashboard and floor with miscellaneous tools, plumbing materials, tabloid newspapers and decaying items of food. The van's number plates were noticeable by their absence.

The three occupants watched the house without a word, as they had for the last hour, wondering when to make their move. It had been a quiet evening, hardly a soul had passed. They withdrew back into the vehicle when the front door opened.

Kate walked out, paused, then shouted something back into the house. A moment or two later, they saw Anna. She gave her mum a hug, then closed the door as she went back into the house. Her mother walked down the path to the road, unlocked the door to a Renault and climbed in. After a couple of false starts the engine sparked into life and she pulled away. *Sweet. Fucking sweet. She's all alone.*

Scud began to open the passenger door, when an approaching figure caught his eye and he paused. He watched as the figure walked to the gate, but, instead of carrying on its journey, it walked up the path and knocked on the door. *Fuck*, thought Scud as he watched the waiting figure. A minute later the door opened, illuminating the gloom, to reveal an Asian youth standing on the step. Anna beckoned him in, giving him a quick hug before shutting the door. *Ugh*, thought Scud. Racism could also be added to the rich mosaic of charm that Scud was blessed with.

"I wasn't counting on two of them, but now's our best chance while her mother is out. Come on." They pulled ski masks over their heads and ran down the path. Scud's accomplices stood one either side of the door as Scud knocked.

"Just a minute!" a voice called back. A moment later the door opened and Anna's eyes widened in shock as she saw the stocky figure standing there before her. Before she could say anything, all three burst in and shut the door.

"Don't say a word and nobody will get hurt!" Scud yelled. He was lying of course. Scud did intend to do harm. It was in his nature. As long as he still got paid though. His accomplices grabbed Anna, one on each arm.

"Run Umar!" Anna yelled.

"Don't think about kid!" said Scud, "or the girl will get hurt. We wouldn't want to damage your white girlfriend would we?" Umar had no choice. He froze in his tracks. A few minutes later they were tied up. "Now, before we go for a little ride, I'd like you to tell me where you put that little something that was stolen earlier from a house in Church Meadows. We know you brought it here, no point denying it. You tell me now and nobody gets hurt!" Scud was bluffing. He didn't know that it was there at all. Anna stared at him defiantly. "I haven't time for games. If you don't tell me now. I'm going to start slicing off pieces of your Paki friend here until you do tell me." He produced a knife from under his jacket.

"Don't tell him Anna!" Umar shouted bravely. The knife was pressed against his throat. "Maybe you ought to tell him Anna." Umar revised his strategy.

"It's on the bed, first on the left, upstairs," Anna said with resignation.

Scud nodded to one of the two accomplices and he ran upstairs. A moment later he returned with the recorder.

"Well well well," Scud said as he stuffed it under his jacket. He put away the knife and while the accomplices held Umar and Anna, he taped over their mouths. Jason, the larger of the accomplices, cautiously opened the front door and, seeing the coast was clear, nodded to the others and the captives were quickly bundled out and thrown in the back of the van. Their captors leapt into the front, started the engine and set off, laughing.

Mission accomplished.

Chapter Five – Hyde and seek

What I think any of us who have children, and who want to share the love of growing vegetables with them need, is to cultivate something the kids will love to help grow, harvest and eat. You can't grow anything more impressive and tasty than sweet corn, especially after 10 minutes in the oven and served with a knob of butter! Sow the seeds in individual small pots, or seed trays separated into individual cells. Cover each seed with half an inch of compost. I find the trickiest bit is keeping them damp and warm but avoiding overwatering, as they may rot before germinating. When the seedlings are around 4 inches high, carefully remove them from their pots or trays without disturbing their roots, and plant outside after the risk of frost has passed in blocks, with each plant around one foot apart. Any closer and they will crowd each other, any further apart and they won't pollinate their neighbours effectively. Don't harvest too early. Wait until the tassels at the end of each cob turn brown, then harvest by gently bending the cob down until it snaps off the stalk of the plant.

Mmm, perfect on a late summer evening with a barbeque.

"Graham. Graham, is that you?" Kate's anxious voice came out of Graham's mobile.

"Kate? How... how are you?" Graham hadn't spoken to her since he went on the run.

"I'm okay, but Graham, is Anna with you?"

"No, no I haven't seen her for a while. She doesn't know where I am. I had to relocate suddenly, earlier today. What's wrong?"

"I popped out earlier to see Richard, look that doesn't matter, the point is I left her in the house and she made a point of saying she was going to be in when I got back. She's not there now." Graham looked at his watch. It was nearly 9pm.

"Look, it's not that late. Maybe she got a call from a friend or something. Why not give her a little more time."

"There's more. When I got back the coat stand in the hall had been knocked over, and there was a smell, stale and sweaty, when I walked in, and mud on the carpet. Graham, something's wrong." Graham's stomach tightened. Anna had not hidden her presence from Frieda, and Frieda knew he had a daughter.

"Kate. Look, just keep it together. There might be a logical explanation. I'll make some enquiries at this end."

"Graham... I'm scared."

"It'll be alright. I promise Kate."

"What's wrong Graham?" Becky asked, seeing Graham's anxious face after he came off the phone.

"I don't know, maybe nothing. But I'm not sure. Anna's disappeared."

"Disappeared?"

"Yes. Kate went out to see her... friend... earlier in the evening and when she came back, there were signs of a disturbance and no sign of Anna."

"It's still early Big G. I know what I was like at that age. Something will have kicked off in her circle of friends. There'll have been some 'crisis' or other. Try ringing her. I won't be surprised if she's at her best friend's, comforting her after she was dumped by a boyfriend."

"Yes... possibly. Yes, I'll try ringing." He brought her number up on his phone and rang it. After what seemed like an eternity, her voicemail answered. "No reply," he said.

"Look, there's nothing you can do right now. Just keep trying, and phoning Kate, and I'm sure you'll get hold of her."

"I need a cuddle Becks."

"That's what I'm here for; it goes with the job description."

*

169

It was a rough and uncomfortable ride in the back of the van. After what seemed like an eternity, the vehicle finally ground to a halt. The doors to the rear of the van opened and the captives were roughly moved across what looked like a building site into the shell of some sort of derelict mill building. They were taken up two flights of stone stairs and pushed into a room that, as far as Anna could tell in the dark, was newly breeze block lined on three sides. It still had a familiar cement smell to it Anna recalled from her earlier childhood days, when her dad used to tinker with DIY jobs at what was her mum's house now. Across the room a recently glazed window covered most of the fourth wall, from floor to ceiling.

"This will be your new home until my boss decides what to do with you. Make yourselves comfortable," he added with a laugh. Scud was enjoying himself. Much as he despised Hyde, the criticism he'd received after the Tomo fiasco hurt. *What the fuck was I thinking giving that job to those Polish half-wits?* Needless to say, they'd paid the price. They were back at work now after a few days off (unpaid of course) to recover from the beatings Scud had administered to each of them in turn.

Anna and Umar sat down with their backs to one of the walls. Umar was terrified. Anna was defiant. *These animals will pay for this.*

Scud roughly pulled the tape from their mouths. "Just in case you're thinking of calling for help, don't waste your breath. You're well out of earshot of anyone up here. And if you try anyway, one of my associates or me will give you a good kicking. Understand?"

"I," said Anna, not averting her penetrating gaze from Scud.

"What?"

"One of my associates or I," she clarified. Scud move towards her, his hand raised. He just stopped short of striking her.

"You are going to pay for your cheek. When the boss gets here..."

"Hyde," Anna added.

"What?" Scud looked confused. How did you...?

"I know who your boss is monkey man. I know he framed my dad along with that tart Frieda. I don't know why yet, but I'll find out."

"Anna. Shush, please," urged Umar.

"You're a brave one aren't you? We might single you out for special treatment. I was going to arrange something nasty for the Paki, but..."

"How dare you talk to him like that you shit bag, you're not fit to..." Anna was silenced by a hard slap across the face.

"I'd suggest you keep your mouth shut from now on little girl." He reached into his jacket. "Is this what you've got your evidence from?" He pulled out the recording device and dropped it on the concrete floor, grinding it into pieces with his boot. "Oh dear, it seems to be broken. What a shame." Anna stared at him impassively, her face stinging from the slap. "We'll decide what to do with you in the morning. Daz, you keep first watch. Jas, you take over at 4."

*

After a sleepless night, Kate decided at 6am that enough was enough. No call or text. Nothing. She rang Graham. A sleepy voice answered.

"Hello. Kate? Is that you?"

"Graham. Have you heard anything?"

"No. No, nothing." Graham sat bolt upright in bed, rubbing his eyes with his right hand. Becky stirred in bed next to him and, sensing something was wrong, woke up quickly and looked at Graham.

"I'm going to phone the police Graham. If she's in danger because of you, because of this situation you got yourself in, I'll never forgive you."

"Kate... Kate I'm sorry. Look, I'm sure she's fine, but yes, phone the police. We can't take any chances now." Kate put the phone down. "It was Kate. Anna didn't come home last night. You don't think..."

"Don't think what?"

"You don't think he's got her, Hyde?"

Becky opened her mouth to say something reassuring, but nothing came out. She stared straight ahead at the wall opposite and, after a pause said, "I know where he lives.

"Hyde?"

"Yes. I found it, a while ago now, with Anna, remember?"

"I'm going there."

"When?"

"Right now."

"Now?"

"Now. Becks, can you drive me there?"

Becky pause, looked at him and held his hand tightly.

"Of course I will. Come on, we'd better get dressed."

*

"Police please. I want to report a missing person, my daughter." Kate gave the officer her name, address and all sorts of unnecessary details that as far as Kate was concerned, were just wasting precious time. There were the usual suggestions that a girl her age would probably be at a friend's, may have had a fall out with someone, or needed a little space for other reasons. It was still early days and she would more than likely call her or just turn up out of the blue later that day. The girl at the end of the phone, who Kate thought didn't sound much older than Anna herself, only seemed concerned when she realised who Anna's father was.

"Oh. Graham Pilgrimm's daughter! So you're Graham's wife?"

172

"Ex wife. Yes."

"I see, sorry. Yes, right. We'll send out detail to all units in the area Mrs... Ms. Pilgrimm, right away, and we'll keep you updated with progress. I'm sure she's alright, but we'll take no chances."

Kate spent the rest of the morning phoning Anna's friends and friends' parents, and then waited. The silence of that Sunday morning, alone in the house, was agonising.

*

Graham already had an inkling that Becky's driving was a little on the racy side. The evening she picked him up from the allotment had often been unnerving and, at times, terrifying. This morning it was something else. Every now and then the brakes would be thumped on as they approached a traffic light, junction or speed camera. Graham wished he'd used the bathroom before setting off. There was no greater laxative than sitting in the front seat of Becky's Fiesta.

Nevertheless, thanks to no horses being spared and the absence of traffic, they made the journey to the Beeches in just under 40 minutes. They pulled up 50 yards south of the electronic gates guarding the property.

"Sure you don't want to call the police?"

"No Becky. I can't take that chance. If she's not here, it's going to look even worse for me. I've nothing on him, no hard evidence. Can you wait here in the car? I'm going to try and find a way in."

"No way Graham, I'm coming with you."

"Becky, it's too dangerous. I can't take that risk. Besides, it might be better having you out here in case... well, in case anything goes wrong. Keep your phone to hand." He opened his door, paused, then leant over to Becky and kissed her lovingly.

"Good luck Graham, and Graham..." she called out just before he shut the door, "take care please."

Graham smiled and nodded. He tapped on the window, then disappeared out of view as he walked towards Hyde's drive.

*

Anna and Umar barely slept that night. They were cold, uncomfortable and scared. Anna's face still stung from the slap Scud had given her. They had no idea what time it was. It was light outside and deadly quiet. Anna shuffled on the concrete floor to keep the circulation going in her arms and legs.

"Don't try anything!" the gruff voice of the one called Jason called out from the chair at the opposite side of the room. Anna stared back defiantly, but said nothing. There was no other furniture. They were in what looked like the shell of what would probably be an office in an old mill building when finished. It was hard to tell. Sitting on the floor in the far corner of the room, she could see little out of the window, despite its size. Maybe a building site and beyond that a river or canal?

The silence was broken by the sound of footsteps and voices coming up the concrete stairs. In walked Scud, Daz and one other. He was medium build, but muscular like Scud, with close cropped hair and a tattoo of what looked like a spider's web on his neck. He was wearing grubby denims and work boots, giving the impression he'd just finished a night shift somewhere. He had as such. He'd been digging a deep hole in a patch of woodland just outside Leeds. All that was needed was something, or someone, to occupy it.

Anna was drawn to his eyes. They were cold and black, like the gates to an empty soul. He frightened her more than Scud and his two accomplices.

Scud spoke to Jason.

"Any problems last night?"

174

"No, nothing." Scud nodded back and wiped his nose on the back of his finger. He turned to the newcomer.

"I've phoned him and he's on his way over." He looked down at Anna and Umar, who stared up at him. Scud smiled when he saw the fear in their eyes. "Now, we wait," he said to them.

*

Graham examined the gates. There was an intercom on the right hand side, with what looked like a small camera built in. More reassuringly, as he looked around the gated entrance, there were no other obvious signs of cameras or other surveillance equipment.

Either side of the gates, a high wall, maybe 10 feet or more tall, extended beyond his view, possibly surrounding the property entirely. Scaling the wall would be difficult. It was stone built, but with clean faced stone which didn't offer enough purchase. He looked back at the gates. Again, they would be difficult to get a foothold on. More worrying were the spikes at the top. Graham instinctively felt his crotch. He was finding that particular organ in more demand recently, so despite the urgency of the situation, he wasn't going to take any risks with the gates.

He followed the wall to his right to see if there were any other opportunities to scale it. After a while it turned a corner and a hawthorn hedge prevented further access to it. He retraced his steps and followed the wall extending from the left hand gate and he stopped when he noticed a mature sycamore tree in front of him, with a limb that extended over the wall. *Bingo*, he thought to himself.

Climbing the tree wasn't easy, but somehow he managed to find enough fissures and scarring on the trunk to climb, so he could peer over the wall. There, maybe a hundred or so yards away, he saw a gothic looking stone built Victorian property, standing in lawned gardens. He sat on the limb overhanging the wall, and shuffled along it, until he was over the garden. Below him were a mixture of rhododendrons and laurels at the lawn edge. He began to ease himself down, when he realised he'd snagged his trousers on part of the limb. *Oh fuck, fuck fuck! Not again! Please, not now!* He shuffled and somehow managed to free himself, though in the process, lost his grip and fell into the shrubbery below.

He lay there for at least two minutes, aware the noise might have alerted someone in the house to his presence. When he realised he'd got away with it, he rubbed an emerging bruise on his elbow and planned his next move. He realised if he followed the line of the shrubbery, it would lead him to a yew hedge bordering a path that would offer him a safe corridor to the house itself.

When he reached the hedge, he got down on his hands and knees and started crawling towards the house with the path and its bordering hedge to his right, hiding him from view from the property. Despite the noise of the blood thumping around his head, he listened intently for any sounds that would alert him that he'd been spotted. So far, so good.

At the end of the hedge he broke cover, leapt up a couple of stone steps and flattened his back against the wall of the house. The only sounds he heard were the low hum of traffic on the A61 where Becky was parked, and the ominous cawing of rooks in a copse of sycamores on the south side of the lawn.

To his left was a large sash window. He edged close to it and peered in, tentatively. There was nobody there. He saw a rather old fashioned oak panelled room, with a desk and leather chair in the middle. Rows of old leather bound books filled shelf after shelf; a study, or library perhaps? He tried the window. No joy. It was firmly secured.

He skirted back along the wall to the south side of the house, crept round to the corner of the building and saw a large sash bay window, looking out onto the sycamore copse. He froze as he heard a male voice inside. He heard only the one voice though, so guessed that whoever that belonged to was on the phone to someone. He heard a laugh, then silence. He waited, then cautiously moved closer to the window. Tentatively, he peered into, what seemed at first glance, a lounge or drawing room. Despite the sunshine outside, this also looked as gloomy as the first room. It was similarly panelled, with a dark green carpet. The combination seemed to suck all the light out of the room. On the other side of the bay window stood a large state of the art television, perched on an antique chest of drawers. It looked out of place in a house that seemed frozen in time.

Graham looked deeper into the room once he realised the coast was clear, although he was conscious that the door on the far side of the room was still half open. There were two armchairs and a sofa, visibly sagging in the middle from evening after evening of accommodating the corrupt frame of James Hyde, Graham presumed. He tested the sash of the bay window. His heart leapt when it gave a little. Once he managed to get his fingers underneath, he carefully lifted it, just far enough so that he could squeeze through. He arched his back up to avoid catching his trousers on the sill. *Not this time*, he said to himself as he wriggled through the gap onto the carpet inside.

He crouched on the carpet and listened, not just for the sound of the male voice he heard earlier, but for any signs that Anna was there. The only sound he heard was the pulsing of the blood rushing round his head. He was aware that he'd been running on adrenaline since he'd had the call from Kate earlier. He tried to take slow, deep breaths to keep calm and avoid giving himself away by doing something stupid.

The silence was broken by the sound of a substantial door shutting somewhere in the house, well away from the room he was currently in. He listened again. Silence. Graham guessed it was Hyde leaving the house. The call was probably from someone he was arranging to meet. This was his chance to leave the room and have a good look round for signs of Anna. *Oh please let her be here and okay*, he prayed to himself as he cautiously left the room and entered a rather grand entrance hall.

He saw a door that he guessed led to the study he saw earlier. Then noticed a door behind the staircase that looked like it might lead to a cellar. He tried it, but it didn't budge. Then, looking down, he saw a large key in the lock which he carefully tuned. He tried the door again and it opened. He walked to the top of the cellar steps, his heart pounding. He reached for a light switch to his right and flicked the light on, half expecting to see a bound and gagged Anna peering back up at him from the gloom below. Nothing.

He slowly started to descend into the musty smelling cool void, looking around as more and more of the cellar revealed itself. There was little to see at first; then a work bench, various old tools, an old stone sink and an old rocking horse. *Did that belong to Hyde once?* Graham smiled. *Even someone like Hyde must have had a childhood, must have been innocent. Once.*

He was half way down the steps when the blow to the back of his head knocked him completely unconscious.

*

Constable Dirker shuffled awkwardly towards DS Hopkins as he watched Graham's friends file past at the station.

"I'm not getting this Ray. I mean, look at them. They're teachers, computer nerds, librarians. The only one who's got any edge to him is that James Roberts bloke and he's just basically a layabout who sells a bit of weed to local students." He rubbed his chin and continued. "If this Pilgrimm is anything like them, how the bloody hell is he going to kill anyone?"

"Don't let him, or them, fool you. Believe me, I've seen the texts that he sent the victim's wife. He is sick. Anyone who

178

writes that kind of stuff has a serious fuckin' problem there." He tapped the side of his head to emphasise the point.

Constable Dirker shrugged his shoulders and wandered off. Hopkins watched him go then wandered to his desk and looked at the statements in front of him. Hopkins, perhaps for the first time, was also beginning to have his doubts.

*

Becky peered out of the Fiesta's windscreen, looked at her watch and checked her phone. *Come on Graham. A text, anything please.* She decided, after ten minutes that it might be safer if she pulled further away from the drive. She found a field entrance further down the road on the opposite side so that by reversing in, and nearly killing one of the local feral cats in the process, she was out of sight but still had a view of whoever came or went from The Beeches.

She sat in the car and waited. After 45 minutes without a word she made a decision. Another quarter of an hour and she was going to call the police. She'd rather face the consequences than risk any harm coming to Graham.

She'd already come to the conclusion some time ago now that, despite knowing him for such a short time, she was in love. She'd fallen for the gardener, big time, and it scared her a little.

*

"Well, now. Who do we have here? We are indeed honoured to have a genuine celebrity in our presence." Graham awoke to find himself in the cold, damp gloom of the cellar. He felt like he'd been unconscious for hours, though in reality, it was minutes. He looked up and tried to focus his eyes on the two figures standing facing him with their backs to the cellar steps, which rose up towards the light and safety. He tried to prop himself up, but a jolt of pain told him his shoulder was injured. His forehead hurt. He touched it and felt the slippery warmth of his own blood. He also had a rising bump on the back of his head.

"You must be Hyde?"

"That's Mr. Hyde to you, just like the monster in the book, and I can do monstrous things you know Mr. Pilgrimm. I can be a very bad man, especially when it comes to people who get in my way.

"Where's Anna? Where's my daughter?"

"Well wouldn't you like to know? She's being looked after by some employees of mine and I was just on my way to see her when my friend Mr. Carter here, who does a marvellous job of looking after the gardens, saw you climb into my drawing room window. That was a bit careless Pilgrimm wasn't it?"

"If you harm a single hair on the head of my daughter, I will kill you Hyde."

"Hmm, alright. Here's the thing Pilgrimm, I really think you need to use a bit of logic. You see I can do what the hell I like because you are a prisoner in my house and you'll notice that my friend Mr. Carter here has a shotgun and knows how to use it." Carter raised the weapon and pointed it at Graham. "Now I am going to have to go. As I said, I have an appointment with your daughter elsewhere. So no Pilgrimm, she's not here. Sorry," he shrugged his shoulders and raised his palms upwards as he mocked Graham. "While I'm away, Mr. Carter will keep an eye on you and, if you try anything, he will kill you. It's really convenient that you called. The deranged murderer breaks into the house of a man he thinks is seeing the girl he's been stalking and is saved, thanks to his heroic groundsman who, by the way, does have a licence for this weapon. That would be a disappointment though, because when I return, I would like us to get better acquainted, you know, share a bit of quality time down here in the cellar." He smiled at Graham then said to

Carter, "keep an eye on him. Don't let him get up or try anything on. If he does, you know what to do." He started up the steps then turned to Graham. "Goodbye for now Pilgrimm. We'll have some fun later, eh?" He then continued up the stairs and disappeared from view.

Graham knew he had to act fast. The only way to find Anna was by following Hyde. Although he was in pain, he managed to sit up and rest his back against the cellar wall. All the while he was aware that Carter was watching him from the other side of the cellar, cradling the shotgun as he sat on a stool. Graham subtly patted his trouser pocket with his left hand.

"You looking for this?" Carter's voice broke the silence. He produced Graham's mobile from his own pocket, then shook it in Graham's face. "Sorry pal. You're cut off from everybody here, he said as he replaced it in his pocket. You're just going to have to sit patiently and wait until Mr. Hyde gets back."

"You know he's going to kill me don't you?"

"Yep, I guess so. Not a problem for me though pal." Graham realised reason was out of the question. He was going to have to fight. He felt the ground around him. His right hand felt something cold and hard. It was a metal object. As he explored it with his fingers, he realised it was an old hammer head, minus the shaft. It was now or never. Hyde would be setting off any moment now. His heart pounded as he gripped the hammer head. He'd never been great at throwing accurately. He remembered skimming a stone a couple of years ago while on holiday in Whitby. He missed spectacularly with the result that the stone struck the side of a fishing boat. He had to cover Anna's ears when the boat's owner called him a 'useless f***ing c**t!' This time he knew he couldn't miss. There would be no second chance. He waited until Carter averted his eyes then, palms sweating and heart thumping in his chest, he threw the hammer head.

Carter only just ducked in time, but it bought Graham just enough time to run at him and get a grip on the barrel of the shotgun. They both wrestled with the weapon. Graham fought against the pain in his shoulder, adrenaline masking the worst of it. He struggled to keep the barrel away from him.

There was an ear splitting explosion as one of the cartridges went off. Momentarily dazed, Graham relaxed his grip and Carter broke free with the weapon. He took aim at Graham, who reached for an object next to him. It was the rocking horse. He grabbed its neck and swung it at Carter, knocking the barrel to one side as the second barrel discharged. Fuelled with adrenaline he leapt at Carter and, ignoring the pain in his right shoulder, punched him on the jaw. Carter fell to his knees. By now a bloodlust had taken over him. Graham picked up the horse, raised it above his head with both hands, and brought it down with dull thud on Carter's head. Realising Carter was out cold, he retrieved his phone from Carter's pocket and climbed up the steps. He paused for a moment, then turned back and approached Carter, kicking his prone body. "Twat!" he added.

At the top of the stairs, he ran to the front door and looked through a window at the side. He caught a glimpse of a Range Rover heading up a winding drive fringed on either side by an avenue of beech trees, leading to the entrance gate.

*

Becky decided she couldn't wait any more. She picked up her phone and was just about to make the call to the police when her ringtone sounded.

"Graham! Is that you? Are you okay?"

"Yeah, I'll be fine Becks. I got into some bother but was saved by Champion the Wonder Horse. I'll explain later, there isn't much time. Hyde is just leaving now. Anna's not here, but he's got her somewhere and he's on his way to where they're keeping her. He's in a Range Rover. Can you follow him?"

"Yes. Yes, I can see him now." She ducked down to avoid being spotted.

"Please be careful Becky. Don't get too close or take any chances. These are dangerous people. I'll catch up with you as soon as I can. And Becky..."

"Yes?"

"I don't know how to thank you. I owe you so much."

"Hey, you don't owe me anything kid. Look, I'd better go. I've got a Range Rover to follow."

*

Earlier that morning, the police took a call from an anxious middle aged Asian man whose son had failed to return home after going round to a friend's house the night before. No, it wasn't like him, Sohail explained to the lady taking the call at the other end of the line. Whose house? His friend Anna, the daughter of Graham Pilgrimm, the murder suspect on the run from the police – but we all know he's innocent, that you're after the wrong man...

The connection with Graham Pilgrimm's missing daughter resulted in a call to DI Smithson. He wasn't supposed to be in work that day, but sat on the edge of the bed he'd shared with his wife of 31 years, and thought. Two 15 year old kids disappear the same night, friends who'd known each other for years. The conclusion you draw is obvious. They'd run off together. The lad was Asian. His parents disapproved of the relationship, so for both 15 year old kids the logical thing to do is run away. Except this was Graham Pilgrimm's daughter. Perhaps they were both helping Pilgrimm? After all, he'd had to leave his hiding place quickly, so maybe they were both assisting him, wherever he was hiding now. Why did they both just disappear though, without even a cover story? Why not say they were going to stay at a Friend's? Easier probably for Anna. It might be more difficult for this Asian lad, especially if his parents were more traditional in outlook.

Even so, to just disappear without leaving a note or message, that would cause even more suspicion. It wasn't going to help her dad if she was going to be reported as a missing person, with even more police out looking for them... so many questions. He turned to his wife, who was also wide awake now.

"I'm sorry Rachel, but I think I should go in today." She nodded and smiled. She'd lived with him long enough to know that look. It was that stage of an investigation when the momentum finally gathers pace towards a conclusion. You don't know how it will end, but you can't stop or slow it. Something was going to happen soon, and the question was, did you want to be there at the end of the journey, or hear about it later?

Smithson got dressed.

*

Becky followed Hyde to a site she immediately recognised as Riverside. She watched the car pass a security checkpoint and enter the site. She parked up and got out of the car. There was no obvious way in except through the checkpoint. She rang Graham. Graham jumped as the phone rang.

"Graham, it's me. Can you talk?"

"Yes, I'm still here at Hyde's place, but I'm going to get over as quick as I can. Any news?"

"He's gone to Riverside. I can't get in. It's fenced off all round and the only way in is through a gate with a security guard."

"Okay. Look, phone the police. I can't take any more chances now, not with Anna there. I'll get over as soon as I can. Let me know if there are any developments. And for God's sake, please keep out of sight. Hyde is a very bad man Becky. Phone the police and wait there. Don't go near that place."

"Ok Boss."

"And thanks Becky. You are one amazing lady."

"You know, for a gardener Big G, you're full of surprises yourself."

*

After a cup of black, freshly ground coffee, Smithson set off to the station. He made a hands-free call to let them know he was on his way, and should be there in 20 minutes. Then, after a few minutes, he pulled to the side of the road and made a second call.

*

Graham's instinct as a father was to get over to Riverside there and then, but he also knew this was a golden opportunity to look around and find something, anything that could help him clear his name. He went to the study, paused and looked around. *Where the hell do I start?*

He went to the old fashioned desk in the middle of the room. One by one he opened the drawers; household bills, receipts, pens, writing paper. Nothing obvious leapt out at him. One drawer had a couple of magazines of an adult nature, with the emphasis on S & M. *Interesting, but probably not illegal,* Graham thought.

The bottom drawer on the right hand side was locked. It was the only locked drawer in the desk. *Hmm,* thought Graham, *he didn't mind his bondage mags being found by a curious cleaner, but he wanted whatever was in there to stay safe.* He pulled hard on the drawer, the jolt of pain reminding him of his shoulder injury.

It was a beautifully made fine old walnut desk, a valuable piece of furniture, but hey, what the fuck? He had been assaulted by this man and he was holding his daughter as well. Time was also of the essence. He wandered over to the fireplace, picked up a poker and smashed it into the slight gap at the top of the locked drawer. He picked up the front piece of the fire grate and, using it like a hammer, forced the poker far enough in so he could finally lever the drawer open.

Inside, he found two DVD's in plain plastic cases. One had 'Neil' written in marker on the case, the other 'Vicarage Mead'. Graham's heart leapt. *Vicarage Meadows, Frieda?* There were a couple of brown envelopes; inside one, a photo of an ugly looking muscular man with a shaved head. Clipped to it the name Simon Cudworth, with information about his address, family and associates. Graham's blood ran cold when he looked in the second envelope and noticed a photo. It was him, plus a similar list of contact details, friends, family and all sorts of other details that Graham couldn't believe Hyde could possibly know. His eyes widened when he spotted a third envelope and peered inside to find bundles of £20 notes that must have added up to tens of thousands of pounds. Who was this for and who was this Simon Cudworth? What was his connection with Hyde? Underneath the envelopes was a mobile phone.

He gathered the contents of the drawer together and put them in a plastic document case he found in one of the drawers. A final look through the desk revealed nothing more of interest. Just as he was about to shut the top left hand drawer, a set of car keys caught his eye. He picked them up and made his way outside.

A little further away from the house stood a modern, stone built garage. There was no obvious way to open the garage door, but a closer examination of the key revealed two fobs. He pressed one and nothing happened. When he pressed the second one, the garage door rolled up to reveal a racing green E-Type Jaguar. *Oh yes,* thought Graham. *That'll do.*

The car started straight away. He pulled out of the garage and turned right, heading away from the house, up the beech lined drive to the gate he'd stood the other side of earlier that morning. He reached down to the other fob and pressed that. The gate opened.

When it was just wide enough, he drove through and, seeing a gap in the traffic, turned right and headed for Leeds.

*

After Becky finished the call to Graham, she sat back in the Fiesta and looked at the mill complex through the wire fence. Somewhere in there was Anna. It was time to lay their cards on the table. The game was over. If somehow they were wrong and Anna wasn't there, there would be consequences for her and Graham to face. But the welfare of a fifteen year old girl was at stake. She had to call the police. She dialled 999 and was waiting for the connection when a large hand reached in through the open window and snatched the phone.

"Well that was good timing." a muscular figure with a tattoo on his neck stood at the door side, examining the phone. He dropped it on the floor and crushed it into the tarmac with his boot.

A momentarily stunned Becky sprung into life and started the car. The figure reached in and grabbed Becky round the neck with a powerful left hand, turning the engine off and removing the keys with his right.

"You're coming with me love." He opened the door and forced her out, dragging her across the road with his left hand over her mouth. She struggled, but it was useless. He was too strong, too powerful. The security guard on the gate came out and grabbed her legs. They carried her horizontally onto the building site and towards an entrance to the old mill building. *Oh God, I'm going to die,* she thought.

*

Kate felt she was going to go mad. There had been no further calls from the police, friends, anyone for a couple of hours now. *Oh Anna where are you?*

She wanted to go out, drive around the streets looking, just to feel like she was doing something. But that wouldn't be logical. Anna wasn't wandering the streets. She was somewhere she didn't want to be, and the best place for Kate to be was to wait there, in the house. She wandered into the kitchen and had just filled the kettle for yet another cup of tea, when there was a knock at the front door. Someone with news! She ran to the door and hesitated briefly before answering. What if it was the police? They'd found Anna but... She took a deep breath and opened it.

"Anna..." except it wasn't. She had the same long mousy blonde hair and a similar face, but she was taller and older. "No. No, it can't be."

"Hello Kate. It's been a long time."

The hallway started to spin and Kate felt an arm support her as she fainted and fell to the floor.

Chapter Six – A pane in the a**e

Glass can be a wonderful ally to the gardener. Our frequently damp and cool summers limit the range of crops we can normally grow outside. However, if you've space on your plot, get yourselves a greenhouse and a new world of opportunity opens to you. The sunshine that penetrates the glass is trapped inside as heat, giving you a warm, humid and wind free environment, perfect for growing those more delicate and warmth loving plants that would struggle outdoors. This week, let's have a go at tomatoes. You won't need many plants to give you and your family a bountiful and tasty crop throughout the summer. Let's say six plants. They are easy to grow from seed, or even easier to buy as young plants. If you do the latter, get a mix of varieties. Kids particularly seem to love cherry tomatoes. I know from personal experience. They are the only kind my daughter Anna likes. I like to plant in grow bags, three to a bag. If you do the same, please do your bit for the environment and use those filled with peat free compost! Keep the plants well watered and attach to stakes before they are a foot tall or otherwise they will fall over. When the flowers appear, gently tap the plant to aid self pollination every couple of days and when the first fruits appear, beginning feeding with liquid tomato feed. As the plants grow, carefully pinch out any side shoots that appear between the leaves and the main stem as they will take energy away from the crop. When the fruits turn red, harvest them carefully so you don't damage the fragile plant stem and enjoy. If the only tomatoes you've experienced before have been from the supermarket, the taste of your own, fresh from the greenhouse, will blow your taste buds away.

As Kate regained consciousness, she started to put the pieces together that led to her lying there on the hall carpet. There was a knock at the door. She opened it. She saw a ghost. Then she fainted, as you would if the same thing happened to you.

All was quiet. She propped herself up on her elbows, then started to get up. She was almost there when a voice from the past piped up from the kitchen:

"Don't get up too quickly. If you do, you might go over again. Sit down on the carpet and rest your back against the wall until your head clears. I'll make some tea and be over in a minute."

Kate, as if in a trance, did what she was told. She was being ordered around by a ghost. That's fine. This ghost was making tea. How do they do that if they don't have a physical presence on this earth? Well, they've got no real hands have they? No, of course not. That's crazy. The best thing is to go to sleep, because this is some sort of dream.

Unfortunately, she was rudely awakened from the dream by the ghost shaking her. She looked at the ghost and then came to another conclusion. The woman standing above her wasn't a ghost at all. She was dead, yes. But then so was she, Kate. She'd died and was being met at the gates of Heaven (thank God for that at least) by her long dead sister in law. That's fine then. Except Heaven looked like her hallway, smelt like it and felt rather like it too.

"Kate. Kate! It's me. It's really me. I've been away. Oh look, I can't explain now. Later, yes, but at the moment I need to find Graham. Kate, Kate! Are you listening to me?"

"Yes, yes of course. Annie! Is that you? Are you... alive?"

"Yes. Look, I'm sorry; not sorry I'm alive, but sorry I've... I really can't explain. I promise I will, all in good time. I need to find Graham. Do you know where he is?"

"No. No, but Anna's missing. The people who did this to Graham, could they have taken her?"

"I don't know Kate, but if I can find Graham, then..." Just then Kate's phone rang. She crawled to the kitchen, reached up to a worktop and answered it.

"Yes?" she croaked.

"Kate, it's me Graham. Listen, I know where Anna is. Someone has phoned the police and they are on their way."

"Graham? Where is she? Is she alright?"

"She's being held in a new development called Riverside. It's that re-development down from the Royal Armouries. I... I'm sure she's ok. I'll make sure she is. I'll ring you when I know more. Take care."

"Was that Graham?"

"Yes. He's gone to rescue our daughter. They've got her. She's in a place called Riverside..."

*

Graham drove the E-Type with a vengeance back to Leeds. His goal was Riverside but the logical part of his brain that still just had the upper hand, told him to make the short detour to his flat. He had priceless evidence. He couldn't take the risk of losing everything if things went wrong at Riverside.

He pulled up opposite his flat. A quick look around didn't reveal any sign of the police.

It felt strange going back to the flat. It was cold, and had begun to smell of damp, but the fact that this was the first time he had been back since his arrest in September was the strangest feeling. Things looked to have been moved. A drawer was open. He wouldn't have left it like that. He assumed it was the police but then again, it wasn't only the police who had been looking for him. He sighed and looked around the flat, his home over the last 18 months. There wasn't really much to show for 45 years on the planet.

The reality of Anna's predicament brought him back to earth. He put the envelopes at the bottom of the wardrobe in his bedroom and went down the flight of steps leading to his front door at the side of the dry cleaners below. He locked the door and got into the E-Type, then drove to Riverside.

*

Becky kicked and struggled, but it was impossible. The tattooed assailant had a grip of iron. She managed to break one foot free from the guard holding her legs and kicked him in the genitals, which briefly was rather satisfying. He released her legs, but the tattooed man twisted her arm up behind her back with a force that made her nearly faint with pain.

"You try anything more, and I will break your arm. Now walk, up these stairs, here!" She climbed the same concrete steps Anna and Umar had the night before. There was no more resistance. She did as she was told.

When she walked into the room, she couldn't believe her eyes. She saw Anna and an Asian boy, tied up with their backs against the wall on her left. Anna's eyes widened with recognition when she saw Becky, but she said nothing. On her right were three males, around 30 years old, dressed in the work attire of builders; in the middle of the group stood James Hyde. She recognised him at once. He didn't look comfortable.

"Who's this?" asked Hyde. The tattooed man threw Becky on the floor.

"Caught her outside, just about to make a call to the police."

"Who are you?" Hyde asked, with a mixture of anxiety and exasperation. How many more people were going to turn up? How many more people were going to have to be killed?

"Fuck, you!" replied a Becky, who was not going to co-operate.

"It's... it's immaterial. Look," he said, turning to the tattooed man, "are you sure she didn't call the police?"

"I told you. I caught her before she made the call. No one knows she's here," he added ominously. Hyde nodded. He knew what would have to be done to all these captives.

Just then, all went quiet as they heard footsteps approaching the room. The one they called Jason, or 'Jas', picked up a pick axe handle and stood to one side of the doorway.

In walked a tall, smartly dressed, late middle aged figure, who ignored everyone except Hyde.

"What on earth is going on here James?" He said in his clipped Rotherham accent as he looked at the bound figures leaning against the wall. "I presume that is Pilgrimm's daughter and the missing Patel boy. Who's that though?" he looked at the prone figure of Becky stretching and rubbing the arm the tattooed thug had twisted.

"I don't know Leslie. We found her outside. She was obviously looking for the girl, or that boy."

"Her mother, perhaps?"

"No, no I don't think so."

"Hmm, this isn't going too well is it James?" Becky suddenly gasped.

"I know you. You're one of the police officers at the press conference, the day Graham escaped."

"Very perceptive little girl. Unfortunately, it won't do you much good. James do you have a plan, or are we thinking we just wait here for a few others to join us perhaps? Maybe make a party of it here in this...?" Smithson raised his hands in a questioning manner, looking with disdain at Hyde.

"The boy and girl will disappear. I'm sure you can 'find' some evidence that they're young lovers who ran away. Their families disapproved of their relationship. The woman..." he looked down at Becky. "If her car's outside, we'll arrange a car accident. Tragic, but these things happen." Hyde took out a handkerchief and wiped his perspiring brow.

"Hmm, I'm not happy it's got so messy James. Our ventures have always gone so smoothly in the past. But I supposed it can't always go without a hitch can it? Yes, I think that's achievable. I presume we can trust all these people?" He glanced at Scud and his three associates.

"Yes, completely. They'll all be well paid for this." Scud still hated Hyde but, well, money talks. He said nothing, but nodded back towards Smithson.

"Alright, then let's get on with it shall we?" said Smithson coldly.

The piece of scaffold pole knocked Jason out completely. Everyone turned to the doorway to see Graham, brandishing the pole and advancing towards them. Darren made his move. Graham stepped back, pursed his lips and swung the pole sideways. It struck Darren just above his left ear with a sickeningly loud clang. He dropped down, also unconscious. Hyde stared open mouthed and backed off towards the window. *Where did he come from? How did he get out of the cellar?*

"Dad! I knew you'd come! I knew it!"

Graham squared up to Scud and the tattooed thug. Fixing his eyes on them, he held the pole in his right hand while he drew a pocket knife out with his right, and tossed it to Anna.

"Anna, take this and cut yourselves free, and get out. Quick!"

The knife fell from her lap and onto the floor. She shuffled towards it, but it was difficult to get hold of it with her arms bound behind her back.

"I can't reach it!" she cried.

"Quick Anna! I can't hold them back...!" The tattooed thug grabbed the pole. Graham tried to twist it free, but it was impossible. He was too strong. He wrenched it from his hands and struck Graham on the side of his left knee, felling him instantly.

"I'll take that. The thug said with an ugly smile on his face as he picked up the pocket knife. His eyes fixed on Anna making her blood run cold. "Well boss man. Looks like all your problems are going to be finally sorted this morning."

"I told you he was good didn't I?" Scud boasted to Hyde, as he put his arm around his cousin's shoulders. Hyde reluctantly nodded and rubbed his mouth nervously.

"Are you okay dad?" Anna whispered to Graham, who was massaging his left knee. It felt like nothing was broken at least.

"I'll live. Are you alright?"

"Better now you're here. I knew you'd come. You're a real hero dad. Despite their predicament, Graham smiled. That meant a lot to him. He leaned over to Umar.

"How are you Umar?"

"I'm fine Mr. Pilgrimm, thanks. Well... actually... not great. I could really do with a pee. What do you think they're going to do to us?" Graham said nothing. He scanned the room and caught Becky's eye from the opposite corner. *Oh fuck!* His heart sank. *They've not got you as well.* He'd arrived at Riverside from the opposite direction to Becky and driven unopposed straight onto the site. He'd not seen her abandoned car further down the road, past the gates. *Are you okay?* he mouthed to her. She smiled and nodded. He smiled back, then looked up at the spectrum of low life before him. Hyde stood with his back to the window, almost putting him in shadow. Next to him a figure he'd seen before. *Oh my God,* he thought. He was one of the police officers that interviewed him the day he'd made the escape. Was he working under cover? The question was answered straight away.

"I'd hoped we'd be meeting earlier than this Mr. Pilgrimm. You've proved more resilient that we could possibly have imagined. In case you're wondering, I've known James for a good many years. Our Masonic lodge was always useful for business connections, and our relationship has been mutually beneficial for oh, how many years now? 15...16? The police pension is a generous one but, well, I'm sure you can imagine Mr. Pilgrimm, a little top up every now and then is always welcome." He smiled benignly at Graham.

Graham sighed and leaned back against the wall, banging his head against it twice in frustration as he looked up at the ceiling. The two thugs he'd felled with the scaffold pole were beginning to stir. Helping them to their feet were the tattooed man who'd knocked him to the ground and another who seemed to bear a resemblance to him. But there was something more. He'd seen him before, but where? He rubbed his knee as he tried to remember.

The two he'd felled fixed him with murderous intent as they regained their feet. Graham was in trouble now and his next move was proving elusive. *What now?*

He'd done well to get so far, he thought. He'd actually surprised himself, found things out about himself he never thought he was capable of. He looked at his daughter, who he loved as only a father can love his daughter; young Umar and then Becky. Becky, he'd only know for a few days, but felt, knew, if they survived this, they would be together. Anna, Becky, Umar, they were all innocents. They shouldn't be involved in this. This was nothing to do with them. If he was going down, he was going to go down fighting. He was going to go down fighting for them.

What was it about that stocky thug though? He had seen him somewhere... wait a minute. He suddenly remembered.

"Simon. Simon Cudworth." Scud turned suddenly to face him, unable to conceal his surprise.

"How do you know my name?" Inspiration flooded through Graham, a moment of epiphany.

"Because I've seen your file in Hyde's office." Hyde stopped talking to Smithson and looked at Graham with, and no doubt about it, a look of anxiety on his face.

"What do you mean file?"

"The file alongside my file. The file with all the information he had to give to the man who came to kill me, down at the allotment. Looks like his arrest let you off the hook Simon.

Looks like you would have been next." Scud stared straight ahead, his jaw set resolutely. There was silence in the room. Scud slowly turned to face Hyde.

"Is that true?"

"No! No way Scud, Simon. He's lying. Can't you see what he's trying to do? He knows he's finished. He's desperate. I've had enough of this. Finish him Scud."

"Your name is Simon Cudworth, you live... oh where is it? Burmantofts. That's it. You go to the local working men's club every Friday and Saturday night and, importantly, you always leave bang on 11.45pm. I'm guessing that's when you'd be most vulnerable. A mugging that could have gone wrong perhaps?"

"How does he know all that Hyde?"

"Now look here Mr. erm... Scud. I'm sure this is some sort of trick..." Smithson stepped between Scud and Hyde, but it was pointless. Scud had realised the truth and the fear in Hyde's eyes confirmed it.

"Scud, no, it's a lie. It's..." Scud threw Smithson to one side and lunged at Hyde, grabbing him around the throat. He forced him against the window. Hyde stared backed in terror. He pressed himself back against the glass.

All became aware of, what could be best described as, a grinding sound, like metal against stone then, was it an optical illusion? The window seemed to tilt back. Scud let go of Hyde, as Hyde and the plate glass window tilted back and, ultimately, fell out of the frame towards the ground below. A moment later there was a muffled crash and... silence. Scud, Smithson and the abductors peered down.

Hyde lay on a bed of shattered glass, staring up at them. Hyde just uttered one word. "Oh," was all he said.

"James! James! Are you alright?" Smithson asked anxiously.

"I don't think I am Leslie. I can't move and I think a large piece of glass is stuck in... somewhere."

"Oh, this is all a terrible mess," said Smithson, rubbing his forehead. He turned to Scud and his cousin. "Look, I'm sure we can sort all this out. I think the first thing we need to do is dispose of Mr. Pilgrimm and all these people. He gestured around to indicate Becky, Anna and Umar.

"I'm not sure I agree with your proposal, Mr...?"

Smithson turned to the doorway to see the figure of a tall, attractive and somewhat stylishly dressed woman, with long straight mousy blonde hair.

"Smithson. And who the hell are you?"

Anna and Graham knew. They knew as soon as they heard her voice. They stared, literally open mouthed. This wasn't possible. *She's... she... died. Is this a dream?* Graham felt he'd finally gone insane, gone insane or was dreaming. Yes, that was it. This was a dream, had been all along. If he pinched himself, he'd wake up. Then she spoke to him in his dream.

"I'm sorry Graham. There was a reason I had to disappear. I'll explain... try and explain later. First, we've got to get you all out of here."

"And how do you, Miss... how do you propose to free these people when you appear to be outnumbered somewhat?" Smithson queried, with a really annoying air of superiority.

"Pilgrimm. My name is Annie Pilgrimm. Graham is my brother."

"Your...?"

"Yes, my brother. So before anyone else gets unnecessarily injured, would you all mind giving yourselves up. I think this has gone far enough, don't you?"

"Sis, Sis, what are you doing?" interjected Graham in a hoarse whisper. Annie Pilgrimm carried on.

"Look, whatever you are up to stops now. Nobody else needs to get hurt." Scud and his cousin looked at each other and laughed. Scud nodded at one of the two thugs Graham had felled. He lunged at Annie. With barely a glance at him, she grabbed his arm, turned gracefully to her left and flipped him on his back. Still holding his arm, she repeated her earlier request. "Will you please give yourselves up immediately?"

Suddenly Scud, his tattooed cousin and the third abductor attacked at once. Graham watched, mesmerised. It was like a scene from a film, one of those that if you watched it, you would go *yes, but in the real world... that wouldn't happen.* But it was, and it did.

Scud was struck on the jaw and dropped to his knees. Annie spun round and delivered a kick to his cousin's midriff. He fell forward. She delivered a fist to his back that put him face down on the ground. The other thug Graham had struck earlier picked up the scaffold pole and brought it down hard, aiming for Annie's head. She sidestepped gracefully and the pole struck the back of the head of the kneeling Scud. Momentarily stunned by what he had done, he took his eye off Annie, just long enough for her to step forward and deliver a couple of blows with her fists, followed by a turn and a kick, that knocked him unconscious. She immediately turned to Smithson, who backed off towards the space where the window had once been. He reached into his jacket and pulled out a small firearm.

"Enough now Miss Pilgrimm. Enough please." Annie paused and fixed him with a cool stare.

"There's nowhere for you to go. Give up now."

"Unfortunately, I can't Miss Pilgrimm. I have far too much to lose. I'm sorry, but I'm afraid..." He paused as he saw a look in Annie's eye. She wasn't even listening. She was looking directly behind him. He turned to look, then pain. The pistol flew across the room. He turned back in shock, then instinctively held onto his broken wrist. The distraction and the kick were timed to perfection. Smithson fell to his knees, as Annie casually drew out her mobile phone. A minute later, Annie spoke.

"It's Willow, yes. I'm at a new development called Riverside. Can you send some assistance? Yes... that's right. Oh, and send

an ambulance please. There are a couple of injured personnel."
She glanced outside and down to where Hyde was trying to
crawl away, slowly and painfully, from the shattered window.
Annie winced, then added, "it appears that one of the casualties
has a large piece of glass impacted in his rectal area..."

Chapter Six – Back from the dead

I love growing courgettes. They're so versatile and great in pasta dishes. Why not bring your growing season to a close with a hearty pasta, cooking your courgettes in a sauce made from your own freshly harvested onions, garlic and tomatoes? Once courgettes start cropping there's no stopping them. You'll find all sorts of other ways to use them in your cookery. Luckily, you can fry them, steam them, roast them, stuff them and even bake them in cakes. You can even eat the flowers as well! Start them the same way as your sweetcorn, taking care not to overwater the seeds or keep them too cold to avoid the risk of rot. When the seedlings have 3 or 4 leaves and the weather has past all risk of frost, plant them out, taking care not to disturb the root ball too much. Space at intervals of 3 feet and keep the growing plants watered in dry weather. Harvest the courgettes with a sharp knife at the base of the fruit, ideally when they are still only 5 or 6 inches long. That's when they are at their tastiest. Unless you have a very large and hungry family, you won't need any more than 6 plants to keep you going right through the summer.

While Graham freed Anna and Umar, Annie kept watch on their assailants. Despite all the questions that needed to be asked, they carried on with their tasks in silence. Annie leaned against a wall, checked Smithson's firearm and, realising it was loaded and working, pointed it in the direction of the assailants, several of whom were groaning from the blows Annie had delivered earlier. Umar broke the silence. "Thank goodness for that, I really need a wee." He discretely left the room.

Graham hugged Anna and Becky together, then finally looked at Annie.

"Where have you been this last year? What happened? The accident. Mum and dad..."

"I know, I know Graham. I'm sorry. Look, there's a lot you don't know about me. I work for a government agency, have done for over 20 years now. I can't say too much at the moment, not here anyway." She looked at the sorry bunch before her, including the pathetic figure of Smithson sat on the concrete floor, nursing his broken wrist. "It was my last case. I was due to retire. 45 is a bit old for this sort of thing."

"You still look in pretty good shape to me."

"Thanks bro. There was someone who'd evaded us for years, a deeply unpleasant character. A lot of people around the world had suffered because of him. Anyway, he suddenly reappeared on the scene. He knew I was on to him. I'd nearly caught him earlier last year. I needed to go undercover, disappear for a while. I'm sorry Graham. There was no other way."

"Did you catch him?"

"Oh yes, we've got him and now I'm back, just in time to come home and rescue my little brother."

"You're only older by 10 minutes." They smiled at each other.

"Aunty Annie," Anna interrupted the silence. "I think you are awesome! And dad... you are my hero." Graham sat back against the wall and smiled back at her.

The growing sound of sirens could be heard in the distance. As they looked up and listened, Scud's cousin ran past them and leapt out of the space left by the missing window and landed awkwardly on the ground outside. He stood up and shook himself, looked up at the Pilgrimms for a brief moment with those disturbing, penetrating eyes, then ran off.

*

Hyde had just about got himself in a position when he could start to crawl away from the shattered glass to... he didn't know where, just somewhere away from here. Why in the name of God did he trust Scud as his bunch of morons to fit his windows? What was he thinking? Next time, if there was going to be a next time, he would employ legals for the more complicated building tasks. As for Scud, he was a dead man. *God, my arse hurts!* he thought to himself as he started crawling.

He heard the sound of sirens approaching. Trouble in the city centre; football hooligans probably. The sirens got louder and louder, and then the realisation struck, they were coming to Riverside. *Oh fuck!*

Suddenly a loud thud alerted him to the figure landing next to him. He turned to look and saw Scud's cousin who, despite the drop, managed to pick himself up almost straight away. He ignored Hyde crawling on all fours only a few feet away and, instead, looked back up at the building, to the figures leaning out and watching. *God, he's hard,* thought Hyde, as the figure ran off, just in time to avoid the emergency vehicles arriving on site.

*

The vehicles pulled up close to Hyde. Paramedics ran to his aid. The first to arrive crouched down to reassure Hyde.

"It's alright mate, you'll be fine." Then he noticed his backside, winced and added, "that's going to sting in the morning though."

Police officers climbed the stairs and were met with the astonishing spectacle before them; a tall and rather attractive woman brandishing a firearm at a group of surly looking workmen sat on the floor, together with a man they recognised at once. Detective Inspector Leslie Smithson, cradling an injured limb. As soon as he saw them he yelled "get that woman, she's dangerous. Quick! She's with that murderer Pilgrimm... there." He pointed at Graham.

The officers were obviously confused. They stood in the doorway and looked at the man sat on the floor with two kids and another woman. He clearly resembled the fugitive they'd been looking for, but why...?

A plain clothed officer walked past the uniformed officers and looked around the group, then looked at Graham's sister.

"Annie Pilgrimm?"

"Yes." Annie replied.

"It's an honour to meet you. Are you alright if we take over now?"

"Absolutely, and I could murder a cup of real English tea."

*

Hopkins sat back in his chair and stared at the notice board across from his desk, without really seeing it. The bottom of his world had fallen out. His boss, a man he'd known for over ten years, was in custody, a suspect in the abduction of two minors and, together with an old friend from his lodge, a prominent and upright member of the Leeds business community, was implicated in a murder plot. The suspected 'killer' Pilgrimm, though back in custody, could be innocent, freed by his sister, who held an important position in the civil service working for national security. He hadn't seen that in Pilgrimm's file.

Worst of all, the useless bunch of Pilgrimm's friends and associates, including that fucker James Roberts, had been released.

*

Hyde lay face down on the hospital bed. The idea of lying on his back was not even worth considering at this stage. He was dreading the idea of taking a shit. A short, sweating bald headed man with wire framed glasses puffed into the room.

"Hello Derek," Hyde spoke into his pillow.

"Hello James. I got here as fast as I could." Derek Grant was James Hyde's solicitor and been called into action on a number of occasions over the years, mainly to protect Hyde's name following his implication in several sex scandals in the past. Hyde's name had been cleared in all cases. He had of course been guilty in each of them.

"How do we get out of this one then?" mumbled Hyde.

"How do we get you out of this one?" corrected Grant as he mopped his brow.

"Don't split hairs. How do I get out of this?"

"Ooh, a bit touchy aren't we James? It's quite simple really when you think about it. What have they got on you?" He answered his own question. "You were on your own property, Riverside, when you were assaulted by one of your employees, who had kidnapped two kids and was holding them there. This... Pilgrimm... turns up, with his girlfriend and sister to, presumably, rescue the kids and you're caught up in the middle, very much the injured party."

"What about the evidence that Pilgrimm found at my house?"

"Yes, that's another thing. This killer, still on the run, breaks into your house, jealous of your friendship with Frieda. Your groundsman did a remarkable job to capture him. He deserves an award for his bravery. As for evidence, a couple of photos, some money? Proves nothing. You were doing your best as the good citizen you are to try and find this man who'd killed a close friend of the family yourself. After all, the police were getting nowhere. As for the photo of this Scud character, well doesn't what happened down at Riverside prove your suspicions about him already? When this is all over and, with the right amount of topspin, you could really enhance your profile in the city even further. It all actually bodes very well James. I'll let you get some rest." He patted him on the rear, dangerously close to the injury, then departed.

Hyde, despite the pain, began to smile as Grant shut the door to his room and headed back to his office.

*

"It is really great to see you Becks. I thought you were never coming."

"Not a problem with you Big G."

"There's a time and a place for that sort of thing." Graham smiled at her.

"Anyway, it's great to see you as well. How are you?"

"I'm fine, but I could do with getting out of here soon."

"Surely that's not going to be a problem, is it? I mean they must believe you. What about everything that happened at Riverside? I've given a statement as well..."

"I'm sure it will be fine Becks. It's not just about me being cleared though, it's about nailing those that planned this. I think I have one or two things that may help. Listen, can you pick up some stuff from my flat?"

*

"Can I help you?" A kindly looking WPC asked Anna as she approached the front desk.

"Yes, please. I'm here to see my father, Graham Pilgrimm."

"Oh!" The WPC's eyes widened. "You're Anna. Are you alright after what happened? Is your mother with you?"

"I'm fine, thanks. I wanted to come on my own because I also have something I'd like to share with someone who's looking into the case."

"Oh." She looked at a diary in front of her. "Well, it looks like you might be in luck. Chief Inspector Reynolds is in. He's the man who led the team that brought everyone out of the Riverside Development." Anna remembered him.

"Could I see him, please?"

"I'll ring through, but he may be busy," she warned. Anna wandered around the reception area, reading the various public information notices. She was just reading one about when to dial 999 and when not to, when a voice called over, "Anna, Chief Inspector Reynolds can see you now if you want?"

"Oh, yes please, the sooner the better. Thank you." She followed the officer down a busy corridor and knocked on a door to her left. A chipper voice responded.

"Come in!" The WPC opened the door into a modern office and sitting behind the desk with, amongst other things, a photo of a golden retriever, was the figure that had greeted her aunt at Riverside. "Ah! Anna. Please sit down. It's really good to see you. How are you today?"

"I'm great thanks. I just needed a good night's sleep, and the toilet of course." Reynolds emitted a loud booming laugh.

"You are something else. My goodness though, you look just like your aunt. She's... er, she's something special as well." He blushed and looked down. Anna had never seen a police officer, especially one as important as this, blush. Then, with a smile to herself, she realised that he fancied his aunt. *God though, she's over 40. That's a bit weird.* "Anyway, how can I help?"

"Well. It's a long story, but, erm... I sort of acquired something that might help my father's case and prove who did the original murder."

"Oh?" Reynolds, suddenly intrigued, looked up at the WPC who returned the look and shrugged her shoulders. "What have you got?"

"Have you a CD player somewhere in the station?"

*

For Annie, the journey to her parents' house gave her more anxiety than any mission she had been on over the last 20 years. They knew nothing about her return. As far as they knew, and had eventually accepted, she had died overseas in a climbing accident.

She noticed their car was in the drive. She pulled up outside the property and walked up the path to the front door. The roses on either side were past their best now, but must have looked, and smelled, beautiful over the summer. He was always so proud of his garden, her dad. She stood outside the door, took a deep breath and knocked. A few moments later, the door was unlocked and opened. Her mother stood before her, looking tired, but well. She stared at the visitor, not comprehending what she saw. Her mouth opened to say something, but nothing came out. Annie broke the silence.

"Mum, it's me. Annie. I've come home."

*

As the disc played, Anna discretely watched the face of Reynolds for signs of a reaction. He stared stony faced at the player, only raising his eyebrows at the sexual interplay between Hyde and Frieda. Anna was convinced she heard a snigger at one point from the WPC behind her, though this was masked by a cough from Reynolds. Thank God she'd made a copy before that thug had smashed the device, she thought. When the disc had finished, Reynolds looked at Anna and smiled.

"It's not conclusive proof and I'm not sure it would be admissible in court, but you know what Anna, it gives us something we can use to start putting the squeeze on Mr. Hyde. More importantly, I think it gives us enough evidence to support the release of your father on police bail. Thank you Anna. I fancy a trip out this afternoon. I think I'm going to call into a hospital and pay a visit to a sick friend." He winked at

Anna and got up from his desk. "Oh Anna, give my regards to your father will you please? When all this is over, I'd like to buy him a drink."

"I will Mr... err, sir."

"Call me Mark. Look after yourself Anna." He smiled as he picked up his coat.

"I will, thanks, and Mark..."

"Yes?"

"He drinks crappy real ale."

*

Reynolds was just leaving the station as an attractive brunette in her mid 30s entered the building carrying a shoulder bag, gripping it perhaps a little tighter than she would normally. He briefly met her beautiful brown eyes but, not wanting to stare, carried on. If he had looked closer he would have remembered her as one of the hostages down at Riverside.

*

Hyde was already making plans. Grant was right, if you thought about it all logically and didn't panic, and that would be the worst thing to do in the circumstances. He could actually get away with this.

Anna Pilgrimm and that Asian lad had been kidnapped by Scud and his cousin. It would be their word against his. Where was the proof he'd asked them? He'd phoned Scud, but then as his employer he'd phoned him about all sorts of things over the years to do with work... and other matters, but there were no recorded messages or texts. If he could get hold of Scud, he could persuade him and his cousin to take the blame for the kidnapping. They would go down for a few years and potentially come out very rich men if they kept their mouths shut. They were going down anyway, they had nothing to lose. Besides, he had a trump card, footage of Scud killing Frieda's husband.

He had to talk to Scud's cousin though. He had to persuade him to turn himself in. What if he didn't want to though? Well at least he could persuade him that if, and when, he was caught he stuck to the story, did the porridge and behaved himself, he'd be set up for life afterwards. He felt nervous with him on the loose anyway. He had a look about him that was disturbing to say the least. No, come on, be positive. If he could just get a message to Scud, he could reach him that way. What was his name anyway? Mick, that was it. Scud would know where he was hiding.

Another thought entered Hyde's head; Pilgrimm had been in his desk and found those files. Could he have found the DVDs as well? No. No, it would have come to light now. No, he must have just picked up the files and that wasn't proof of guilt either. As Grant said, he'd have files on his employees anyway, especially the ones he had concerns about. And why not on the psycho that was still on the loose too after killing his friend McArthur? Of course he might and of course he was going to hand everything over to the police, like the good citizen he was. He had to get hold of Grant, get him to talk to Scud and the others before they talked. Unfortunately, Hyde knew he was unlikely to be in a position to talk to anybody in person for a while. The only other unknown was the assassin. He wouldn't talk though. He was a professional.

Just then, the door opened and a nurse came into the room. "Mr. Hyde, you've a visitor."

Excellent, thought Hyde. *Grant.* "Show him in please," he said into the pillow. Footsteps crossed the room to the chair at the side of the bed his face was turned to. He saw a pair of trousers, then knees, as the figure sat down. By turning his face upwards, he saw a man he'd seen before somewhere, but it wasn't Grant.

"Do I know you?"

"We met briefly at Riverside Mr. Hyde. You were in a... somewhat uncomfortable position at the time. My name is Reynolds, Chief Inspector Reynolds. I've taken over the investigation from DI Smithson. And how are you today?"

"I could be better."

"I'm sure, sounds like it was a rather nasty and deep cut." Reynolds tried his best to hide a smirk.

"How is Leslie by the way?"

"He has a broken wrist and nothing more. He's just taken some... err... leave until we get to the bottom of why he was there before the rest of us arrived."

Fuck. I'd forgotten about Smithson, the stupid prick. "How can I help you officer? I'll give you as much on those psychos who kidnapped the kids as I can. Are they alright now? I've been really worried about them."

"They're fine, thanks. They've both been fantastic, considering what they've been through."

"I can't help feeling responsible for this."

"Oh?"

"Well, yes. The abductors were my employees. God knows what they were thinking. I'd had some concerns over Simon Cudworth for a while now; so much so, I'd even started to have him watched. There was something not quite right about him. Do you think they were after some sort of ransom with these kids? It sounds like this Pilgrimm has connections with the underworld. I think he's had a lot of people fooled."

"I never thought about that James. You don't mind me calling you James?"

"No, not at all. It's good to meet you and well done for turning up on time like you did."

"Oh, I can't take the credit for that."

"No?"

"No. I got the call via a secret government agency... all very James Bond, isn't it?"

"The Secret Service?" Hyde's buttocks clenched and he winced in pain.

"Yes, it turns out Pilgrimm's twin sister is some sort of government agent. Amazing that, isn't it?"

"Yes. Yes, the family are full of surprises aren't they? That was lucky," he said through gritted teeth.

"Anyway, to other matters James. Do you mind if I ask you about your relationship with Frieda McArthur?" Hyde's buttocks clenched together again.

"Are you alright James? You appear to be in pain."

"I'm... fine, thank you. Frieda, yes Frieda. I've known her and her husband for years. The construction industry is a small world. They were a lovely couple. What happened to Peter was horrific. Pilgrimm should be hung by his knackers for what he has done. I told Frieda I'm there for her and... wait a minute... do you think that's why Pilgrimm broke into my house? Do you think he was after me next, because I was some sort of threat to his fantasy relationship with Frieda? God, the man is truly insane."

"Do you know, I never thought about that either? I'm really pleased I've come to see you James. This is all really enlightening. I hope you don't mind me asking this though, is your relationship purely platonic?"

"I don't mind at all. She's a beautiful woman, but I'm 30 years older than her. I think of her more as the daughter I never had. I really care for her, but purely in a fatherly way. Why do you ask though?"

"No particular reason James. I suppose to eliminate all possibilities, so all we're left with is the truth. Oh...!" Reynolds jumped slightly when he realised a call was coming in on his mobile. "Excuse me James, I'd better take this outside, you understand."

"Yes of course. Unfortunately, I can't go anywhere at the moment."

"No, I suppose you can't." Reynolds smiled back and left the room. *And if I get my way, you are going to be going anywhere my friend for the next 20 years. We just need to find the missing pieces.*

*

Becky was not expecting this. She thought she might be led to a cell to find Graham, head in hands, unaware of the fate that awaited him. Instead, here he was, with a large mixed group of police officers, some uniformed, others plain clothed, sharing a coffee and chatting.

"Graham?" Graham leapt up.

"Becks, Becks! It's ok. I'm free to go."

"What? That's fantastic... but, how? What...?"

"My daughter, my bloody brilliant daughter. She found enough evidence to set me free, on bail at least, until this is sorted." Becky stood there, not believing what she was hearing. As the reality sank in, a smile, the broadest she had produced in weeks, spread across her face. She walked towards him, then broke into a sprint and, despite the location, she leapt into his arms and they kissed with a wild passion, oblivious to all around them.

They only came back into the real world when they became aware of the spontaneous applause of the police officers surrounding them in the canteen.

"Graham!" she tried to make herself heard, despite the noise around them. "Graham, I've got the things you wanted from your flat. What do you want me to do with them?"

"We, my beautiful, wonderful Becky, we are going to share some of this with my new found friends here. But I think we'll have a quick look at what we've got here first, back at your place, just in case there's something we might want to save until later, for a special occasion."

*

Reynolds was delighted with the news of Graham's release. The timing of the call was perfect. His plan after the hospital visit was to meet up with a female colleague and pay a visit to someone he hadn't yet met. After hearing her recorded conversations with Hyde and 'performance', he was somewhat curious to meet her. Receiving the news in the hospital of Graham's freedom though, presented him with the opportunity of being able to share the good news with the patient he'd just visited first. He went back into the room.

"I'm sorry about that James. I think I've got everything I need for the moment anyway. Oh, by the way, that call..."

"Yes?" the muffled voice of Hyde replied.

"It was from HQ. Graham Pilgrimm has been released." More pain as Hyde's buttocks clenched again.

"Released?"

"Yes. He's still being investigated of course, but new evidence has come to light that has shed considerable doubt on his guilt and, instead, implicated some others."

"Oh?" said Hyde weakly after a pause. "Some others?"

"Yes. I'm afraid I'm not at liberty to say any more at the moment." Enjoying the moment he continued, "Anyway, I'm afraid I'm going to have to head off now. I have a rendezvous with a colleague and one or two other people I'd like to see this afternoon. I hope you are feeling much better soon James. I think we are all going to be having a busy few weeks. No rest for the wicked, eh?"

*

The drama of Riverside had bypassed Frieda completely. She checked her phone regularly enough for news from Hyde but beyond that she paid no attention to the news bulletins that talked vaguely of abductions and arrests at the site of a prestigious new development near the Royal Armouries, while she enjoyed the saunas and tanning booths of the expensive health spa.

The stresses and strains of waiting for the long overdue demise of Graham were taking their toll so this was just what the doctor ordered. Seducing a 23 year old muscular black masseur called Ryan was the icing on the cake. True to form in terms of racial stereotyping, he reached places that hadn't been reached in years. She decided there and then that when she'd eventually got what she needed from Hyde, in other words bled him dry in a year or two, a long break in the Caribbean would suit her very well thank you very much.

Back at her house and feeling much refreshed, she was just unpacking from the weekend when there was a knock at the door. Her first thought was Hyde. *I told him to ring first!* She looked out of the bedroom window and saw a car she didn't recognise. She went to the front door and spoke through the letterbox.

"Yes? Who is it please?"

"Is that Frieda McArthur?" A softly spoken voice enquired.

"Who wants to know?"

"It's the police miss. Do you mind if we come in? We won't take up too much of your time."

"Oh. Yes, yes of course. Where are my manners? Just a minute." She briefly angled herself so she could get a better view through the letterbox and caught a glimpse of a uniform, just to verify they were genuine. She opened the door to reveal a plain clothed officer around 50 years old, wearing a suit that had clearly seen better days, accompanied by a female uniformed officer in her mid 20's.

"Come in officers, please."

"Thank you. Oh, what a lovely house. Do you mind if I call you Frieda by the way? I don't like to be too formal," Reynolds smiled.

No, I can tell by the way you dress. "Frieda is fine."

"I'm Chief Inspector Mark Reynolds and this is WPC Griffin. May we sit down please?"

"Yes of course officers. Would you like some coffee? Tea?

"I'm fine, thank you," replied Reynolds. "What about you Catherine?" He turned to the young WPC at his side.

"Nothing for me, thank you."

"Well, how can I help officers? Have you some news of my husband's killer?"

"We do indeed Frieda."

"Oh. Oh? Have you... caught him, or...?"

"Well now, Frieda, and I'm really sorry you are having to go through all this, I can't imagine the stress you must be under. The thing is we have had a gentleman in custody..."

Pilgrimm!... "Had him in custody?" Her demeanour suddenly changed. Reynolds caught a fleeting glimpse of something unpleasant behind the exquisite façade opposite him.

"Yes. Unfortunately for this case Frieda, we don't believe that Mr. Pilgrimm was the killer. Some other evidence has recently come to light. *Ah, there you go again. That was a squirm if ever I saw one.* I say unfortunately only because the real killer has yet to be identified. Truth to tell Frieda, we're really pleased for Mr. Pilgrimm. He's become quite a hit with my colleagues down at the station. A bit of a Robin Hood figure, so to speak."

"Really... right!" Frieda was genuinely lost for words. Hyde was finished as far as she was concerned. He had not only fucked her, but fucked around with her, and she did not appreciate that at all. Think, think. What if she helped nail Hyde instead? What connection was there with her? Where was the proof they had planned it together? They had spoken on the phone, but then they were old friends. That night he spent here though, could anyone have seen him come or go? He said he'd been discreet but then, he was pissed at the time. Reynolds interrupted her thoughts.

"I do appreciate this is distressing Frieda, but can you think of anyone else who could have done this to your husband?"

"My husband was a lovely man officer. I can't think of anyone other than this man Pilgrimm. He had the murder weapon though, are you saying he was framed?"

"It certainly looks like it."

"The poor man, hiding in a shed for all those weeks. I can't think of... wait a minute..."

"Yes?"

"I'm sorry but... no. Sorry, forget it."

"What is it Frieda?"

"Look, I... erm." Frieda looked down and rubbed her forehead with her right hand.

Come on, come on. You know you want to. "Frieda, if someone's come to mind, you must let us know. If they are innocent, well all that can be cleared up pretty quickly but, if they are guilty, it means we've caught a dangerous person who could hurt others." Reynolds looked her with a reassuring sincerity.

"There's a friend of mine, very important in the construction industry and, well, someone who gives such a lot to local charities. Look, I..."

"Frieda, it's alright."

"His name is James Hyde. The thing is, well, once at an industry event a couple of years ago, he got a bit drunk and, well..."

"Yes?"

"He told me how much he wanted me. He said he loved me and, well, I said it was really flattering, but I was in love with my husband and wasn't going to leave him. Afterwards he kept, you know, pestering me. Oh, you don't think..."

"I don't know Frieda but, you know what? I think you've been really brave. We'll look into this Mr. Hyde character. I'm sure he's innocent but, well, you never know. Thank you Frieda, thank you for your honesty." He smiled at her and Frieda smiled back, a little nervously. *It's just a matter of time Frieda. You and Hyde are going to hang for this. I'll get you. I'll get you both. I just need that final piece of the jigsaw. In the meantime, a little divide and conquer can't do any harm.*

*

"Oh Becks, it is so good to be here again with you." Graham leaned back on the leather sofa.

"And free."

"Free, as long as I can conclusively prove my innocence."

"Do you want to have a look at these DVDs?"

"Oh, okay." Graham suddenly felt a rush of anxiety. What if there was nothing of any use on them? All there was to help him at the moment was the recording taken by Anna and Umar at Frieda's, and that was probably inadmissible in court.

"Hey, big man, cheer up. Come on, let's see what we've got."

Graham picked up the plastic case marked 'Vicarage Mead', paused for a moment, took a deep breath, then put the disc into the player. There was a bit of fuzz and accompanying white noise, then darkness. Graham thought that was that, then a glimmer of light. It was a street light. He then began to make out a road, with houses set back a little behind manicured lawns. It was a modern housing estate. It was Frieda's road. Then he saw a figure, a silhouette walking, skulking down the road. They couldn't make out who it was, but Graham could see it was heading towards Frieda's house, that much he was certain.

The picture then wobbled. He realised that was because whoever was filming was following the figure with a handheld recorder. It was really difficult to see again. The darkness increased as the figure moved away from the street light. Then more light, from a house, Frieda's house. Now Graham could clearly make out the figure. It was the one they called Scud he'd encountered down at Riverside. That was him alright.

"I recognise him." Becky confirmed. The figure went to the back door, Graham remembered all too clearly what that looked like, then appeared to knock. There was no sound on the recording. Dread began to build inside Graham. His palms began to sweat. He knew what was going to happen. The door opened and a man appeared. They briefly exchanged words, then Scud raised his arm and brought a weapon down, Graham's billhook, onto the head of the figure, that fell to the ground immediately.

"Oh God!" exclaimed Becky, and put her hands to her mouth. Mercifully, the poor lighting spared them the gory details. Suddenly the image turned away from the murder scene as the figure filming moved back into shadow, then towards a vehicle, a Range Rover. The film then fleetingly picked up a number plate. Neither Graham, nor Becky, recognised the vehicle but, one thing was for sure, the police would find it. "Graham," said Becky, "we've got to get this to the police." Graham had already pulled out his mobile.

"I'm calling now."

*

Frieda stared at her suitcase, still half packed from her spa break. She chewed the side of her finger as she paused and thought for a moment, then began to re-pack.

It was over. She was leaving. She quickly found her passport, then booted up her laptop to look for a flight... anywhere.

*

Scud sat in his cell, plotting revenge. That bastard Hyde was going to get it. He'd find him then make him talk. He was going to find out where that footage of him killing McArthur was first, then smash his skull in. He had a restless night, thoughts of vengeance keeping sleep at bay.

Shortly after 10am, his cell door opened. In walked a middle aged plain clothed officer and two uniformed officers. He recognised the plain clothed officer as soon as he stepped in. He was the one who had walked into Riverside. No sooner had the police entered than the officer spoke.

"Simon Cudworth, I am arresting you for the murder of Peter McArthur..."

Chapter Seven – Sex, lies and a DVD

Unfortunately, Mother Nature isn't always on the side of the gardener. There are many enemies out there. Here are just a few that I've encountered along the way. Public enemy number one for me is the humble slug. This is a ruthless eating machine that will cause havoc and devastation, especially over a wet, warm summer. I must admit I'm too squeamish to squash, but prefer a merciful killing. A plastic glass with a drop of real ale (yes, real ale - they prefer it to lager) buried so the rim is at ground level attracts slugs for miles around. Drawn to the smell, they fall in and drown; dying in the best way imaginable - in a vat of ale. We can briefly envy them this way of passing into the afterlife. Public enemy number two is the pigeon, a rat with wings. Unless you take precautions, anything you grow from the cabbage family will be devastated. Unfortunately beer traps don't work here, but netting does. A frame of canes covered by a net will keep them off, otherwise cabbage; broccoli, sprouts and cauliflower don't stand a chance. Public enemy number three, for me at least, is old Benjamin Bunny. Lately we have been plagued by the furry little monsters. The only sure way of keeping them out is to surround your plot with a fence of chicken wire, buried to a depth of at least 6 inches, to keep the critters out. It's either that or get yourself a 22 and learn how to cook rabbit pie!

Graham's mind was in a whirl. They'd got the killer. He was in the clear for the murder. He was a free man, for the moment at least. There were still questions about his role in all of this. The full story needed to come out. If it didn't, he could still face some charges, but that didn't matter right now though. He hadn't delivered the blow that killed Peter McArthur, it was Simon Cudworth and he was safely in custody.

They spent the day phoning family, friends, everyone they knew. The calls became more incoherent as the wine flowed and, at the end of the day, they collapsed into bed. They didn't make love, but held each other as they talked. There was so much still to do, to organise. There was going to be a party at The Tap – where else? Tomo was organising it. Eventually sleep finally took them. Graham was so busy, he forgot to have a look at the DVD marked 'Neil'. The next morning Graham was awakened by a buzzing noise from the apartment's intercom.

"Ugh." He grunted. He found speech difficult. Someone had apparently stapled his tongue to the roof of his mouth during the night. His head throbbed and he realised he had awoken with the luxury of a hangover. It had been a while since he'd experienced that feeling.

"What time is it?" a voice from under the quilt next to him enquired rather sleepily.

"Shit o'clock."

"What?"

"It's nearly 9. Becky, can you get it? I feel crap."

"No. My head hurts and will probably explode if exposed to ultraviolet light."

"Mine hurts too Becky. It really hurts and I may well have to be sick." He rolled onto his side and noticed half a glass of red wine he must have brought to bed with him. *Dare I?* He thought. *Can I face the hair of the dog?* The buzzer went again. *Go for it,* he thought. *It's now or never.* He sat up, reached for the glass, and downed it in one. "Ugh... oh Lord." He pressed his hands to his head, rubbed his face and got up.

"Yes?" he said into the intercom.

"Hi dad, it's me." Anna's cheerful voice boomed out, causing a momentary stab of pain behind his eyes.

"Hi love, where are you?"

"I'm in the lobby dad. How else am I going to be able to speak to you on the intercom?"

"Oh, right, yes."

"So, can I come in?"

"Erm, yes, yes of course. How do I do that?"

"I don't know dad. You're in there and I'm out here."

"Oh. Yes. Sorry Anna love. My head's a bit, you know..."

"I know dad. I spoke to you last night. You were seriously wasted."

"I was a bit merry, but... look, hang on. Becks!" *Oh, that hurt.*

"What?" a muffled voice replied from the bedroom.

"It's Anna, she's in the lobby and I don't know how to let her in."

"Press the green button on the left," the voice from the duvet replied.

"What, oh right. Yes, I see it. Anna! Come up!" *I must refrain from shouting at the moment.*

"Hi dad, it's great to see you." She gave him a massive hug. "I didn't think we were ever going to get out of there. I can't believe it was only a couple of days ago. You were fantastic and Auntie Annie, she was just... incredible. Is it true she's some kind of secret agent?"

"I think that's a bit of an exaggeration. She worked for the government, but, well, she was involved in things I didn't know about, and neither did grandma and grandad. It's great to see her again though, isn't it?"

"Do want a coffee Anna?" Becky called from the kitchen area.

"Oh, yes please. How are you Becky?"

"I'm afraid I'm suffering a bit like your father at the moment." Anna laughed, then looked around the apartment.

"You've got a nice place here Becky."

"Thank you. I like it. I like things uncluttered and simple, like me."

"How's your mum love?" Graham asked, while smiling at Becky.

"She's great dad. Even she thinks you're a hero." Graham smiled again and looked at his daughter. *It could all have gone so wrong though.*

"Coffee's up!" Becky came into the living room wearing her white bathrobe and carrying a tray. They sat down and chatted. There were so many things to talk about, so much to try and understand. And still so many unanswered questions.

"So what happens now dad?"

"What do you mean?"

"Well is it all over. Are all the bad guys in prison now?"

"Err, well, it's not that simple. I mean as things stand, the police don't think I'm guilty, but..."

"There are no 'buts' dad. The police know all about what happened to Umar and me, and they've got the recording of Hyde and Frieda admitting everything."

"Yes. I know love. It's just... well..."

"What your dad means is that although that's what everyone thinks now and believes to have happened, proving innocence and guilt in court is more complicated. It's got to be conclusive, you know, beyond doubt. Look Anna, the difference now is that because of what you and Umar did, you have given the legal system enough to cast so much doubt on your dad being guilty that they feel confident enough now to let him go. And that is a massive result Anna. If it wasn't for what you did, for your bravery, your dad might not be here at all."

Anna looked down and thought for a moment. "Thanks Becky. This policeman they've put in charge, you know the one that came in and helped rescue us, that's pretty well what he said. By the way dad, he fancies Auntie Annie."

"How do you know that?"

"It was pretty obvious when he was talking to me."

"Well, you know Anna, even people over 25 can still fall in love. Hard to believe I know." He winked and smiled at Becky, who went visibly red.

"We still need to decide what to do now dad."

"We, as in you, don't need to do any more. Look love, you have been incredible, but your part in this is over. It's up to the police and the legal people now."

"I don't think so dad. Not until you are properly in the clear. And there's still one of the gang on the run isn't there?"

That was true. Somewhere out there, probably not in an allotment shed though, Scud's cousin Mick was hiding out.

"Anna, I don't want you to go looking for him. I don't think is a particularly nice man. Please Anna, just stay close to mum for the time being."

"Whatever. Anyway, what's that?" Anna pointed to a DVD on the glass coffee table, marked 'Neil' with a felt pen on the plastic case.

"Oh, that. I don't know yet." Graham had forgotten about that disc. He meant to view it last night, but after the telephone calls and wine had taken their toll he'd forgotten about it. "You are nosy my girl."

"Is that something to do with the murder?"

"Why do you say that?"

"All Becky's other DVDs are neatly arranged on those shelves. It stands out like a sore thumb. Am I right?"

"Look, I don't know yet, but Becky and I will find out later." He was conscious of what they saw on the last disc and after all she had been through, he didn't want Anna seeing anything that could be distressing.

"Okay, okay." Just then the buzzer went again. "Saved by the bell," she added, wandering over to the intercom. Before Becky could say anything, Anna said, "I'll get it." She spoke into the intercom, "Rebecca Andrew's residence, who is it please?"

"Is that you Anna?" a familiar voice piped up.

"Auntie Annie! Yes it is, come up." She pressed the button, allowing Annie into the complex. Anna turned to Graham and Becky, "It's Aunty Annie."

"We'd never have guessed, and please don't shout Anna, I'm still a bit... unwell."

A few moments later, there was a knock at the door.

"Come in!" called Becky and Anna together. The door opened and in walked Annie. It still sent a shock around Graham's system to see her alive and well. Anna ran up and gave her a hug.

"Hello bro, and good to see you Becky. How are you both?" They exchanged kisses.

"We're fine sis, thanks. The last few days just don't seem real. It's only when you see the bruises, you remember it really happened." Graham rubbed his knee.

"Hmm, I was thinking more about after the wine you both consumed. That would have killed a normal couple of human beings and probably preserved their mortal remains for a few decades at least."

"Oh, were we that bad?" Graham looked at Becky.

"You were both completely off your faces."

"Oh." Graham winced as he began to piece together some of the previous evening events.

"Don't you remember offering your undying love to that policeman, Reynolds, for freeing you?" Annie happened to have called round to the apartment, just prior to Reynold's visit. Graham and Becky already were pretty far gone at that stage in the evening.

"Did I?" Graham began to remember. *Oh fuck, fuck, fuck.*

"Did he reply back offering his undying love for anyone else in the room?" Anna asked, mischievously. Graham gave her a look and Anna looked away smiling.

"Well, I don't know what that was all about, but anyway he said he's going to try and call again today, just to get as much info as he can to bring about some convictions. I don't think he got much sense out of either of you yesterday"

"How are mum and dad?"

Annie let out a deep sigh. "Oh, not bad considering they just had a visit from a long dead daughter. I'd say pretty good in the circumstances."

"So what are your plans now?"

"I'm retiring from my secondary employment, so to speak. That was always the plan anyway. I'll probably go back into research. First, though, I'm going to take some time out, travel a bit I think."

"Not planning to do any climbing then?"

"Very funny Graham. You were always the comedian in the family. Anyway, what does a lady have to do to get a cup of tea here?"

*

Mick Cudworth sat in the empty lounge of the boarded up council house. Breaking in had been easy enough. One pull and the board over the kitchen window came off straight away.

He was going to have to disappear for a while, maybe even change his identity. He found a fragment of mirror and looked at his face, regretting the tattoo now.

Scud was Mick's first cousin. Their mothers, Karen and Mollie, were two of ten children who grew up in that tough mining village in South Yorkshire. From the age of 16, Karen lurched from one abusive relationship to another. It was a drunken fumble with a Welsh lorry driver that brought Mick into the world. He disappeared pretty quickly when he found out Karen was pregnant, never to be seen again. The only evidence the child was ever his were those penetrating black eyes, the eyes of his father, that began to appear in the young Michael as a toddler.

An assortment of males of all shapes, sizes and colours came and went as Mick grew up. A worthless thug called Darren Scott was the worst of them though. The two years that Scott was in their lives was a living hell for the boy and his mother. It was rare for the young Michael not to turn up at school with a fresh bruise while he was around. Nothing was ever done though, because that's how it was where he grew up. Unfortunately, it was the same for Karen as well.

There were periods of respite from his company though. A pattern began to emerge where he'd stay a while then just disappear, for a few weeks or sometimes months. No one knew where he went, or what he got up to. When he returned though, the troubles began again.

Mick was fourteen when he first came into their lives. He was a skinny and sickly looking youth, with dark circles around those black eyes. He looked younger than his years and was an easy target for a punch from Scott. When he reached fifteen he began to grow, not particularly tall, but stocky and muscular.

He was six months into his sixteenth year when Scott came back drunk from the club one Friday night, waking up the household and demanding that Karen made him something to eat. She complained that it was late and consequently received a slap. That was enough for Mick, he jumped at Scott and knocked him to the ground and began hitting him. Blow after blow rained down despite the pleas and cries from both Scott and Karen. Scott managed to crawl to the front door and, despite his injuries, got to his feet and ran off, never to be seen again. From that day onwards, nobody pushed either Mick, or his mother around.

People realised the lad had a talent for violence and he forged a career in the criminal underworld of South Yorkshire. He was close to his cousin Simon and they would sometimes work together, although when Simon moved to Leeds to work for James Hyde, this happened less frequently. But there were still occasions they got the chance to work together, such as Riverside.

He was good at what he did, and was always in demand. He'd stay with his mother for weeks at a time, then disappear for a while, returning with money. Karen was always relieved to see him back, and he was always good to his mother, but in other ways it sometimes felt like she was living with Darren Scott all over again.

Mick had enough money after the escape to buy food and a few provisions, but only enough for a couple of days. He had contacts who could help him disappear, that wouldn't be a problem. The problem was his pride. He wasn't used to being on the run. This was supposed to be a simple, straightforward job. He was just hired to make a couple of people disappear. Nothing could or should have gone wrong. Now he was on the run, his cousin had been arrested and he hadn't been paid. This made Mick very angry.

*

Reynolds tried numerous times over the following days to contact Frieda, without success. His instinct told him he was going to be unlikely to either, without drastic action. Once he'd got the appropriate paperwork, he descended on the house at the end of the cul-de-sac and knocked on the door. Nothing.

His colleague broke the lock on the back door and they entered the house. All seemed in order, except there was a plate with the remains of a meal in the kitchen. That would have been cleared and washed up days ago under normal circumstances. It was a tidy house. He'd noticed that on his first visit.

He realised he may have made a tactical mistake when he'd called round earlier. He'd meant to unsettle her, trip her up and unlock secrets that would fill in the gaps. Instead, it looked like she'd run.

Reynolds phoned his colleague back at HQ to alert all units to find her. They were to check airports and ferry terminals as well. He then spoke to his colleagues in the house. "Search the house from top to bottom. I want you to bag up any paperwork you find, however unimportant it might seem."

"Are you sure about this Mark? Don't forget she's the victim's wife," his colleague reminded him discretely in the kitchen.

"She's as guilty as Hyde. And somewhere in this house, there'll be something to prove it."

*

"Well, shall we see what's on this." Graham picked up the disc marked 'Neil'.

"What are you afraid of?" Becky asked.

"It's not what you think. Seeing the murder was bad enough though. I suppose I'm more worried that there's nothing on it and we never actually find out why all this happened."

"Maybe we never will Graham, but you are free and that's the important thing. That footage of the murder means nobody can convict you of that."

"That's not good enough for me now Becky. I want to get to the bottom of this; find out how all this happened and why. It still doesn't make any sense."

"Maybe it's you who should have been the reporter my lad."

Graham smiled back at her. "Come on, no time like the present." He put the disc on and they sat back, rather anxiously, in the leather sofa.

The footage lasted approximately half an hour, but it was pure gold. Graham recognised Frieda straight away, despite the grainy footage at the start. He had no idea who the figure was being led around on a lead around the room. Becky did, though. She knew straight away.

"Oh... my... God, it's Neil." She put her hand to her mouth. They were transfixed by what they saw. Graham was even a little aroused. Frieda still had that effect on him, despite everything. He crossed his legs to avoid giving anything away.

"Who's Neil?"

"Councillor David Neil. I think he's called David. Anyway the man being led around and whipped on the screen before us just happens to be the chair of the development agency that commissioned Hyde to build Riverside. Don't you see Graham? Hyde got the commission through blackmail. Can you imagine what this would do to Cllr. Neil if it ever got out?"

"Hmm," said Graham. "Well, I think this also needs to go to our friend down at the station with the other evidence we submitted."

"The officer you were offering your undying love to? What are you going to be like after the party in the Tap next week?"

"Yes... yes, thank you for reminding me Becks. Anyway, before we submit it, could you make me a copy please?"

"Graham, what are you up to?"

*

Grant sat opposite Scud, contemplating his bulky form on the cell bunk. *Dirty job this, but someone's got to do it.* "Good morning Mr. Cudworth."

"Who the fuck are you?" Scud replied.

You're a little charmer aren't you, Grant thought. "My name is Derek Grant and I'm James Hyde's solicitor."

"Then you can fuck right off back to Hyde and tell him he is a dead man."

"Yes... I, we understand how you must be feeling, about the little misunderstanding earlier..."

"Don't use fancy words with me. I know what that prick was planning on doing."

"Can we just lower our voices a little bit, please?" Grant gestured with his hands as he looked nervously at the cell door, aware of the police officer stood outside. "My client denies ever planning to arrange for any harm whatsoever to befall you. As I say, it was a complete misunderstanding. Anyway, I'm here with an offer that might be of mutual benefit to you and my client."

"What?"

"Something that might help you both," he clarified, increasingly frustrated with Scud's clumsiness and stupidity. *Why in the name of God did you hire him in the first place James?*

"What's he offering?"

Ah, interested now are we now? "My client has given this situation a great deal of thought. Unfortunately, it appears highly likely, looking at the evidence the police have, that you will be convicted for the killing of Peter McArthur..."

Scud stood up and loomed over Grant, who visibly shrank back. "He made sure of that, the bastard. He paid me to do the job and then filmed me. He was going to set me up for this all along!"

"No, no, not at all. He filmed it, yes, but it was never going to be seen by anyone else. It was an... erm... insurance policy, only found by chance when Pilgrimm broke into his house. Please, calm down. There is a solution to this."

Scud sat back down, without taking his eyes of Grant. "Start talking and this had better be good."

Grant took out his handkerchief and mopped his sweating brow. "My client is going to suggest that the disc was in the possession of Pilgrimm all the time. There were no witnesses with Pilgrimm when he says he found the disc in my client's house anyway. It won't stand up in court."

"So?"

"So Simon, we propose you confess to the murder, on the instructions of Pilgrimm. We'll arrange some possible meeting times between you both prior to the murder. These are minor details. But my client would look to ensure you would be generously compensated for the inconvenience."

"That's a pile of shit. Nobody is going to believe that."

"Why not? The police had evidence he'd been pestering Frieda prior to the murder. She wouldn't accept his advances, so instead of killing the husband himself, he found someone else to do it." Scud could see the logic. "There's another thing, you will also need to confess to arranging the kidnap of the daughter and her friend. Again, there can be no disputing you did it, but there must be no indication the orders came from my client. You planned this yourself because you knew Pilgrimm had the video evidence that you were the killer and you needed to trade the daughter for the disc."

"You've both got it all worked out, haven't you," Scud sneered. Grant smiled nervously.

"There's one final thing as well. Are you in touch with your cousin?"

"Why? What if I am?"

"My client is further proposing that he... err... pays a visit to Pilgrimm and... erm... disposes of him." Grant mopped his brow again with his handkerchief and wiped his hands as well. By now he was sweating profusely. "He should be easy to find, now he's no longer in hiding. With him finally... err... removed from the equation, I would suggest we have every chance of getting away with this completely."

"What's in it for us?"

"You will be convicted and serve a sentence. We all know life can mean just a few years, with good behaviour anyway. Then, when you are released, the sum of £100,000 will be waiting for you in cash, and the same will be paid to your cousin.

"£200,000."

"Yes, £200,000 between you."

"No, £200,000 each."

"Pardon?"

"£200,000 each, or you can forget it.

"Err, well. I don't know. I'll have to talk to my client." Inside, Grant was smiling. He's taken the bait. Grant knew Hyde had no intention of paying Scud or his cousin a penny. But still, best to play the game.

"I'll talk to my client," he reiterated, "and I'll get straight back to you. In the meantime Mr. Cudworth, I'd be grateful if you didn't discuss this matter with anyone other than your cousin, for obvious reasons, and I'll be in touch in 48 hours."

"48 hours?"

"Two days, it means two bloody days" clarified Grant, a little more impatiently than he'd planned.

*

"Mark, come and look at this." DI Jones called to Reynolds from a small room at the top of the stairs. Reynolds walked across the landing and met his colleague in a bedroom that had been converted into an office. He guessed this was where Pete McArthur would have run his business from. There were filing cabinets, a desk with a phone, fax and PC and, poignantly, a framed photo of a smiling Frieda and Pete on the wall. *If only you knew what you were marrying,* thought Reynolds.

One of the filing cabinet drawers was open and crouching next to it was DI Jones.

"Look at this," he repeated to Reynolds.

"What am I looking at?" Reynolds asked. Jones pointed to one of the dividers in the cabinet. It was labelled 'Hyde Constructions'.

"I think this could be worth looking at Mark, don't you?"

*

Meanwhile, in the derelict council house where Mick was hiding, the silence was interrupted by a mobile phone ringtone.

"Yes?"

"Is that you Mick?"

"That you Scuddy lad?"

"Yeah, can't talk long though. Are you okay mate?"

"Been better kid. Pissed off though. I don't know what the fuck happened back there, but I wasn't going to hang around."

"Listen, I can't talk long. Hyde's mouthpiece came to see me. He's making us an offer. I keep quiet about Hyde and take the shit for the murder and kidnapping, and you finish off Pilgrimm. We both get £200k when I get out."

"£200K each?"

"Yeah. What do you think? I'm going down anyway mate. But I won't mind the wait if there's £200K at the end of it. Interested?"

"Think I'd better pay a visit to this Pilgrimm then. I was thinking of calling to see him before I disappeared anyway."

*

Hopkins paused in front of the large 1920s semi-detached in a respectable part of north Leeds, just off the York Road. It had a mock Tudor appearance, with the white render of the first floor contrasting with fake black timber framing. He paused in front of the drive, before walking up to the front door.

There was a definite nip in the air. The first winds of autumn were blowing from the north. He felt chilled to the bone. He hadn't really felt himself for a while now. His colleagues kept asking if he was coming down with something. He was. It was disappointment.

He'd looked up to Smithson for most of his career; always respected his decisions, his judgement and integrity. And now this.

He walked to the front door and knocked. There was nothing for a good minute or so. It gave Hopkins the excuse he was looking for. He was just beginning to turn and return to his car when he heard the door opening. When he looked, he saw a tired looking DI Smithson with at least a couple of days of stubble on his face.

"Oh, it's you Raymond." Smithson looked surprised. "I thought it might be... well, it doesn't matter. Come in." He sounded different, detached somehow.

"How are you Leslie?" Hopkins had a pretty good idea though, looking at the shuffling figure with his bandaged arm leading him through to the lounge. He looked 20 years older than a month ago. As they went into the room, the piles of clothes and clutter told him that he'd been alone for some time as well.

"I'm fine Raymond. I just feel tired, really tired at the moment you know." He sat heavily in an armchair and beckoned Hopkins to sit on the settee opposite.

"Where's Rachel?"

"Oh, she's gone away for a few days. I'm sure she'll be back soon. She just needed to get away..."

"Is it true Leslie? Is it true what they're all saying down at the station?"

"What are they saying Raymond?" Smithson asked, rather absently.

"They're saying Pilgrimm was set up by James Hyde and that you were in on it."

"Are they? Is that what they're saying?"

Hopkins just had to look at his mentor to know it was true. "Why Leslie? Why in the name of God?" In any other situation like this, Hopkins would have been fuming. Fists might even have been flying. Instead, he looked at Smithson with no discernable feelings at all. He felt betrayed and dead inside.

"I've been on the make for years Ray. I've taken thousands from Hyde over decades, getting him off the hook for all kinds of things. This was just one in a long line of business dealings

236

with James. Why? There's always room for a little more money Ray; a couple of weeks with the wife and children in Florida, a new car, the landscaping of the back garden. Everything comes at a price." All the time he'd been speaking he'd focussed on the wall opposite. Then he looked at Hopkins. "I'm sorry Ray. I've not always approved of your methods, but you're a good copper. You'll always do what you've got to do to get the bad guy. And today, the bad guy is me."

"This Pilgrimm... he's innocent?"

"Oh completely yes. He was the fall guy who refused to fall. We chose the wrong man there. Not only was he the wrong man, but he had the wrong daughter and, God only knows where she came from, the wrong sister as well."

"Leslie..."

"Don't say anything Ray. I know why you're here. Just leave me a little while longer, here in my house - just five minutes or so before I have to go. Somehow, I don't think I'll ever be coming back here, do you?"

"No Leslie. No, I don't." Hopkins looked at Smithson and finally started feeling something. At first he couldn't put his finger on it. Then finally he realised what it was.

It was pity.

*

"Bloody hell Becky, you nearly killed that cyclist!"

"Oh man up for God's sake!" Becky barked at Graham as the Fiesta narrowly avoided the cyclist who swerved off the road and hit an advertising board in front of a newsagent's. Luckily the board came off worse.

"Why are you having a go at me anyway? What have I done?"

"It's what you've not done. You promised you were going to take that DVD to the police. You're now withholding evidence and we could get into trouble for that."

"Not we, me. If anyone's going to get into trouble, it's me."

"I don't want you to get into trouble Graham. We're trying to clear your name in case you've forgotten. What part of not getting you into any more trouble don't you understand?"

"Look, I will. I promise. There's just something I have to do first that's all."

"Why did you need a copy? What are you up to Graham?"

"I can't tell you Becks. All will be revealed later."

"You are so fucking infuriating sometimes Graham."

"Yeah, but you still love me though don't you."

"That isn't fair. I'm not answering that. All I'll say is this; until you hand that DVD into the police, there'll be no more sexy time happening with us."

"You can't do that!"

"I bloody well can - and I will. I mean it Graham."

"Not even that... you know... that special thing you do with your..."

"Not even that, lover boy. So put that in your pipe and smoke it." Becky ended the discussion just as they pulled up outside the launderette underneath Graham's first floor flat.

Graham looked up at the windows facing the road. It seemed a lifetime since he'd lived here. In many ways it was.

"Do you want me to come up and give you a hand packing?"

"No love, thanks. You get off and do your shopping. It'll do me good to be alone here for a while and exorcise a few ghosts.

"Are you okay?"

"Yeah, I suppose. I just feel... Did you ever see 'My Fair Lady'?"

"Oh, yes, with Audrey Hepburn. It's one of my favourite films."

"Yes, me too." Graham smiled. "It's just that bit near the end when she realises that she's changed. She's been transformed into this beautiful high society lady and she tries to go back to where she came from, realising she can't. She's caught halfway between lives and feels like she doesn't belong in one world or the other. I feel like that Becks. I feel like things have changed and can never be the same again."

"Oh Graham. You are a sensitive man and I do love you. Perhaps you've not changed. Perhaps for the first time in your life, you realise who you actually are." They looked at each other. "You know what Graham, despite what I said earlier, if you get in the bath I'll do that thing after all."

"Thank you Becks. That will be really appreciated. In the meantime..."

"No. Now get in there and start packing. The sooner you're finally out of that place the better. How long do you need?"

"Oh, I'm not sure. I guess to pack enough to fill this car, maybe an hour?"

"Okay, lover boy. See you then." She blew a kiss, then shot off down the road; nearly taking out a dog and its owner in the process.

Graham shook his head as he watched the car disappear, then went to the door at the side of the launderette, unlocked it and climbed the stairs up to the flat. It felt even colder and damper than the last time he popped in with the packages he'd rescued from Hyde's office. *I can't wait to get out of here,* he thought. They'd made the decision the previous week that they were going to live together in Becky's apartment, at least in the short term, until all this was over and then make longer term plans. Until then, they couldn't really see beyond the short term.

After five minutes of pottering around, he got down to the task of packing, starting with the important stuff like his CDs and DVDs. He tried to pack them so their alphabetical orders remained intact.

Ten minutes later, he heard the front door open and close. *Becks is a bit early. She must have forgotten something.*

He looked up from the floor and saw at once it wasn't Becky that had entered the flat, it was Scud's cousin. He could never forget the tattoo and those black eyes.

"Oh," was all Graham could say.

"Hello Pilgrimm. Bet you didn't expect to see me again, did you?" he said as he leaned against the doorway leading to the staircase down to the front door.

"No, no I didn't." Graham replied, his voice heavy with resignation. "Are you here to kill me?"

"That was the idea."

"Can I at least ask why?"

"Hard cash old love. Hard cash."

"From Hyde, presumably?"

"That's right. You're on the ball you are."

"Do you think it's wise?"

"Well, it seems a perfectly good decision to make in the circumstance pal."

"How much has he offered you?"

"Oh, are you going to try and outbid him?" Mick Cudworth mocked.

"No. I'm just curious to find out what I'm worth. That's all."

"Two hundred big ones old love."

"Two hundred, thousand?"

"That's right."

"Do you think you'll ever see the money?"

"What do you mean?"

"Don't you think Hyde will make sure you and your cousin are taken out before you see a penny?"

"I'm not going to fall for that again. You tried it on at the building site and everything went tits up. You're the one that's playing games pal."

"What have you had from him to prove he's going to pay you?" All the while they were discussing Graham's demise he sat on the floor of the flat, next to the box he'd been carefully packing, while he looked over at the bulky and somewhat scruffy figure standing before him.

"What do you think he's going to give me Pilgrimm, a written contract?"

"I bet the assassin he sent to kill me down at the allotment had a contract. He was a professional though. He'll have used him before and would have used him again in the future. That won't be the case with you." All the while he was talking, Graham carefully manoeuvred his mobile phone on the carpet next to him so it was behind the box he'd been packing his CDs in, just out of view of his adversary. He deftly unlocked it with his thumb, and hit the dial button, knowing the last person he'd called was Becky. *Come on Becks, pick it up!* "He will betray you, like he did with your cousin." A glance down at the phone showed Becky had picked up the call. He allowed 10 seconds for her to have spoken her greeting, then tapped the symbol on the bottom right hand side of the screen that activated the speakerphone.

"That's bollocks Pilgrimm. It worked for you then, but it's not going to work for you now."

"I saw the file!" Graham raised his voice. He wanted the mock anger to be heard over the phone. "He was going to have Scud killed and will do the same to you. It's you that is walking into a trap."

"It's not going to work Pilgrimm."

"What's your name?"

"What?"

"What's your name? If you are going to kill me, it would at least be nice to know your name."

"Mick Cudworth, for what it's worth to you pal." Graham glanced down at his phone, just in time to see the call terminated at Becky's end. *Come on Becks, come on.*

"Mick you have got to realise what this man Hyde is like. If you kill me he will be the only winner. You won't see a penny.

Think about it Mick. Is there anything you have that proves Hyde has planned this?"

"Don't fuck with me Pilgrimm!"

"And don't you fuck with me!" This time, Graham really was beginning to lose his temper. The fact that he could be dead within minutes somehow gave him a freedom to express himself. What had he got to lose? He'd originally planned this conversation as a delaying tactic, but all the while he was talking, he realised himself that this poor fool in front of him really was just going to be just another fall guy as he had been and Mick's stupid cousin Scud had been as well. "If you do this, we will both be the losers. The only winner will be that slimeball Hyde. Mick, I saw the file in Hyde's desk. There were photos of me, with stuff on my family, friends, job, everything about me. I saw the same information on your cousin, all in the same format. It was everything an assassin would need to know. Don't you remember the look on Hyde's face down at Riverside when he realised I knew? He was scared Mick. He knew I'd found out." *Come on. I really need the cavalry right now.* "Mick, Hyde is a bully. He's a bully of the worst kind. He's not physically strong. You'd kick the shit out of him in a one to one fight. But he doesn't need to do that. He doesn't need to get his hands dirty, because there are always others to do it for him for a price. He's rich, has influence, he's respected. People like him will always get away with it, as long as people like you and your cousin are there to do his dirty work, the sacrificial lambs, the shields he can hide behind. And guess what Mick? When it hits the fan, he'll always walk away whiter than white, because there are always people like you, your cousin and even me he can use. We'll be the ones who'll take it Mick. I can do nothing if you want to kill me. But just think who will be the real winner here. Do you think it will be you after Hyde tells you to piss off without a penny? I really don't think so. It's up to you now son. Do you really fancy being a puppet Mick, a plaything for bullies like Hyde, or are you going to decide your own future?"

Mick looked at Graham, deep into him. It felt like those black eyes were looking into his very soul. Then he seemed to focus on something beyond, a distant memory. It was something from his past, a time when he did take control of his life.

What are you thinking Mick? What are you going to do? "Mick, you're not going to be able to run away forever. Give yourself up now. You'll have to serve time for abduction, or assault, or whatever, but it won't be much. It won't be anything like the time you'll serve for murder. Mick, stop running away. Stop running away from yourself and put the real bad guy behind bars."

Graham didn't know what was going to happen next. Neither moved, or spoke, for what seemed an eternity. Eventually Mick slowly opened his mouth, about to speak. Graham tensed, then both paused and listened. There it was, the sound of a siren, getting audibly louder.

When it became obvious the sirens were pulling up outside, Mick glanced behind him, down the stairs to the front door, weighing up whether to make a run for it. Instead, he looked back at Graham and then the strangest thing happened. Despite having the option of running, he stayed where he was. He looked at Graham and slowly nodded. A man who only moments ago was going to kill him, now acknowledged him with a sign of respect. Both looked at each other, lost in time.

Moments later the door to the flat burst open and uniformed officers ran up the steps and entered the lounge. Mick raised his hands in surrender, turned slowly to face the officers and was duly handcuffed and taken away.

Graham followed them down the stairs and outside where he watched Mick being bundled with no resistance into one of two police cars, before being driven away. One of the remaining uniformed officers went up to Graham.

"Are you alright Mr. Pilgrimm?"

"Yes, I think so. Thanks."

"Will you be able to come to the station and make a statement?"

"Yes... oh wait, my girlfriend, Becky. I need to see her first, make sure she's okay." At that moment Becky's car pulled into view and came to a sudden stop, inches behind the second police car. The officer visibly jumped back. She leapt out and ran to Graham.

"Oh, thank God. Graham, are you alright? What happened?" They hugged each other.

"I'll tell you down at the station Becky. I've got to go and give a statement. You saved my life, again. I don't know what to say. God Becky, I love you."

"I love you too, sweetheart." She held his head between her hands and kissed him. "Officer, can we follow you to the station in my car?"

"Yes miss, of course, only..."

"What is it?"

"Please don't drive too close will you?" he said, looking anxiously at the narrowest of gaps separating his car and Becky's Fiesta.

*

Reynolds was riveted to his desk, mesmerised by what he was reading. There were pages after pages of photocopied contracts, letters and other documents, together with photos and even financial records that painted a damning picture of Hyde and his empire. It was clear that the private and public persona were poles apart.

Hyde had cheated, lied and intimidated his way to the top and here was the evidence to prove it. Sometime over the previous year, Pete McArthur had stumbled across something or had his suspicions aroused enough to start an investigation that, if he had gone public, would not only have destroyed Hyde, but sent him to prison for years.

Was he going to blackmail Hyde? Reynolds gave him the benefit of the doubt. By all accounts McArthur was a decent man. This seemed to be the consensus from friends, family and colleagues who were interviewed after the murder. He ran a successful business, but would probably never be a millionaire. By all accounts, he was honest and did everything by the book. More likely, Reynolds thought, he was probably going to go public with this to simply expose him for the crook he was.

Perhaps this was the motive for his murder. Had he confided in Frieda, unaware of her seedy relationship with Hyde? Any husband probably would in those circumstances.

It didn't take a massive leap of imagination to guess that knowing this was about to happen, Frieda and Hyde could have arranged the murder to keep him quiet. This would also then allow Frieda and Hyde to legitimise their relationship over time. Frieda could achieve her financial ambitions and Hyde would have his massive ego enhanced with a trophy wife who could, judging by the recording Anna obtained, also satisfy his more primeval urges. All they needed to do was find a killer, the hapless Scud, and someone to put in the frame. Graham Pilgrimm.

Reynolds sat back in his chair, contemplating his next move. If only he hadn't frightened Frieda off. That was a mistake. He looked down at the papers on his desk. There was a folder in the pile marked 'Riverside'. *Now that looks interesting*, he thought. He opened it and started to leaf through when there was a knock at the door. "Come in."

A somewhat breathless uniformed officer walked in. "You're not going to believe this boss."

"What is it?"

"We've just picked up Michael Cudworth."

"Where was he?"

"In Pilgrimm's flat, about to carve him into slices with knife he had concealed on his person."

"Was Pilgrimm there?"

"Yes, but get this. He kept Cudworth talking while managing to get a message to his girlfriend to call us. Can you believe it?"

"Nothing this man does surprises me anymore. Is he okay?"

"Yes, he's fine, tired, but otherwise okay. He's given us a full account and gone to her place. He can be contacted there if we need him."

"And of course, this Cudworth character has denied it all."

"No Mark, that's the funny thing. He's admitted it and even confirmed he was acting under the instructions of Hyde himself and would receive £200,000 on completion of the job."

"What? He's told you that?"

"Yep, and guess what. He's going to make a formal statement and is prepared to stand up in court and say the same."

"Why. What stopped him from killing Pigrimm?"

"I have no idea. Tell you what, I'd pay a few quid to have been a fly on the wall when they were having their little chat in Pilgrimm's flat."

*

"Mr. Hyde, you have a visitor." From his peculiar position on the hospital bed, Hyde could just make out the pretty ankles of the Irish nurse. *God, I like to see what's underneath those tights.*

"Who is it nurse?"

"It's me James." Hyde caught a glimpse of a somewhat less attractive pair of ankles, mercifully covered with the crumpled pair of brown suit trousers."

"Hello Grant, pull up a chair. Do you have news?" Grant sat down on the red plastic chair next to the bed. Hyde turned his head so he could just about make out his face. He was nervously rubbing his chin.

"What's the matter with you? What is it?"

"It's not good James." Grant pulled out his handkerchief and started wiping his hands with it."

"Well?" said Hyde. "Start talking. What in the name of God am I paying you for if you're just going to sit there like a dummy."

"That's the thing James. You don't need to pay me anymore."

"What the fuck are you talking about Grant?"

"The thing is, James, I'm resigning."

"What?"

"The police have got Mick Cudworth."

"How? Has he killed Pilgrimm?"

"No James. He went to his flat to do the job and, well, he seemed to have changed his mind."

"He changed his... what are you talking about?"

"He's given the police a statement James. He's told them you were paying him to kill Pilgrimm. And there's more." Hyde felt like he was descending into a dark tunnel, perhaps on his way to hell, earlier than scheduled. Grant's voice seemed to disappear into the distance. It was only the pain in his rear end that brought him back to reality. "James. James, are you listening?"

"Yes." Hyde replied weakly.

"James, the word is Simon Cudworth is also going to make a statement."

"Yes?"

"A statement to confess to the murder of Peter McArthur, that you paid him to do it and that Pilgrimm was framed."

"The money. What about the money I was going to pay them?"

"The money you said you were going to pay them, but weren't going to."

"They didn't know that."

"It didn't matter in the end. The word is James, they all just want to see you put away now, even low lives like the Cudworths." Hyde wiped his hands even more vigorously. "James, it's all collapsing around us. The ship is sinking and I'm sorry, but I can't go down with it."

"You bastard!" Hyde tried to get up, but the pain put him back down on the bed.

"I'm sorry James. I'm afraid it's all over." He got up quickly, anxious to be away as soon as possible. He was just leaving the room when he paused, turned and spoke to Hyde's rear end. "I will have to bill you for the last couple of weeks though James. I won't charge for today, but..." The sound of the animal like snarl growing audibly louder from Hyde's bed cut him short and he rapidly departed from the room.

*

"It's over Becky. It's really over. That was Reynold's colleague. The Cudworth cousins and others have confessed to everything. They're dropping all charges. I'm free Becks. I'm free." He stared out of the apartment window towards the river as he spoke. Even as he was saying them, the words didn't feel real. It felt like the day Hopkins and Smithson had him down at the station when he realised he'd been framed. He was detached from the reality, watching a performance on the stage with someone who looked like him playing the main character. Yet it was him then, and was now.

"Oh Graham!" Becky stood across the room and put both her hands over her mouth. She started to cry. They moved towards each other and met with a tight hug in the middle of the room. Graham said nothing. He couldn't. He was crying too.

Chapter Eight – A bit of Yorkshire hospitality

I like the autumn. Don't get me wrong, the joy of planting, growing and harvesting over spring and summer is what it's really all about. But autumn allows us time to start to catch our breath again, take stock and start planning for next spring. To keep your plot in a healthy state, make sure you don't grow the same crops in the same ground over successive years. Plan to rotate the crops around the site to avoid the build up of disease. Also, each crop has a specific nutrient demand. This same crop in the same place may deplete certain nutrients. Part of your planning should involve thinking about what grew well over the summer and what didn't. You might want to try different crops or not bother with those that don't work too well on your plot. I can't grow peas. I've tried on and off over the years, so now I don't bother. Sounds defeatist, but the way I look at it, maybe the soil conditions aren't right or I'm prone to certain pests. Either way, other things grow better, so I'd rather work with nature and grow the things that want to grow there. As well as planning on paper, there's still work on the ground. Dig over the cleared plots and spread your home made compost. You can leave the soil in course lumps. The freezing weather and winter rains will break up the soil and mix in your compost naturally, ready for your spring planting. I can't over emphasise how important your home made composts can be. There are a few basic rules for making successful compost. More on this later. Compost replaces lost nutrients naturally, adds organic matter which helps retain soil moisture and promotes an excellent soil structure. And it also means you're not adding to the pressures on landfill with your garden waste.

Councillor David Neil put the phone down and licked his lips nervously. The call from the police officer didn't give too much away. They would appreciate his assistance in an investigation they were currently undertaking so yes, tomorrow afternoon around 2pm would be fine. All very civilised and polite.

He stared at himself in the mirror, at his crooked tie. The call had interrupted his preparations for a presentation he was delivering at a rather prestigious event later in the evening. His wife Sarah walked in with a pile of ironed clothes she started putting away in the bedroom.

"David, you look miles away love. Are you alright? You're not nervous about tonight are you?"

"No, not at all. I was just going through my speech in my head."

"Well, you'll be fine. What do you think is going to happen about this Riverside project now? Can you believe that James Hyde has been arrested for the murder of Peter McArthur? It's unbelievable. They must have made a mistake. He's such a nice man and he's a good friend of yours as well, isn't he?"

"No! No... he's more of an acquaintance, that's all." Sarah stopped sorting the clothes and stared at him. His response had come out a bit firmer than he'd hoped.

"Are you sure you're alright David."

"Yes, I'm fine." He tried to sound reassuring. "I'm just a little tired and yes, Riverside. I don't know what we'll do now. I suppose nothing until the investigation into Hyde is complete."

"There must be some mistake. I can't believe he would do anything like that. And look at that poor man Graham... Pilgrimm? Something like that. It looks like he was innocent all along. It's a funny name though."

"What is?" asked Neil, absently.

"Pilgrimm. Aren't you listening David?"

"Sorry love. I'm miles away."

"Look, I can see your mind is elsewhere. I'll let you get ready in peace." She left the room, much to Neil's relief. He looked back into the mirror and stared at his reflection.

*

"Where are you going love? You're being very secretive this evening."

"Um, what?"

"Where are you going tonight?"

"Oh, it's just a catch up with the lads. I won't be late."

"You'll be seeing them tomorrow."

"Oh, I probably won't get time to talk tomorrow. It could be a bit crazy, you know."

"Well, don't forget I'm working tonight so it'll be late when I'm home. Do you normally dress as smart as that when you go out with the lads? I'd have thought overalls or some other form of protective clothing would have been more appropriate for the Tap."

"Most amusing. I feel any moment my sides may well split. Anyway, what's wrong with dressing up occasionally? I don't always need to look like I've been sleeping under a hedge."

"I'll take that as a compliment. Must be my influence."

"Anyway, I'm expecting you at the Tap tomorrow night."

"Wouldn't miss it for the world. Graham's coming out party."

"Steady on, wouldn't want people to get the wrong idea."

"No danger of that lover boy. So what's the plan tomorrow night?"

"The Lord only knows. It's been organised by Tomo and Jim-Bob, so don't be surprised if there are strippers or worse."

"I can't wait."

"I'm sure it will be fine. Even those two can organise a piss up in a brewery, so to speak. What have you got on tonight? Anything exciting?"

"Just some local government thing. I have to do a write up for the Post."

"Sounds thrilling. You get all the sexy jobs, don't you?"

"Tell me about it Big G. Anyway, I'll see you when you get back. I'm hoping it's not going to be a late one. I don't feel that great to be honest."

"Are you going to be alright tonight?"

"I'll be fine. I just feel a bit Moby Dick and tired as well. I just need a good night's sleep - that's all."

"Ah, so no...?"

"Absolutely not Big G. Don't wake me up when you come in and if you're on the ale, please open the window before you come to bed."

"How romantic. So it's come to this." Graham mocked.

"Just have a good night and don't talk to any strange blonde women please?"

"I'll do my best kidda."

Half an hour later, Graham's taxi pulled up outside Kate's house.

"Just blow the horn will you please. She'll be straight out."

"No problem mate," the elderly Asian driver replied. A couple of short blasts quickly brought out Anna. She said a quick goodbye to her mum and ran to the taxi. Graham waved out of the window to reassure Kate he was in the taxi. After everything that had happened over the last few weeks, Kate was understandably a little anxious whenever Anna went out, especially in the evening.

"Hi dad," she said as she got in.

"Hi love, you look great. What did you tell your mum?"

"Just that I'm out with you for a curry following your release back into society."

"Great." Graham turned to the driver. "Can you take us to the hotel, please?"

"On our way boss," he said as they set off.

"What have you told Becky?"

"I'm out with the lads tonight."

"A bit smart for The Tap aren't you?"

"Don't you start. I've had enough of that from Becky."

"Have you got the disc?"

"Yes, it's here." He passed the DVD to Anna. "It is going to be compatible isn't it?"

"Should be."

"So how are you going to get it into the machine?"

"Jack says he'll sort it. We just have to meet him at the kitchen door near the wheelie bins. We can get in that way as well."

"Isn't he a bit young to work there?"

"He's 16 dad. You can serve and wait on the tables, but can't serve alcohol. He's legal. It's us that aren't."

"I know. Are you alright? Six months ago I wouldn't have dreamt of asking you to get involved in anything like this."

"I think after everything I've been through dad, this will be a piece of cake. Besides, I can't wait to see this myself. You've never shown it to me."

"There's a reason. I think it would be appropriate if you turned away when I indicate."

"Are you joking? I am seriously looking forward to this."

The taxi pulled up outside the impressive entrance to the hotel. Various well heeled guests were coming and going, but nobody paid any attention to the middle-aged man and his daughter who slipped down the alleyway at the side. When they got to the door next to the bins, Anna took out her mobile and phoned her friend Jack. A few seconds later he answered. "Hi J. It's us. We're just outside now. Aha, yes. Great, see you." She put the phone back in her pocket. "He's on his way."

A couple of minutes later the door opened outwards and a pale looking skinny youth with red hair peered out anxiously. Seeing Anna he smiled.

"Hi Pilly." Seeing Graham he added, "Oh, hello Mr. Pilgrimm sir. Everyone at school thinks you're pretty cool by the way."

"You didn't have to say that," Anna reprimanded him, deeply embarrassed.

"Hey, no problem. Thank you Jack and nice to meet you as well."

"Have you got the disc?" he asked Anna.

"Yes, it's here. Do you know what you're doing?" she asked as she handed him the DVD.

"No problem. Greasy Paul is going to load it and all you need to do is give him the nod when you want it on."

"Who's Greasy Paul?" Graham asked.

"He's the IT technician who works here. I'll point him out but you'll recognise him straight away. He's got long, straggly hair and round glasses. He's a bit of a perv, but brilliant with IT."

"Thanks Jack. Are we going to be okay to come in this way?"

"Hang on. I'll check the coast is clear first." He disappeared for a minute then came back. "We're fine now. Just follow me."

They walked through a brightly lit, hot and steamy kitchen, busy with a spectrum of staff of all nationalities rushing around and shouting in a multitude of different languages, then down a more subtly lit, red carpeted cream painted hallway, into a large dimly lit function room. On the left, a raised area of staging overlooked numerous round tables, tastefully decorated with flowers and tea lights. *God this is posh*, thought Graham.

Jack took them round the side of the room to avoid drawing any attention to them. Graham had suddenly found himself back in the public eye with news of his release and the implication of the true culprits in the murder of Pete McArthur. He certainly didn't want to be recognised here, not yet anyway. Jack seated them at a small table at the rear of the room.

"I'll be right back," he said.

Graham looked around and noticed others sat at the back. It was difficult to make them out, but they seemed far more underdressed than the assembled great and good sat around the tables before them. He looked towards the stage and noticed a small table directly in front with a couple of laptops and what looked like a projector. He could just about pick out the figure of

Jack talking to a large woman connecting cables and plugging equipment in. He handed something over to the woman. It was then he realised it wasn't a woman at all, but a chubby male with long hair. *Greasy Paul.*

Graham suddenly felt the hot flush of nerves in his stomach as he saw the disc Jack handed over. No going back now. Graham and Anna sat in silence, taking everything in, when Jack suddenly appeared with a bottle of wine and two glasses.

"Here, this will help you blend in better," said Jack.

"Thanks," said Anna."

"Have you got a coke instead for Anna?" asked Graham.

"Dad, get a life will you? I'm nearly sixteen. I've been drinking this stuff for a couple of years now."

"Does your mother know?"

"I usually have a few glasses with her at the weekend when I'm not with you."

"I'm not sure I'm happy about that. I'll have a word with mum about this afterwards."

"Dad, shut up and pour the wine will you? I think there are other more important things we need to think about at the moment, don't you?"

"We'll discuss this later." Graham then looked at Jack. "Do I need to give you a signal?"

"It's fine Mr. Pilgrimm. I've had a word with Paul. He knows when to put it on. I'm looking forward to this."

"Are you and Paul going to get in trouble for this?"

"I'm not bothered to be honest. I'm sick of working here. The pay's shit and my boss is a twat. Paul is quitting anyway. He wants to start his own internet porn business." *He might find the presentation of interest then,* thought Graham.

*

Becky sat at her table, nursing a coffee she didn't really want. She really did feel sick and just wanted to go home. All she wanted was to get back to her bed and cuddle up to Graham. *Oh please don't be farting all night when you get back will you Graham?*

She exchanged a bit of small talk with an old friend opposite who worked for the Express, looked towards the stage and watched a skinny youth chatting to a fat lady next to the projector stand, then down at her cold coffee on the table in front of her, wishing the evening away.

*

Graham was just beginning to settle down and relax a little after his second glass of wine, when a chance look over to his right revealed Becky, no more than four tables away. *Fuuuccckkk! I am dead!*

He realised the only course of action now was to get the DVD back, but it was too late. A smartly dressed woman took to the stage and welcomed everyone to the event. After the usual health and safety information she introduced the chair of the development agency. Councillor David Neil bounded onto the stage with an outward confidence that hid a deep anxiety.

"Ladies and gentlemen, it is wonderful to be back here again. I cannot believe it is a full year since we first confirmed, in this very room, we were able to provide the funding for the new 'Destination Yorkshire' promotional film; a film that will be showcased all over the world, including several major cinema chains I'm delighted to be able to announce as well, (applause) that will showcase the unique sights, sounds and welcome our visitors can expect to receive here, in the heart of God's Own Country. This will also be the first time I've seen this as well, so I am looking forward to it with baited breath. It will last about 20 minutes and then afterwards I'd like you to welcome the director, Greg Davies, onto the stage to share with you what it was about our county that inspired the imagery you are about to see. Greg, can you just stand... ah, there you are."

A figure stood up from one of the tables near the front of the stage and turned to face the crowd, offered a modest bow to the applause he received and then sat back down again.

WhatthefuckhaveIdone? Graham sat staring ahead, a look of pure terror on his face. He looked at Anna as she sat back in her chair, laughing her head off in anticipation. She was loving every minute of this. He looked over towards Becky. She hadn't spotted him there. His beautiful Becky. It was over. In less than a minute, all his hopes and dreams of a new life with Becky would be all over. He'd blown it. He might as well have let the Baltic assassin finish him off at the allotment, or Hyde's groundsman, or Mick Cudworth. He was finished as far as Becky was concerned. The voice of Councillor Neil brought him back down to earth.

"It gives me great pleasure to start the film with the words – make Yorkshire your destination!"

The lights were dimmed and the projector sprung into life. Many of the audience were expecting a burst of patriotic or evocative music, perhaps a brass band. Instead, the film showed a somewhat grainy image of a hotel bedroom. It looked an expensive one though. Ah, perhaps the director was going for an arty look? Interesting.

The director, meanwhile, was looking extremely confused. *What the hell is this?* He started looking round, but in the dark of the function room, nobody noticed his expression or anxious looks towards the projector. *Someone's put the wrong bloody film on.* His eyes were drawn back to the screen by the gasps of the audience. He joined them with a gasp of his own. *Oh, my sweet Lord...*

A tall blonde in thigh length boots, carrying a whip strode onto the screen. She cracked it a couple of times and a naked figure, wearing nothing but a dog collar and an erection crawled into view.

"You are a bad dog!" She cracked the whip again. "You are going to be punished for this." She whipped him twice on the bare buttocks and he started whimpering. "Bad dog! Bad dog!" The tall blonde repeated.

Graham suddenly felt a strange mix of emotions in no particular order:-

Resignation – there was nothing he could do now to stop this.

Satisfaction – exposing the corruption that had gifted Hyde Riverside.

Arousal – Bloody Hell, she was good, a real pro in all senses of the word.

A few people around the room started laughing, others cried out in protest and indignation. What kind of tourism was this going to promote? Neil made an attempt to leap off the stage and stop the film, but caught his foot on a rail and went sprawling all over the floor.

Graham turned to look at Anna. Tears of laughter were rolling down her cheeks. It was pointless telling her to look away. Nervously, he looked over towards Becky and the rest of the press. He couldn't make out Becky initially. Her colleagues were having a field day though. Their fits of laughter were interspersed with frantic scribbling. Then he saw her.

He couldn't believe what he was seeing. Becky was clutching her sides from laughing so hard. At one point she nearly fell off her chair. *Fuck me,* he thought. *I might actually get away with this.*

*

Back at the main event, Greg Davies, together with a couple of stewards, had managed to unplug the projector. Davies looked towards Neil, who by now had managed to get to his feet.

Davies shouted at him. "What the fucking hell have you done to my film? You fucking pervert. I've never been so humiliated!"

Neil just stood there, in a catatonic state. He opened his mouth to say something. Then, after a pause and to nobody in particular, "I think I'd better go now."

The room lights were switched back on revealing a room full of people whose expressions ranged from shock and horror to pure joy, especially those who had never liked or trusted Neil. Becky stood up, looked briefly around, then caught sight of Graham. A look of surprise spread over her face. She picked up her bag and marched over to him and Anna with purpose, and addressed Anna first.

"Anna, what are you doing here?"

"Hi Becky," she replied a little sheepishly. "I've a friend who works at this hotel who could let us in. I only agreed to help if my dad let me come along."

"I see, and you were happy about this, knowing what was on that film?" She addressed Graham like he'd been a naughty schoolboy.

"Err, well. I did suggest she looked away when it got a bit, well, you know."

"Graham, within 20 seconds of it starting, you could see Neil's thingy."

"Was it 20 seconds?"

"Yes. I timed it, but that's not the point. And what about everyone else here who had to sit through that film? There were some old people in this room."

"Well they don't seem too traumatised." Graham pointed out a couple of elderly ladies in their 70s who was giggling as they left the room. One of them put her hands out in front of her, palms approximately 6 inches apart. They burst into a fit of giggles again.

"Graham, I knew you were up to something and I warned you."

"I know Becks. I'm sorry. The Devil made me do it."

"Graham..."

"Look Becky, I spent six weeks in a shed. I have nearly been killed on at least three separate occasions, my daughter and her boyfriend were abducted..."

"Friend." Anna corrected.

"Right. Okay, friend. Becky, look what could have happened to you? These people, and I include Neil in this, made our lives hell for weeks and why? Greed. They were rich, had more than enough, but always wanted more. And it wouldn't have stopped with us. Others would have suffered in the future. Those that could have been bought would have been used for a while until they were no longer needed. Those who got in their way, stood up to them, would have been crushed, like... like..."

"Ryvita."

"Ryvita! Thank you Anna. Becky, I'm sorry this isn't a very Christian philosophy, but you know what? Revenge really does taste pretty damn sweet at the moment. And another thing, I've missed every bloody home match over the last couple of months. I don't even know where we are in the table!"

"Oh Big G. What am I going to do with you? Take me home. I'm too tired to argue. I just want to go to bed." She looked at him with pure love in her eyes. He didn't half come out with some crap, but she still loved him.

"Err, can I hitch a ride?" Anna asked.

"Of course you can. We'll drop you off on the way back." Graham replied.

"Can't I come back with you two? Life's pretty interesting with you at the moment."

"No. You are going back to mum's. Just at the moment, until all this settles down, mum likes to have you around. It's been really difficult for her."

"Okay, I understand dad. Can I come out with you tomorrow night?"

"Lord, I'd forgotten about that. Yes, I guess so, if it's early on and mum brings you."

"Thanks dad." Becky looked a little anxious in the background.

*

Later, after Anna had been dropped off with Kate and they were driving back to Becky's, she spoke about the next day.

"Graham, is it going to be awkward for Kate with me around tomorrow?"

"Sorry love, I never thought. It's not just about Kate though. Are you going to be okay as well?"

"I think so."

"Look, I'll ring her tomorrow and talk to her about it. If she's okay about it, will you be?"

Becky smiled back. "Of course I will. I'm with you all the way now Big G, for the whole journey."

*

The knock at the door awoke Reynolds from his thoughts.

"Come in." The door opened and a uniformed officer came in.

"Sir, we've found Mrs. McArthur, or at least we know where she went."

"Where?" He asked with some urgency.

"Miami. It looks like she flew out the day after you called round sir."

"Oh... fish." Reynolds rubbed his forehead. He'd blown it. She'd run. "I suppose there's no trace of her now?"

"I'm afraid not, sir. She's disappeared without a trace... sorry."

"I'm sorry too. That was one person I really wanted to put behind bars. Hey, thanks for finding that out at least."

"No problem sir. You okay?"

"I'm fine, thanks. What time is it?"

"It's coming up to six sir. Why?"

"I've got an engagement this evening. I owe someone a pint of 'crappy real ale'."

"Pardon sir?"

"It doesn't matter. Thanks again."

*

"You've got a visitor Mr. Hyde" No pretty ankles to look at this time. Instead, Hyde caught the polished shoe and pressed trousers of a uniformed officer as he entered his room in the hospital.

"Oh?" was all Hyde could muster.

A second pair of shoes, brown brogues this time, came into view. The trousers above them looked in need of a good iron. Hyde looked up from his awkward position on the bed. He had been lying like this for such a long time it was beginning to feel normal. Perhaps he would spend the rest of his days like this, lying face down on a bed, unable to experience the pleasure of a fuck or a good shit. He recognised his friend Smithson as he sat on the plastic chair next to his bed.

"Hello James." The voice was that of an old man. Hyde turned his head enough to get a good look at the face of his friend from the lodge.

"Hello Leslie. How are you?" He knew the answer before he asked the question.

"I'm... not that great James."

"Well, you might be surprised to learn that things are not wonderful here either."

"James. It's all gone wrong. Everything we've worked towards. It's all... gone. I'm under investigation at the moment."

"Have you told them anything?"

"Yes. Yes James, I have, because they know anyway. They've found things out about me, about things I've done for you. They've found money that has been paid into accounts that are impossible to explain."

"So you've betrayed me Leslie?"

"James, they know. They know everything. We're going to go to prison, both of us. I'm not sure I'll survive that."

"I... don't... give... a... fuck about you Leslie!" Hyde snarled through gritted teeth. "Do you know why?"

"I can guess." Smithson said, weakly.

"I'll fill you in. One month ago, I had everything. The business was booming. Recession? What recession? People loved me because of the charity work, because I was transforming this shitty city. I was a fucking hero Leslie. There would probably have been a statue to me in years to come. I had a girlfriend 30 fucking years younger than me that was the sexiest woman you will ever meet. She was finally going to be all mine because her fucking husband with his little vendetta against me had been wiped off the face of the earth because, like the utter pathetic fool he was, he trusted Frieda. Two birds with one stone as they say. I would have lived in luxury Leslie until my dying days, with a woman who would be the envy of all who saw her. How I would have loved that, to see the faces of all those grey business people looking at me, with her on my arm. I had it all Leslie."

"James. I wish you hadn't told me all this."

"What are talking about?"

"I think he's referring to me, sir." With a sinking feeling, Hyde realised the officer hadn't left them alone in the room. How could he anyway with Smithson under investigation?

Oh Fuck!

"I'm sorry James. I'd better be going."

"Then fuck off Smithson. Fuck off back to your wife!"

"There is no wife anymore James. She's left me. She left as soon as everything came out. Don't you see James? There's nothing left for me either."

Smithson got up and headed towards the door, where the officer was standing. He turned back. "Goodbye James."

It would be the last time they would ever see each other again.

Chapter Nine – A night of surprises

And so, more on compost. As we've already said, compost replaces lost nutrients naturally, adds organic matter which helps retain soil moisture in our increasingly dry summers and promotes an excellent soil structure, perfect for healthy vegetables. So, how do we make the stuff? It's really like baking a cake. You need all the right ingredients, in the right proportions. You also need a bit of mixing, and time. Many people come up to me and say they've had a go but either ended up with a disgusting, slimy, smelly mess, or a dry pile of barely degraded material. The former is the result of too much kitchen waste or grass clippings; the latter, too much in the way of bulky waste, twigs, leaves or other dry materials. However, get the balance right, mix them well and allow a bit of time, and wow. The way I do it is to have two bays, made of old pallets side by side. The first bay will be the active one. I'll use that for all the kitchen waste, blended with allotment waste, under the cover of an old carpet to keep the moisture in. That one I'll keep topping up over the summer. At the end of the year, this will be shovelled into the second bay, mixed up in the process, and again covered but this time left undisturbed for a year to rot down. I'll then start again with the first bay the following summer. Meanwhile, the earlier contents of the second bay will have been spread across the plots, having had the benefit of the best part of two years to decompose. I find the whole process so satisfying. It's like taking all that has happened in the past and breaking it down to build something new, something better for the future, like a phoenix rising from the ashes. It's a metaphor for life in many ways...

"Graham, I have to say I'm getting a bit nervous about this evening." Graham and Becky were getting changed in their bedroom.

"If I'm honest, so am I. I really have no idea who's coming, or what to expect," he replied, looking for a sock in the drawer to match the one in his hand.

"I said you should have paired them up. Oh, let me look." As Becky was rummaging around in the drawer, Graham looked at her. She looked fantastic in her black dress. It hugged her figure beautifully, accentuating the curves around her bottom and her full breasts. *How did I get here?* He thought to himself. *How did I end up with such a beautiful woman?*

"Here." She turned with a look of triumph on her face. "Found it. Now stop daydreaming and hurry up!"

"Yes boss, won't be long."

"And no more cheek from you, my lad, or you'll feel the back of my hand."

"Oh yeah baby."

"Graham!"

Half an hour later they were heading for Leeds city centre in Becky's Fiesta

"We could have got a taxi you know."

"Why? You're not scared of my driving are you?"

"I'm bloody terrified, but that's not the point. It's just you can't have a drink. That's not like you."

"What are you trying to say? Anyway, I told you earlier. I'm not feeling great. I'm happy to stay on the soft stuff and drive, as long as I don't end up driving your drunk mates home."

"Well, one thing's for sure they'll soon sober up." Graham gripped the side of his seat as the Fiesta pulled back into the nearside lane just in time to avoid the oncoming white van. "Are you going to be okay this evening?"

"Oh yes. I'm probably just coming down with a cold or something. Hey, I'm fine. Don't worry." Graham looked at her. She was holding something back.

Ten minutes later they parked down a lesser known back alley, a short walk from the Tap. On the rare occasions Graham ever drove to the Tap, he was always sure he could park there. Graham hadn't driven much over the last six months though, since his last car, a rather sickly Ford Escort, had finally passed away before it had to face the humiliation of an MOT test. His finances being the way they were, resulted in the car never being replaced.

They walked hand in hand between the shops and down the alley to the Tap. All seemed quiet as they approached, even the lights seemed off.

"You've got the right night, haven't you?"

"Course I have – though it seems a bit strange."

Graham tried the door. Thankfully, it opened and as they went in the doorway, the lights flickered on and a crowded pub greeted them with a loud rendition of, "There's only one Graham Pilgrimm, one Graham Pilgrimm, there's only one Graham Pilgrimm!"

"Oh no! Guys. Oh!" Graham was overwhelmed. They were all there. The lads, family members, even some of the local constabulary that he recognised from down at the station. There were rudimentary decorations around the walls and ceiling. The lads had plans for more but the temptation of ale had got in the way and they'd been somewhat distracted.

"Free the 'Farnley One'!" yelled Kev.

"I. We don't know what to say. Thank you guys... I'm... speechless."

"Well thank fuck for that. Let's get on with some serious drinking!" added Tomo. A pint was thrust into his hand. Graham and Becky then spent the next hour circulating, talking to as many people as possible. He was conscious that he ought to do this sooner rather than later, when he might be less coherent. There were hugs from family. His mother and father were there, happy to share the celebration with their son, though mildly anxious about some of the characters in and among the crowd.

After they'd chatted for a while, Annie strode up to him and they hugged.

"Hey sis, what are you going to do now?"

"Well, I'm retiring from my secondary occupation if that's what you mean. I've got to go down to London to tie up a few loose ends, then I'm coming back and will stay with mum and dad over Christmas. After that I'm going to travel for a while. Mark's going to join me for a couple of weeks in Australia.

"Mark?"

"You know, Mark Reynolds, the nice policeman who came to our rescue. He scrubs up well, don't you think?"

"I'm pleased for you sis. He seems a decent guy. Anna had her suspicions he fancied you."

"The feeling is extremely mutual bro." She winked.

"Hi Graham." A voice interrupted. Graham turned, and there stood a rather sheepish Dave. Becky made a tactical retreat.

"Hi Dave."

"Look. Mate. I'm really sorry... about...well."

"Dave. It's okay mate, really. How can I stay mad at you? We've a history going back what? It must be nearly forty years. You don't just throw that away."

"That Hopkins... he just got to me."

"It's fine Dave, honestly." Graham held out his hand. "It's fine, but there will be a penance to pay for your absolution."

"Oh? What's that?" Dave asked with a hint of anxiety.

"You've got to buy all the lads and my family a drink.

"It will be an honour mate. Only, can I make any shorts singles rather than doubles... money's a bit... you know."

"That's fine Dave." Graham stood up on a chair to address everyone in the pub. "Ladies, gentleman and Tomo, can I have your attention please? I just wanted to let you know that my good friend Dave here has kindly volunteered to buy everyone here a drink." A loud cheer erupted around the pub and Dave suddenly looked like a rabbit caught in the headlights.

"Wait! No! Hang on..." His protests were halted by a swarming crowd of drinkers pressing up to him, eager to place their orders.

"You are a bad man Mr. Pilgrimm." Becky chastised him, with a smile on her face."

Half an hour later, Graham perched himself on a stool in the corner of the pub and took stock of the evening. He was aware that for the first time in years he was feeling truly happy. Here he was, surrounded by friends and family. Not only had his name been cleared, but he had become a local folk hero. Earlier in the day Look North had contacted him to invite him for a TV interview. It wasn't just the BBC either. All the regional media were interested in his story. He'd actually achieved something in his life and it gave him a sense of achievement he'd never felt before. What he was going to do after this, he had no idea. The thought of another twenty years sitting opposite Geoff did not appeal in the slightest. No, it would be different now, it would have to be. But what was he going to do with his life?

That was for another day though. For the moment, life was good, really good. Even his sister had returned from the dead. He saw her sitting at a table near the fire with Reynolds. They looked close. He smiled. Good for you girl.

A voice interrupted his thoughts.

"Hi dad."

"Anna! Hey, great to see you." He stood up and gave her a hug. Behind her stood Kate. She smiled at Graham. He smiled back. They looked at each other for a moment. *If all this had happened earlier, would we have still been together?*

Graham felt a squeeze on his arm. He looked to his side. It was Becky. He smiled at her. *I guess we'll never know. But one thing I do know is I love you Becks.*

"Becky, this is Kate. Anna's mum."

"Hi, it's good to meet you." They shook hands and exchanged a fleeting look that hinted at unspoken jealousies and rivalries. The moment passed. "You have a remarkable daughter Kate."

"She is something special. We are all really proud of her." Anna blushed and mouthed a silent 'Oh mum.' "It looks like I appear to have a remarkable ex-husband and sister-in-law as well. There must be something in the Pilgrimm genes."

"I can vouch for that." Becky confirmed. Then realising how it came out, she looked down, embarrassed. Anna smirked.

Graham was distracted by the sight of his sister coming over with Reynolds.

"Hey bro. Can I properly introduce Mark?"

"Hello Graham. It's good to meet you under slightly better circumstances." They shook hands.

"It's good to see you too, and err... well, I'm glad you're here. I wanted to say thanks for, well, everything you've done to clear my name."

"Graham it was you, your family and friends that did all the hard work, especially your daughter." He looked at her as he spoke. "Anna, there's a career in the police force waiting for you if you want it girl."

"Thanks Mark, but I think I'd prefer to operate on the fringes of society in my future quests for truth and justice."

When Reynolds had stopped laughing, he turned to Graham. "I did rather promise your daughter I'd buy you a drink. I gather you like real ale?"

"Well, thank you for that. I do indeed. Shall we go over to the bar and look at what's on the menu?" As they walked over, Graham asked Reynolds how the investigation was going.

"I can't say too much Graham, as I'm sure you'll appreciate. But it's looking like we've pieced everything together now and have most of the perpetrators in custody. I say most, because unfortunately Frieda McArthur seems to have slipped through the net. It looks like she fled to the States. As to her whereabouts now...?" Reynolds shrugged his shoulders. "Your guess is as good as mine. Oh, and by the way Graham, that stunt the other night..."

"Ah!"

"Ah, indeed. Graham, that could have got you into a lot of trouble. I had to pull a few favours to stop charges being brought. Can I ask what the idea behind that was, when we had the evidence down at the station to pull him in anyway?"

"I'm afraid nothing more than pure revenge. Any associate of that sleazy bastard Hyde was fair game as far as I was concerned. Thanks though Mark."

"It's okay Graham," said Reynolds wearily. "Just don't do it again please?"

It was the first time Graham had stood at the bar of the Tap since that fateful September evening, a lifetime ago. As he approached the bar George jumped slightly once he recognised him.

"Oh! Hello... Graham. It's err... great to have you back. We were all behind you. It's good to know justice has finally been done." He looked somewhat anxious as he spoke, then looked down at his fingers; tapped a rhythm out on the bar with them, coughed a nervous cough, then looked back up. "What can I offer you both, and these will be a 'welcome home' gesture from err... me?" George's unusually deferential and somewhat nervous behaviour was lost on Graham, as he was beginning to succumb to the five pints of real ale so far consumed.

"That's really good of you George, thank you. Can I introduce a new friend of mine? This is Chief Inspector Mark Reynolds. He led the cavalry that came to my rescue. Can we have two pints of that one please? Is that alright with you Mark?" Graham pointed, with a slight hint of a wobble, at a new pale ale on the bar. George looked anxiously at Reynolds and subconsciously lifted his left hand up to his throat.

"I'm supposed to be buying you one Graham, but yes, thanks. That's great with me. But I still owe you one. I won't forget."

"I'll hold you to it." Suddenly a crashing noise made them both turn back to the bar.

"Sorry about that," said George. "That was me being clumsy. I accidentally knocked a tray of sandwiches on the floor. I'll get them cleared away in a moment. They were freshly made as well. Oh well, these things happen." He smiled nervously as he pulled their pints.

"He's a strange man," said Reynolds as they left the bar.

"Oh, George? He's alright in his own way. He's not normally that polite though. He's usually a right twat."

"Hey Graham!" Tomo called to Graham from across the pub. "Look who's here?" He pointed at half a dozen men who'd just turned up. Graham looked puzzled. He'd never seen them before. He shrugged his shoulders back and shook his head. 'Who are they?' he mouthed to Tomo. "It's Stefan and Jacek!" Tomo yelled back. "They've brought some friends as well."

Graham momentarily sobered up. Weren't these the guys who abducted Tomo? Before he could decide his next move, the group approached and stood before him.

"It is so good to finally meet you Mr. Pilgrimm!" Stefan exclaimed, hugging Graham and finishing with a kiss on the cheek. "We will buy you a drink. Does this place do vodka?"

"I'm not sure," said a stunned Graham as he looked at a beaming Tomo.

"We will find out. We will be right back. Please don't go away."

"Tomo. Are these the men who...?"

"Yes, yes, I know. Look, I've explained all that. It was that Scud and his thugs who made them do it. These are beautiful people at heart Graham and they have been consistently bullied, overworked and paid fuck all by Hyde and his cronies. Trust me. I am so glad they have been able to make it. They haven't got

272

much money but they insisted on buying me and you a drink. Let them Graham. It's important to them." Moments later the Poles appeared with a bottle of vodka and eight glasses.

"Here!" They gave a glass to Graham and then Tomo and divided the rest between them. The vodka was poured out and after a toast in Polish that was lost on Graham, they all knocked the drink back.

"Graham," said Jacek, looking Graham squarely in the face, "you have removed two great evils from this world. Hyde is no more. Scud is no more." Clearly the worse for drink already, he leaned close to Graham. "We obtained access to the office on site, found the keys to the safe and obtained payments that were a great deal owing to us. Justice has been done. Na zdrowie!" He raised his glass to all the gathering.

"Na zdrowie!" They all replied and drank their refills. Graham was beginning to feel the need for fresh air.

"What are you guys going to do now?" Graham managed to slur to the Poles.

"We are all going back to Poland." Stefan said with an air of great seriousness. "There is now much work for skilled builders like us in Warsaw. It is boom city." He raised his arms in a dramatic gesture to emphasise the point. "We are all going back. And besides," he added, "this country is turning to shit."

"Well, good luck to you all and thank you for not bringing any serious harm to my good friend Tomo." As he said this he was grateful that Reynolds had moved out of earshot to sit in a corner with Annie and had missed the entire conversation.

Graham then became aware he hadn't seen Becky for a while. A quick look around the room found her sitting at a table with Kevin and Dave. He moved over to see how she was.

"Hi," he said as he pulled up a chair. "How are you doing?"

"Better than you by the sounds of it," she laughed at him.

"What do you mean?"

"I mean you sound pissed Big G."

"I'm not pissed. I think I'm just a bit... merry that's all."

"I'm not judging Graham." She held his hand. "If you can't let off a little steam tonight of all nights, when can you?"

He smiled a drunken smile back at her. He then became more serious. "Are you alright though love? You weren't so good earlier."

"I'm fine. Just a bit tired, that's all."

"Are you sure?"

"Yes, honestly. Stop worrying." Graham looked at her for a moment, until Kevin distracted him.

"Hey, look who's just turned up." Kev looked towards the door as the figure of Joe walked in. Graham stood up and made his way over to him.

"Joe, am I glad to see you? I owe you my life."

"No you don't kid. You just owe me a beer," Joe said with a wink.

"Well you sit yourself down and I'll get you a beer." Graham went to the bar while Joe joined the others at the table. Moments later he returned with a pint and passed it to Joe.

"Thanks kid," said Joe as Graham sat down next to him.

"Hey up old man!" Tomo exclaimed as he joined them. "It's a bit past your bedtime isn't it?"

"You cheeky fucker. Oh, beg your pardon." Joe added, realising that Becky was also sitting at the table."

"Don't mind me. I work with a bunch of male reporters. I've heard it all before."

"That was pretty stealthy work, sneaking up on that guy down at the allotment Joe. Did you learn that in the army?" asked Dave.

"Aye, the training never leaves you."

"Even after 65 years."

"What do you mean 65 years?"

"Well that's when the war ended, wasn't it."

"What are you saying?"

"Well... you were in the army weren't you?"

"Yes."

"And you did go to war?" Dave was now getting anxious.

"I went to the fucking Falklands you dip-shit. That was 30 years ago."

"Oh... that's what I meant. Yes, the Falklands." Dave looked over at Graham and Tomo.

"How... old are you Joe?" Graham asked.

"Fifty three. How old did you think I was?"

"About that," Graham added hastily.

"Yes, I'd have said that." They all interjected after each other.

Just then Jim-Bob came to the rescue. "Anyone fancy a bit of fresh air?" He furtively put an imaginary cigarette to his lips.

"Do you mind if I pop out for a bit of air Becks?"

"Go on, I'm fine here," she smiled.

Outside, Graham sat on a low wall with Tomo, while Jim-Bob leaned against the pub and rolled a joint.

"That was good timing Mr. Roberts. I thought Dave was going to get a slap from Joe back there." Graham said.

"Fuck me. I thought he was a bit older than that. Anyway, I think we got away with it." He lit the joint and inhaled. "Oh... yes, that is good. Here Graham old son. This'll put hairs on your chest." He passed the joint to Graham. "So what are you going to do now?"

"Mmm?"

"Are you going back to work?"

"No. I don't think I can." The thought of another 20 years in that musty old office in the pavilion filled him with dread. Besides that, he'd changed. He needed something more, but what?"

"Why not take a bit of time out? You know, to think about it." Tomo suggested.

"I think I'm going to have to. Anyway, I need a bit of quality time with Becks."

"She's a bit of alright, that one Graham. How do you do it?" Jim-Bob said as he wrestled the joint from Tomo.

"I don't know guys. Wit, charm, hung like a donkey... take your pick."

"Face like a donkey," said Tomo. They laughed, only stopping when Kate and Anna appeared outside the pub.

"Graham! Are you ever going to grow up? This is just you all over, and in front of Anna as well. What sort of example is that setting?"

"Kate! Sorry, wait... no I'm not. Bloody hell Kate after everything that's happened, you're having a go at me for a smoke?"

Kate stormed off. Anna stayed for a moment and smiled at Graham. He smiled back and winked.

"I'll ring you tomorrow love."

"Look forward to it dad. Enjoy the rest of the night."

The rest of the night turned out to be a blur. The combination of real ale, vodka and marijuana left Graham in a daze. He vaguely recalled a few goodbyes and hugs, and being supported by Becky back to her car. Even the journey back in the car failed to sober him up. He only started coming round when they got back to Becky's apartment.

"I love you Becks. I really love you," he repeated, numerous times.

"Yes and I love you as well. Before we go to bed, I want to show you something?"

"Oh yes?" he said with a hint of sleaze.

"It's not what you think Graham." She led him to the second bedroom which she'd converted into a small office. On the desk sat a laptop.

"What...?"

"That's for you Graham and tomorrow... tomorrow you start to write. You write your story. I want you to become the writer you always dreamed of. Do it for me."

"What about my job? What about money?" he slurred.

"I'll support us. I just want you to be the person you were meant to be. You've come so far Graham. Now see it to the end."

Graham looked at her, nodded and smiled. Yes, why not? He would start tomorrow.

"I need to go to bed Becks."

Becky led him to their bedroom, helped him get undressed and eased him into bed. She climbed in next to him and held him close, stroking his hair.

"Graham. There's something I need to tell you."

"Mmm?" a semi-conscious Graham murmured.

"Graham. I think I'm pregnant."

"Mmm. That's nice."

Chapter Ten – Pilgrimm's Progress

Happy New Year readers! It is wonderful to be back in the saddle after a 15 month break. As you are probably aware, it has been quite an eventful period. Thankfully, things have settled down a bit now, and the good folk here at the Post have taken pity on me and offered me back my weekly gardening slot. So, as I sit here and look forward to another year of planting, growing and eating, I would like to wish you all the best for 2012. May all your hopes and dreams come to fruition and, of course, may United finally get promotion back to the promised land of the Premiership this season. Next week, though, it's back to work, and we look at ordering and starting off seed potatoes...

"Graham! Where are you?"

"Mmm?" Graham stared at the laptop screen in the office.

"Oh, there you are. You're up early." Becky padded into the office wearing one of Graham's T shirts. She gave him a hug as he sat in the office chair and he gave a grunt of satisfaction as he buried his head into her warm breasts.

"That is nice."

"Well, enjoy them while you can, they won't be like that for ever." A cry from the bedroom brought them back to reality.

"Speak of the devil."

"Don't talk about your son like that. He's a little angel."

"That's not what you called him at 2am this morning."

"He just needed his supper that's all. Anyway, looks like he's ready for breakfast now. Can you get our breakfast on the go please? I could murder a full English."

"Yup, no problem. I've got a couple of days before I have to send this in." He saved the file, shut down the laptop and wandered through the kitchen. "Fancy a run out today? Little walk and pub meal? Looks like it's going to be a decent day."

"Sounds good Big G. We'll discuss it over breakfast." Becky shouted back from the bedroom.

Five minutes later Graham brought a coffee into the bedroom for Becky and smiled with contentment as he watched her feeding baby Jack.

"Hey, he's a hungry feller this morning."

"Just like his father."

"You mean he can't get enough of those breasts."

"You are so crude sometimes. How's breakfast doing?"

"I'm on with it. Be patient woman. Anyway, I was thinking. Do you fancy a run to Skipton? We could have a potter around and grab a bite to eat there?"

"Yes, sounds good to me. I'll leave it to you. Now... food. Please...?"

*

After a hearty breakfast and a struggle to force a resisting Jack into his warm clothes, they made their way to the car park outside the apartment. Graham unlocked their new Audi A4 parked next to Becky's Fiesta. Once Jack was safely installed and his favourite nursery rhyme disc was located, they were off. Graham kept checking the rear view mirror and once Jack looked like he was asleep, the disc was ejected and replaced with Kasabian.

"Oh, not this again."

"You've got no musical taste."

"This isn't music."

"I can put 'Humpty Dumpty' back on if you'd prefer."

"Do you know what? I think I'd actually prefer it."

"'Ollocks," Graham muttered under his breath. Becky squinted at him. He quit while he was behind.

A beautiful sunny winter's day meant parking proved to be a bit of a problem once they'd got there. Eventually they found a space not too far from the castle and parked up. Once Jack was safely wrapped up in his pram they spent the next hour window shopping and pulling faces at Jack, that left them both in hysterics when he laughed back at them.

"Where does he get that laugh from?" Becky asked, wiping a tear from her eye.

"You laugh like that."

"I don't, do I?"

"You do, honestly."

"You make me laugh Big G. I don't remember laughing much in my old relationship."

"Hey, that was in the past. Do you believe in fate?"

"What do you mean?"

"Well, that things happen for a reason. My dad does. He believes everything happens for a reason. I mean a year and a half ago I was where I was, getting by, but not really doing much with my life. And here I am now, with you. And I couldn't imagine being with anyone else. You complete the picture. You complete me Becky."

"Oh Graham, don't be getting all soft."

"But it's true. It was through that chance meeting in the Tap with Satan-in-female-form and everything that subsequently happened as a result, that I met you. Otherwise..."

"I don't know Big G." She gave him a hug. "I find you sometimes impossible to live with but, you know what?"

"What?"

"I couldn't imagine being with anyone else." Graham smiled and kissed her gently on the forehead.

"Do you fancy making a little brother or sister for Jack tonight?"

"No, but thank you for asking."

*

280

They found a traditional pub with a real fire that served an ale meeting Graham's exacting standards, and had an excellent bar meal.

"Do you know what? I could just sit here in front of this fire all afternoon." Becky said, sounding sleepy.

"I know what you mean. And this pale ale is too much of a temptation when I'm driving as well."

"I'll drive back if you want."

"Oh... it's fine. Thanks for asking."

"Hmm?

"Anyway, there's somewhere I want to call in at on the way home."

"Oh? Sounds mysterious."

"I'm saying nothing more. Are you ready to head off?"

"I am, but have to say I'm a bit curious. Do I need to be worried?"

"No." Graham laughed. "Trust me."

Once outside, they were heading back up the main road to their car when Graham suddenly pulled up outside a bookshop and laughed out loud.

"What is it Graham?"

"Look Becky."

Inside the window, the central display featured a photo of Graham's face next to an image of an allotment shed, with a montage of garden images cleverly interspersed with copies of press cuttings. In front of the graphic several copies of the same book were displayed; some in hard back, others paperback. All bore the same title, 'Pilgrimm's Progress'.

"You did it, didn't you Graham? You really did it." Graham said nothing, but stared at the display, shook his head and smiled. Under the display, a large caption said, 'The true story of an innocent man's fight to clear his name against the odds'.

"I wouldn't have done it if it wasn't for you, love."

"But you did it, you had it in you. It just needed something like that to happen to bring it out. And it's not just the story of what happened to you Graham, it's the way you wrote it. Look at what you're writing now. This new material is nothing to do with real life, but what did your agent say? It's going to be huge. Graham, you've a gift and now you're finally able to express it. I'm so proud of you love."

"Hey!" a voice interrupted. "You're that feller aren't you?" A short, stocky bald man with an earring stood in front of him.

"Yes. Yes, that's me." Graham's chest puffed out with pride and he looked at Becky.

"My Sharon read that book. She said it were a load of shite."

*

A couple of miles out of Skipton and Graham was beginning to feel more like himself again.

"The trouble with you is you take everything so personally Graham. If you're going to write, you're going to have to take criticism. It goes with the territory."

"Yes, well. There are certain people's opinions I value Becky. And that person's I did not. Anyway," he said, suddenly brightening up, "here we are." They had pulled up outside a large stone cottage in a village of similar styled period properties, surrounding a small green. It was set back from the road in a large sloping garden, bounded by a drystone wall. Immediately surrounding the house was a cottage garden with lavenders and roses that in summer would look and smell beautiful. To the right and rear of the cottage garden as you faced the house, a large lawn sloped gently down to a stream that bordered the property and which tumbled beyond the garden to join others that would eventually become the Wharfe.

"What do you think?"

"It's beautiful Graham, but...?" She looked at him, puzzled.

"It's for sale. I fell in love with it as soon as I saw it."

"You mean... you want to buy it? But, we couldn't afford it..."

"We can love. We can. My book, it's selling shitloads. I've got the money. I can afford it. Becky, I want to get out of Leeds. This can be a new start, a new start for all of us. I can write here, and what a place for Jack and his brothers and sisters to grow up in."

"It's beautiful Graham. My job though. It's a long way to commute."

"Pack it in Becky. No, before you ask, not to be a housewife. Becky, I'm turning the tables now. I want you to write, to go freelance. You're too good to be doing what you're doing at the Post. You can work from here. We both can."

Becky started crying. She couldn't help it, but the tears just kept coming and she felt they wouldn't stop. She felt happier than she had ever felt in all her 36 years.

*

As Graham drove back to Leeds in the dark, he reflected on the last 15 months. Becky had indeed unlocked something within him. The day after the party in the Tap, he had started writing. His hangover that morning had quickly disappeared when the reality of Becky's pregnancy sank in. He was going to be a father again!

They kept the news to themselves for a few weeks until they were confident enough to be able to tell friends and family. But that first day of knowing, they shared together in the apartment.

Throughout that day Graham kept wandering into the office and sitting at the desk. He'd look at the laptop Becky had given him and think to himself, *how do I start?* Then wander back around the apartment, finding other things to do instead.

He didn't have a PC or laptop in his flat above the launderette. 'Graham's Garden' was written on his computer at work after 5pm, when he could use it for personal use. Now he had his own machine here in the apartment.

At dinner, that first evening after the party, Graham said little.

"Are you alright Graham?"

"Mmm?"

"You're...happy about the baby?"

"Yes, oh yes Becky. I'm over the moon love. I'm just thinking about other stuff. Things I need to sort out."

"If you want to talk, you know I'm always here." She reached across the table and held his hand.

After the meal had finished, Becky went over to the sofa and stretched out in front of the TV. Graham sat at the table, looked down at what was left of the glass of red wine in his glass and finished it with one swallow. He got up and went over to Becky, knelt down next to her and kissed her forehead.

"I'll be in the office if you want me love."

"Okay. Have fun."

Graham sat at the desk, as he had done several times that day, but this time he turned the laptop on. As it sparked into life, he sat thinking. Once it was ready, he opened Word and started typing.

It was slow going at first and there was a great deal of deleting of text and rewriting. After 20 minutes he nearly gave up. He was about to shut the machine down, when something made him push his chair back, just far enough to reach the door which was ajar, and he peered round at Becky, across the room on the sofa. She saw him looking at her and she smiled back.

He felt her love and belief in him. He smiled back, then moved back to the desk, focussed on the screen for a few moments, then started typing. And it started to flow.

Day after day he wrote. And with each day that passed his resolve increased. He wasn't going back to his old job. He contacted his boss who tried to persuade him to return, but writing aside, it would be impossible. He was famous now as well.

Following all the arrests, everyone and their dog wanted to speak to him; radio, TV, the papers. He could only tell them so much. There were legal restrictions and Annie's role had to be somewhat played down. But on top of that, he wanted to tell his own story. How could he go back to his old job as if nothing had happened?

He wrote right through the trials. One by one, they fell. Scud, his cousin and associates, who all looked impassively at the judge as their guilt was pronounced; Smithson and Neil, who both wept when their sentences were read out; then Hyde, who just stared straight ahead into space at his. He was a broken man. He had lost everything and, as the sentence was read out, he knew he would probably never leave prison again, except in a wooden box.

Only two people never made it to trial. Frieda, who had disappeared somewhere across the Atlantic; and Aleksis, the assassin with the gold tooth. A week before his trial he was found dead in his cell in suspicious circumstances; suspicious in that he'd been battered about the head with a blunt object.

Nobody had seen anything of course, though it was of interest to the police that there were several residents in the same prison building who appeared to have been related to Scud and Mick. Nothing was ever proven though.

Graham worked hard on his book over the spring and summer and had everything completed by July. He bided his time, until he had the legal clearances to try and publish, but had plenty to occupy himself with as Becky approached the time of the birth. Then one late summer evening, Becky woke in the night. She clutched Graham's hand and squeezed as the contractions began.

"Graham, Graham. Wake up! I've started."

They immediately went into automatic pilot; got up, put the pre-packed bags into the car and were on their way to the hospital within 15 minutes.

Becky sat on the edge of the bed and looked scared. Graham was transported back sixteen years to the time of Anna's birth. As she cried in pain he remembered the mad confusion of emotions that flooded through his mind at the time of Anna's birth; excitement, joy, fear, and guilt, because of the pain his act of love nine months earlier was causing now.

Mercifully, the labour was short, and the gas and air had taken the edge of the pain. But it still hurt. Becky came out with a string of expletives that shocked even him, despite 20 years experience of working alongside council gardeners.

The sound of Jack's first cry had both of them in fits of tears. Even the midwife was crying.

Little Jack was a hit with all the family. Annie returned from her work in Australia to be there for the Christening. It was at the party afterwards that she announced her engagement to Mark, so there was a double celebration that night.

The explanation for Annie's reappearance was ludicrous, but her 'employers' got away with it somehow. She's had a climbing accident and ended up with amnesia! It took the best part of a year to identify her. Graham glossed over the details of her disappearance in his book, other than to mention the joy it brought to him and all the family when she finally reappeared. You'd never put that plot line in a book though. It would just be too ridiculous to be believable.

When the time was right, he published.

*

The success of the book took everyone by surprise, everyone except Becky. She had faith in Graham, and had from the start of his writing. She was the only person he trusted to read the

286

pages he wrote, to suggest changes, or just to say, "That's brilliant Graham." His confidence grew with each chapter.

Writing lanced the boils of post trauma from the events that had passed. Even if nothing became of the book, the act of writing was a healing process, for both him and Becky.

The icing on the cake was the success of 'Progress'. He now had the financial return to confirm he could do this for a living. And so it was to be.

*

Graham arrived back at the apartment car park, brought the car to a halt and gently woke Becky.

"Becks. Becks love. We're home."

"Oh... hi love. I must have drifted off. Are we back already?"

"We are," Graham smiled. He loved her when she was asleep. He loved her when she was awake. He simply loved her.

They entered the apartment quietly and carefully put the still sleeping Jack to bed.

"He's going to wake up at 2am again. Just you wait and see."

"That will be your problem, my love. If I had the boobs, I'd take over."

"That is a cop out if ever I heard it. Anyway, I'm off to bed. Might as well get some sleep before it all starts again. Are you coming?"

"In a few minutes. I didn't check my emails this morning. I'd better have a look and see if anything's come through that might be of interest."

"Okay. Try not to wake me when you come through."

"I'll do my best. Night love." He kissed her.

"Night Big G." Becky replied with a yawn as she went to bed.

Graham sparked up his laptop and loaded his mail. There were a couple of messages from his agent and an after dinner speaker invitation. *How much are they offering? And they'll feed me as well? That's just stupid money.* There was something from Look North. *I'm sure that presenter fancies me.* And one from an address he didn't recognise.

Suddenly he felt a chill in his heart. There was something in the email address .

...folin@...

He took a deep breath and, with some trepidation, he opened it.

```
Hello Graham.

I bet you never thought you'd hear from
me again, did you?
Well, as I'm sure your new friends in
the police have told you, I've left the
country and I don't plan to return just
yet, so don't you worry too much about
that my friend. We'll probably never
meet again, but I had to write Graham. I
had to write to congratulate you. I
badly underestimated you.
I chose you because I thought you were a
simple, sad middle aged Yorkshireman I
could use to take the blame for the
murder of my husband. He was an
innocent, like you. He trusted me. That
was his downfall. The thing is Graham,
there's no one who'll ever be more
important to me, than me. People like
him, like you, like that old creep Hyde,
they are all there to be used to help me
get to be where I want to be.
It was all planned so well. You would go
down for the murder, that ape Cudworth
would be erased from the equation at a
```

later stage and I would stay with Hyde,
just long enough to marry him. Once I
knew I would secure at least half of
what he had, I'd be gone. Maybe in his
sad way, he knew that. He would happily
sacrifice his millions for a few
blowjobs and fucks with a younger woman.
Men are pathetic really. Their brains
don't extend beyond their balls.
You were the same though, admit it
Graham. You did what you were told to
earn my little rewards and because you
thought you'd also own me in the end.
And everything was going to go to plan,
except in the end it didn't, did it? I
chose the wrong victim. I underestimated
you and that brat of a daughter of yours
too. And where did that sister of yours
spring from? What kind of family are
you?
So here we are. You've won, you're a
free man. You've proven your innocence.
Not only that, you're a celebrity.
You're famous and probably rich now. My
instinct would normally drive me
straight back to you, to hunt you out
and use you because of it. I don't think
I will though Graham, not yet anyway.
The prospect of a few years in jail
doesn't really appeal to me somehow. But
that's how I work, instinct. I'm like an
animal Graham. I get the scent of my
prey and I hunt it. I usually catch it
in the end as well, and then I use it
until I'm ready to move on to the next
one. That's how I work. Sooner or later
age will catch up with me, but not just
yet.
Graham my friend, I am somewhere in
America. That is all you need to know. I

am with a 68 year old fat, ugly, stupid
old businessman. He cannot believe his
luck that he is with me. He is only
recently divorced and has told me
already how much he loves me. He is
pathetic. He doesn't see how his friends
laugh at him. They've sussed me. They
know I will bleed his fat old carcass
dry - because that is what I do.
Did you ever wonder why I'm like this
Graham, why I'm such a bad person? Let
me tell you some things that I've never
told anyone else. I grew up in what
seemed to all like the perfect middle
class Swedish family. My parents were
both teachers - both very respectable.
Unfortunately for my mother and little
me, my father had a problem; he drank.
And when he drank, he would become a
monster. There would be violence towards
my mother - I'll spare you the details
Graham. I learned to read the signs
early on. I learned to disappear until
he collapsed into a coma. I don't know
how he kept the façade of respectability
going for so long, but sooner or later
these things always catch up with you
don't they? One day he turned up to work
still drunk from an all night session.
He was asked to go home and he became
abusive; the fool ended up lashing out
at a colleague.
There was an investigation. They found
bottles of alcohol hidden in his desk.
He was fired and never worked again. He
drank the rest of our money away.
My parents divorced and I went to live
with my mother. There was little money.
She went from one disastrous
relationship to another. One of them

took a liking to me. He tried to touch
me when my mother was out at work. I hit
him Graham, I hit him hard. He hit me
back and as soon as my mother came home
and saw the bruises, that was that. She
threw him out.

Something changed in my mother that day.
She started to take control. My mother
was beautiful and learned that to
survive she was going to use, rather
than be used. She found men who had
money and used her natural talents to
take what she could, and then moved on.
I learned everything from her Graham.
She was my teacher and I was the best
pupil she ever had. When she began to
realise I was turning into her, she sent
me to England to study, to get away and
better myself in other ways.
Unfortunately, it was too late; the
damage was done.

So here I am Graham and I am sorry. This
is me. I am what I am. Goodbye and good
luck my friend and, as you say in
England, 'I take my hat off to you'. You
beat me Graham. You've done what no
other man has been able to do. You got
the better of me.

There's something else I need to
tell you as well Graham. You were a good
fuck. I hope the woman you are with
appreciates that.

Farewell my Friend.

Frieda.

X

*

Graham sat back in his chair and let out a deep breath. He stared into space for a few minutes, then re-read the email and finally logged off.

He sat in his chair thinking. A mixture of conflicting emotions ran through his mind. Up until now, all he'd felt was anger at her for how he'd been used, chosen apparently at random to take the blame for a murder so that she and others could prosper, without a thought for his plight, let alone that of the victim or his friends and family.

He began to wonder now if it was all as simple as that. Frieda wasn't born bad. Hyde probably wasn't either. He remembered the rocking horse in the cellar and the likelihood that a young James Hyde was probably as innocent as any other child his age. Something had gone wrong along the way, as it clearly had with Frieda. *We are all products of our environment,* thought Graham. Sometimes to survive trauma you have to change, become tougher, otherwise you go under. Maybe Frieda was an extreme example. *It explains but it doesn't excuse. Frieda and Hyde knew what they were doing. They could have changed their lives if they'd wanted.*

Then Graham thought about his own life. How often had he challenged the directions his life seemed to take over the years? There were plenty of opportunities along the way to change his life for the better, before the events of the last year or so forced that upon him; to push himself and do a bit more with his life, to use the talents he was undoubtedly born with. But he hadn't. He would probably have carried on drifting through life on automatic pilot, as he always had done.

"Goodbye Frieda." Graham gently touched the laptop screen and shut the lid.

He quietly got undressed, crept silently into the bedroom and carefully got into bed, snuggling up to Becky.

He kissed her on her back and slowly drifted off to sleep, holding her in his arms.

Acknowledgements

This has been an incredible journey, so I will start at the beginning.

Thank you Fiona. I learned so much from our time together. But of all the things I learned, probably the most important thing was to give this a go. I'm not sure I would ever have got round to telling Graham's story if you hadn't encouraged me all those years ago.

Thank you to all the people I have known or bumped into over the years who inadvertently gave me snippets of their characteristics and personalities to help mould the characters in this book. All the characters in 'Pilgrimm' are of course entirely fictional, but I would be lying if some of their traits weren't borrowed, consciously or subconsciously, from people I have met over the years.

Thank you to my beautiful daughters Ellie and Izzy. You have given me, and continue to give me, so much joy, as well as an empty bank account. You are both such amazing and talented people. Special thanks must go to you Ellie for designing the book cover, as well as being the inspiration for Graham's daughter Anna – so yes I did make one exception to the fictional character statement above.

Thank you to the rest of my family; my father, my brother Colin and his gorgeous wife Carolyn, for their encouragement and support. And especially our much loved and missed mum Doreen. She gave us all her everything, and so much more.

Finally, a huge thank you to Richard at J R Nicholls for having the belief and courage to take this book on. Thank you for putting your faith in both Graham and me.

Happy allotmenting!